BATTLE OF TERRA TWO

Heedless of the blaster and gunfire, the admiral scrambled to his feet. “What’s the matter?!” he shouted at the gangers hugging the hard ground. “You want to live forever?” Blue lightning flashed by, never quite touching him.

The gangers didn’t stir.

“Scum! I should have gassed the lot of you! Watch a man fight for his world!” Turning, he charged the S’Cotar defenses, running zigzag, firing his blaster.

“Bloody bastard. See you in hell.” Malusi rose. “Come on!” he shouted above the din. “We go or he’s right!” Wheeling, he followed Hochmeister, hearing his answer as a roar swept the line. Vipers and Lords, blacks, whites, yellows, browns, all surged after him, charging uphill over their dead and dying.

Irresistible, the wave swept up John, Heather and zur Linde, carrying them along as it broke over the bunkers, smothering the blue flames, sweeping on into the compound, where a gaunt, cold man awaited, content for now.

STEPHEN AMES BERRY

A TOM DOHERTY ASSOCIATES BOOK

This is a work of fiction. All the characters and events portrayed in this book are fictional, and any resemblance to real people or incidents is purely coincidental.

THE BATTLE FOR TERRA TWO

The stanza on page 117 is from John Donne's *A Hymn to Christ, at the Author's Last Going into Germany*.

First printing: February 1986

A TOR Book

Published by Tom Doherty Associates
49 West 24 Street
New York, N.Y. 10010

Cover art by Alan Gutierrez

ISBN: 0-812-53191-4
CAN. ED.: 0-812-53192-2

Printed in the United States of America

0 9 8 7 6 5 4 3 2 1

To my uncle, Willard C. Ames,
a good friend and a gallant man

A big Thank You to my editor,
Beth Meacham, who Waited

1

D'Trelna finished the last line of his report. Sighing, he clasped his fingers over his ample belly and leaned back in the big chair. "Computer, top of text, please."

The desk screen blinked, then presented the first portion of his status report to Fleet. "Scroll," said D'Trelna. He read the report as it slowly rolled up.

TO: Grand Admiral K'Lor L'Guan
FleetOps, K'Ronar
FM: Commodore J'Quel D'Trelna
Special Task Force One Seven, Terra

Sir,

Task force is now at authorized strength, with two capital ships: the Y'Tal-class destroyer, *V'Tran's Glory*, just arrived, and the L'Aal-class cruiser *Implacable*, under the command of Captain H'Nar L'Wrona, Margrave of U'Tria. Task force is ready to proceed to the coordinates of the Trel cache, given by the Imperial cyborg, Pocsym Six. We may not leave the Terran system, however, until the arrival of our relief force.

May I again urge, Admiral, that such a force be sent at once? I realize that with the virtual annihilation of the S'Cotar, many of the liberated quadrants are in a state of near anarchy. I realize that Fleet is scattered on urgent missions of relief and rescue throughout the Confederation. I realize that this expedition, founded on the word of an ancient, possibly demented cyborg, must have a low priority. Yet, Admiral, if there is the smallest chance that Pocsym was telling us the truth, that this universe is in danger of invasion from a parallel reality, it would be utter folly for us to not . . .

The door chimed.

"Computer hold," said D'Trelna, pressing the entry tab.

Captain L'Wrona came in.

"Ah, you're just in time to finish this report, H'Nar. It needs an aristocrat's touch."

L'Wrona sank into the room's other armchair. Younger, taller, much thinner than D'Trelna, his aquiline features and flawless uniform were a sharp contrast to the commodore's double chin and unbuttoned tunic. "Nothing from FleetOps yet?"

"Two ships, H'Nar!" Pushing himself from his chair, D'Trelna paced the carpet in front of the armorglass. "All we need are two ships—a S'Kan-class frigate will do. Just something with missile and fusion cannon to sit up here in case the S'Cotar survivors down there try anything." He turned to look beyond the armorglass to the soft blue-white world below. Three hundred miles beneath *Implacable*, most of North America was wreathed in cloud.

"The Terrans have S'Cotar detectors in most public

buildings now, J'Quel,'' said L'Wrona. ''They're stamping out thousands more every day. One firm's even manufacturing a combination smoke-S'Cotar detector. Don't you think that limits the bugs?''

Shaking his head, the commodore turned from the armorglass. ''I suppose the handful that are left should be cowering in the jungles, yet . . .''

''Yet what?'' said the captain as D'Trelna sat down. ''The S'Cotar high command is dead. The Illusion Master Guan-Sharick is dead. Their fleet is wiped, their warriors killed. Their citadel on Terra's moon is just another crater. The galaxy, J'Quel, is free of the S'Cotar. Let's get on with our mission.''

D'Trelna slapped the desk. ''No, H'Nar. If I felt we could leave Terra undefended, we'd have left last month. And until fresh ships arrive on station . . .''

They looked up as the door chimed. D'Trelna opened it with the flick of a thick finger.

A young blonde yeoman entered, carrying a silver tray with two crystal goblets and a decanter of amber liqueur.

''S'Tanian brandy, gentlemen,'' she said, setting the tray on the light brown traq-wood desk.

D'Trelna's eyes lit. ''H'Nar, you never cease to surprise me.'' Eagerly, he unstopped the decanter. ''I thought we wiped the last of this after the G'Tal raid.''

''We did,'' said the captain, rising, looking at the yeoman.

''Will that be all, sir?'' she asked D'Trelna.

''There are four hundred and seven crew on this ship,'' said L'Wrona. ''We've all been together at least two years. I know every face, every name.

''I don't know you, yeoman. That bothers me. And we're long out of S'Tanian brandy. That bothers me.''

D'Trelna watched, unmoving, a goblet in each hand.

"I'm a replacement, sir," she said, cool green eyes meeting the captain's cold blue ones.

L'Wrona's black leather holster was suddenly empty, his long-barreled M11A pointing at the blonde's heart. "We've had no replacements."

"Your mind's always been slower than your blaster, L'Wrona," said the yeoman. "Your victory over us was a gift from Pocsym. You should be hanging from a meat hook, my Lord."

"It's Guan-Sharick," said D'Trelna, carefully setting down the goblets. "I recognize the sarcasm."

"Impossible," said L'Wrona. "Guan-Sharick died beneath the Lake of Dreams."

"The Margrave would like to see a green carapace," said D'Trelna.

A six-foot-tall green insectoid stood where the blonde had been, antennae swaying, tentacles falling from the base of the pipestem. It shuffled two of its four long, three-toed feet.

A jig perhaps, L'Wrona? hissed a cold voice in both men's minds.

"No," said L'Wrona, grimacing.

"I preferred the woman," said D'Trelna.

The blonde reappeared.

"Any reason the captain shouldn't put a big ugly hole through your big ugly self?" asked the commodore.

"If he kills me," said Guan-Sharick, pointing at L'Wrona, but looking at D'Trelna, "all intelligent life in this galaxy dies."

D'Trelna's bushy eyebrows rose. "Perhaps we should talk," he said. "Is this any good?" He held up the decanter.

"The best, Commodore," smiled the blonde.

Half filling two goblets, D'Trelna held one out to L'Wrona. "Brandy, H'Nar?"

"I'd rather shoot the bug," said L'Wrona, tight-lipped.

"Captain L'Wrona, you will holster your weapon and join me in a drink. That's a direct order, H'Nar."

Reluctantly holstering the blaster, L'Wrona took the goblet in his left hand. "Direct, not lawful," he said, sipping. His right hand stayed on the M11A's silver-inlaid grips, his eyes on the S'Cotar.

"How is it, Margrave?" asked the S'Cotar.

"Potable."

"Why isn't every intruder alarm on this ship screaming?" asked D'Trelna.

"I'm wearing a device that foils your sensors, Commodore. A prototype developed at war's end."

"And the shield?" said L'Wrona, still facing the S'Cotar as he put his goblet on the desk. "You can teleport through a class-one shield?"

"Yesterday's visitors' shuttle," said Guan-Sharick. "I was the well-endowed professor of physics"—the S'Cotar's features rippled, bosom swelling, face becoming oval—"whom you so gallantly offered to guide through *Implacable*." The original blonde reappeared. "An effective technique, I imagine?"

The captain blushed.

D'Trelna put his empty glass down. "Excellent brandy, dear bug. Prewar?"

The S'Cotar nodded. "From the A'Lor vines of T'Kal."

"The best, indeed.

"Now, anthropomorphic v'org slime," D'Trelna continued easily, "what's this about all intelligent life in the galaxy?"

"You don't mind if I sit?" said the S'Cotar.

"I mind," said L'Wrona.

Without apparent transition, the blonde was seated on

the small gray sofa to D'Trelna's left, slender legs crossed at the ankles. "I need your help."

"Help? Us?" L'Wrona laughed bitterly. "You monsters wiped out billions of defenseless people, torched planets, mind-wiped whole populations . . ."

"Not precisely monsters, Captain," said the blonde. "Biofabs—biological fabrications of the Imperial cyborg Pocsym Six. A society of aggressors designed to test your mettle, condition you against the enemy which Pocsym and his long-dead designers believed were coming at you from an alternate universe. A hypothesis your expedition is about to test."

"You'd have wiped us if we hadn't wiped you," said L'Wrona. "Eight billion corpses rotting on scores of planets isn't a conditioning exercise."

The S'Cotar shrugged. "If we hadn't wiped most of your corrupt fleet and your rotting republic, something else would have—the invasion Pocsym predicted, some unpleasantness out of the old Imperial Marches. Life's a quirky gift, Margrave—you often have to risk it to keep it. We reminded you of that."

"Too costly a lesson," said L'Wrona, pulling his blaster.

"H'Nar!" snapped D'Trelna. "No!"

"Please, J'Quel," said L'Wrona softly, weapon on Guan-Sharick. "They killed my world."

"Captain my Lord L'Wrona," said D'Trelna, voice flat and hard, "you will holster your weapon or I will relieve you and charge you, sir."

"As the commodore orders." L'Wrona slid his blaster back into its holster, then clasped his hands behind his back, expressionless.

"If this isn't convincing," said D'Trelna to the S'Cotar, "you're dead."

Guan-Sharick shrugged. "During the war," it began,

gaze shifting between the two men, "we found an Imperial device in this system that could access alternative realities."

D'Trelna mumbled something. The other two looked at him. He shook his head. "Nothing. Continue."

"Gaining a crude understanding of this machine, we used it to establish a base on an alternate Terra—Terra Two, we called it. This covert base was to continue research into the use of the device and serve as a fallback for us in the remote chance that we lost the war." The blonde smiled wryly—an engaging smile. D'Trelna marveled as always at the S'Cotar transmute's flawless mimicry of its dead victims' mannerisms. "As this base was not part of the war, we placed it in charge of a troublesome Tactics Master."

"Tactics Master?" said D'Trelna.

"Ten years you fought us, Commodore," said Guan-Sharick, surprised, "and you don't know what a Tactics Master is?"

"Your command structure was mostly a mystery. Whenever we captured one of you, you'd blow up. Can't interrogate wall scrapings."

"A Tactics Master is—was—roughly the equivalent of a second admiral—the senior-most insystem commander."

"Leader of a heavy task force," said L'Wrona.

Guan-Sharick nodded. "Shalan-Actal distinguished himself early in the war. It was he who planned and executed the assault on your home world of U'Tria, Margrave."

L'Wrona's face seemed graven in stone.

"He was a zealot, though," continued the S'Cotar. "As the war dragged on, we saw the need to conserve resources. Shalan did not. He'd rather torch a planet than capture it, shoot humans rather than use them as labor, burn cities in reaction to minimal guerrilla activity, rather than convert their industrial plant to our war effort. He grew worse and finally was relieved, sent into what we thought was a harmless exile."

"Terra Two," said D'Trelna.

"Terra Two," said Guan-Sharick. "There he conducted unauthorized experiments with the device. During one such experiment he contacted entities in another parallel universe—entities with a similar device. It was like two opposing tunnels meeting."

The blonde stood, pacing in between desk and sofa. "When you won the war, Shalan formed an alliance with these entities. They're silicon-based life-forms—machines of beings long dead. They're now on Terra Two, a small force of them, trying to reestablish the connection between that world and their own universe. When they do that, they'll come pouring through their portal, take Terra Two and then Terra One."

"How do you know that?" said L'Wrona.

The S'Cotar faced L'Wrona. "I was there. I heard, I saw. And I escaped, Margrave. Even now Shalan's transmutes are hunting me."

"Where's their portal on Terra?" asked D'Trelna.

"No." The S'Cotar shook its head. "I don't trust you—you might do something rash. If you attack that portal, you'll spark a counterattack—one you may not stop with two ships."

"Of course we'd stop it," said L'Wrona. "You've said the machines are few. And how many bugs could this Shalan have been allowed in his exile?"

"Few, but they're breeding up to strength. Fast, using an untested growth accelerant."

"Assuming this is true," said D'Trelna, "what do you want us to do?"

The desk commlink chirped. "D'Trelna," said the commodore.

"Engineer N'Trol requests permission to lower the shield for periodic maintenance," reported K'Raoda, *Implacable*'s third officer.

D'Trelna sighed. "What did N'Trol actually say, T'Lei?"

"He said, sir, 'Tell Fatty and the fop to let me fix the number eight shield generator, or we'll be eating meteors next watch.' "

"Seems clear," said D'Trelna. "Thank you, T'Lei. I'll advise N'Trol direct." He turned to L'Wrona. "What do you think?"

"It has to be fixed," said the captain. He looked at the blonde. "As long as slime here doesn't flick an assault force on board."

"I could do that very easily," said Guan-Sharick. "You're well within teleport range of the Terran surface. But I've no force left.

"If Shalan knew I was here, though, he'd try for me."

"Does Shalan know?" asked L'Wrona.

"No."

Commodore and captain exchanged glances. "Let's do it," said L'Wrona.

D'Trelna nodded curtly. "Agreed." He spoke into the commlink. "Chief Engineer."

"Engineering. N'Trol," said a surly voice.

"N'Trol. Fatty here. Fop and I have decided that you may lower the shield."

"About time."

"N'Trol, you'll find this hard to believe, but there are other considerations than the care and feeding of the engineering . . ."

The commlink telltale winked out.

"Cut me off," said D'Trelna, surprised. "He's getting worse, H'Nar."

"Why do you tolerate him?" asked the S'Cotar.

"He's very competent," said L'Wrona.

"N'Trol's the finest engineer in Fleet," said D'Trelna. "He resents having been drafted from a very lucrative job."

"He resents humanity," said L'Wrona. "N'Trol should have been a S'Cotar." He touched the communicator at his throat. "Bridge. Captain. Shield's going down for repair. Go to high alert, coordinate with Engineering on outage and hull-security party."

"All sections, high alert." K'Raoda's voice echoed through the great old ship. "High alert. The shield is going down for repair. Shield will be down. All sections to high alert. All sections acknowledge."

"You won't give us the portal location," said D'Trelna as the alert call ended. "What proof can you offer?"

A small white cylinder appeared in the blonde's hand. "Everything is on this commwand. But all I need"—the S'Cotar smiled ruefully—"all we need, is one man. One special Terran who can stop Shalan-Actal. A man who'd never work for me, Commodore—but he'd work for you."

"The shield is down," announced the bridge. "The shield is down."

Guan-Sharick rose, extending the commwand.

As D'Trelna stepped around the desk, a transmute flicked into existence beside him, firing at Guan-Sharick. The blonde vanished. The blue bolts tore through the sofa, exploding against the bulkhead.

L'Wrona drew and fired, two quick, red bolts, as the battle klaxon sounded and D'Trelna threw himself to the floor.

"All secure, J'Quel," L'Wrona called over the klaxon. The transmute lay dead on the floor, an arm's length from the commodore, viscous green blood oozing from a hole in its thorax, staining the maroon carpeting.

D'Trelna stood, pulling himself up by the desktop, the commwand in his other hand.

The door hissed open. L'Wrona whirled, blaster ready. A reaction squad of black-uniformed commandos surged in, commando lieutenant S'Til leading. Captain and commandos faced each other over the dead S'Cotar, weapons leveled.

"Captain to Flanking Councilor four," said S'Til.

"Concede," said L'Wrona, lowering his weapon.

"Sir." S'Til saluted, M11A to her chest. If L'Wrona had given an I'Wor move, she'd have killed him.

"Clean this up, Lieutenant," said L'Wrona. He spoke briefly with the bridge, then turned to D'Trelna. "Just that one," he said, as two commandos dragged the biofab's body out. "The rest of the ship's clean."

Back in his chair, D'Trelna poured another drink for himself. "Join me, H'Nar.' He indicated the captain's almost untouched glass.

As L'Wrona sat on the armchair, blaster in hand, D'Trelna slipped the commwand into the desktop reader. "Computer," he said, "scan, read aloud and file contents to main memory, command access only."

They listened for the rest of the watch, D'Trelna making an occasional note on his desk pad. When it ended, the shield was back up and the brandy half gone.

"So," said D'Trelna, setting down his pen, "if this is all true, we need Harrison."

"If it's true," said L'Wrona, "yes."

"We'll have to brief the Terrans," said D'Trelna.

"And our ambassador?"

"After the Terrans," said D'Trelna firmly.

"He'll scream," said L'Wrona.

"Let him. Security of the Confederation—military priority."

''Communications,'' said the commodore into the commlink, ''get me the American Central Intelligence Director, Bill Sutherland.'' He ganced at the time readout, doing a quick conversion. ''He's probably at home, asleep. Get him up. Tell him we've one last world to win.''

2

"Hear from Zahava?" asked McShane, helping himself to another cup of John's coffee.

"Early yesterday." Using a fork, he slid the waffles from the little electric oven onto the two plastic microwave plates. "There's a seven-hour time difference between here and Israel."

"How's her sister doing?"

"Better. Cardiac's a tricky thing, though. "Syrup?" he asked, putting a plate in front of McShane.

They faced each other across the breakfast bar; McShane stolid, white-bearded, with red suspenders stretching from the top of his corduroys over his blue flannel shirt; John, thirty years his junior, in faded jeans and a red cardigan.

"No, thank you. No waffle, either." He pushed the food back, thumb and forefinger to the plate edge. "TV-dinner plates, pop-up breakfasts. You're living on this swill?"

"Not worth cooking for one," said John, squeezing a layer of cold syrup across the waffle. The sunlight flooding the kitchen lent the topping the look of thick, yellowed varnish.

"When's she coming home?" asked McShane, adding milk to his coffee.

"It could be a few months. Natie's got two kids and there's no one else to help.

"What brings you to the Hill so early in the day, Bob?"

"Checkup." He tapped his chest. "Iron-poor blood or something. I'm not twenty-nine anymore, but I shouldn't need a four-hour nap every afternoon."

The phone rang. John reached out, taking the receiver from the wall. He listened for a few seconds, then hung up.

"Wrong number?" asked Bob, sipping his coffee.

John shook his head. "My former employer, I think."

"You think?"

"A voice I've never heard hit me with a hot-shit authenticator and the words 'Gather at the river. Thirty minutes.' "

"What, the Potomac?"

"Yes. I know where—it's a stretch along the canal in Georgetown."

"When I was a boy," said McShane, "back in the Pleistocene, kids used to run off to join the circus. Your crowd ran off to join the CIA." He set his cup down. "Are you driving?"

"No." John rose, taking the dishes to the sink. "Car's in the shop for a brake job."

"I can drop you at Foggy Bottom." He tucked in the bar stool. "Wear your mitties—it's cold out there."

"You need a what?" Harrison stared at Sutherland.

"A hero," said the CIA Director. "We need a hero."

"A hero's a sandwich, Bill." He watched as a sudden gust sent a yellow-red cloud of maple leaves swirling into the canal. "Or a word in a eulogy."

A chill October wind had driven all but the hardiest joggers from the towpath. More would venture out later, after work, but for now the two men had the Georgetown riverfront to themselves.

"Guan-Sharick can get you there," said Sutherland, thrusting his hands into the pockets of his camel-hair topcoat. "You have to get yourself back."

"By taking the other end of this Shalan's portal?"

"Yes."

"Why me? Why not a transmute?" As they walked, he turned the collar of his parka against the wind. "Our old buddy Guan-Sharick could just rip out some poor bastard's mind, imitate him, turn this resistance movement against Shalan-Actal and his base." Stooping, he picked up a flat stone. "Find another hero, Bill. I've retired." He skimmed the weathered shale across the brackish canal surface, one-two-three. It sank midchannel.

"There's no one else," said Sutherland. "And Guan-Sharick can't steal a dead man's mind." He took the photo from his pocket. "Here's who you'd be replacing."

John stared at the snapshot. The man was in his midthirties, sandy-haired, blue-eyed, with a familiar ironic grin. He wore a jet-black dress uniform and high-peaked cap with gleaming visor. "Me," said John. "Only not me." He looked up. "My double on Terra Two?"

"Your dead double," said the CIA Director, taking back the photo. "Major Harrison was killed in a motorcycle accident last week. Very T. E. Lawrence, but very bad timing. He'd just finished his doctoral dissertation at McGill and was to report to his new post in Boston."

"Guan-Sharick was going to replace him?"

Sutherland nodded. "He saw the accident and disposed of the body. Then he flicked through Shalan's portal and appealed to D'Trelna and L'Wrona for help."

"Now that I'd like to have seen," smiled John. The smile faded. "So in another reality, I'm a corpse."

He pointed to the photo. "What's that shroud he's wearing?"

"Class-A uniform—CIA Counter Insurgency Brigade. Sort of a yankee doodle Waffen SS, now fighting in Mexico."

"Mexico?"

"But he's been seconded to the Urban Command garrison in Boston as intelligence officer." Sutherland laughed at Harrison's expression. "You're going to love Terra Two, John."

"I'm not going to Terra Two." He looked across the Potomac, watching as a jet skirted the towers in Rosslyn, heading in to National Airport.

The CIA Director's smile faded. "No one else can do it. If you don't go, bugs and killer machines will come swarming into this reality. They have to be stopped on Terra Two. And you're elected. Or rather, Major Harrison with his ganger connections is."

"I won't ask what a ganger is, Bill," said John, facing Sutherland. "And I'm not elected—I wasn't running. I don't work for you anymore, I don't free-lance anymore, and I don't believe anything Guan-Sharick would say."

"We have to assume he's telling the truth," said Sutherland. "To not do so would be criminally irresponsible."

"You're saying I'm irresponsible?"

It was Sutherland's turn to gaze across the river. "You left the Outfit in a tiff . . ."

Harrison's face flushed, not from the cold. "No one pisses my people away."

"And you were getting bored with the free-lance stuff when the K'Ronarins showed up," continued the director. "Then the biofab war, that battle under the moon. Blasters, mindslavers, starships, Pocsym, S'Cotar. Then it ended. Boom." He turned back to Harrison. "You married your Israeli friend, wrote a book about the biofab war and made an obscene amount of money."

"Am making."

"And now that you're the only one in this whole frigging universe that may be able to save it . . ."

"Really, Bill."

"You won't go. Why not?" He snapped out the last two words, like a drill instructor.

"I don't want to die," said John easily. "That's a one-way trip."

"You haven't a choice, buddy. You go, or we all die."

"I have a choice."

"Crock," said Sutherland. He held out the tan attaché case. "Take this. Read it. It's everything Guan-Sharick gave the K'Ronarins. Give it back to me tomorrow at nine, along with your decision. Scholl's Restaurant on K Street—toward the back."

John took it. They walked in silence to the footbridge, crossed it and stepped down into the hilly side street. "Can I drop you?" said Sutherland. "Long walk to Capitol Hill."

John shook his head. "I could use the air."

He was crossing Fourteenth Street and the sleaze strip when the young blonde in the bimbo suit fell into step beside him. "Something soft and warm for lunch, sir?" she asked.

"No." John quickened his pace.

She kept up with him as he moved past a row of strip joints. "It must be lonely, with Zahava away."

Stopping, he turned, seeing her for the first time. "You."

"Indeed," said Guan-Sharick. "The reports of my death . . ."

"I heard."

The S'Cotar appeared to slip an arm through his. "Let's stroll a bit—John and hooker."

"Funny," he said, walking reluctantly beside the transmute. "What do you want?"

"Everyone asks that," sighed the blonde. Her china-blue eyes met his. "You know what I want.

"Harrison, Shalan-Actal's transmutes are gunning for me, so I'll make it short. I know Sutherland just briefed you—laid a moral imperative on you. Will you go?"

"I don't know," he said honestly.

"Harrison," said the S'Cotar urgently, "if those machines establish a bridgehead in this universe, it's all over—for you, for us, for all intelligent life. They'll wipe Shalan the second he's no longer needed. One of their battle units is five times the size of the K'Ronarin fleet. Harrison, they have over ten thousand battle units! Maybe the Imperial Fleet could have stood against them—nothing of this time can."

"How do you know all this?"

"Some few of us can receive their internal communications—cold, alien thoughts, dedicated to the death of all sapient life. The dead hand that programmed them created an undying malevolence. We either stop them now, one reality away, or we're all dead meat."

"We?" John shook his head. "I don't trust you, bug."

"Trust this then," said the blonde coldly. "Your wife's visiting in Israel. She's now seated in the Café Hertzel, on Jerusalem's Dizendorf Street, sipping Turkish coffee from a white, chipped demitasse cup. Her girlfriend tells an anecdote—your wife laughs, her brown eyes sparkling.

I've but to signal and she's dead. And I will, unless you help us."

Harrison laughed bitterly. "Kill her if you want. We're getting divorced. Zahava's gone home to stay."

"Fine," shrugged the blonde.

"No!" John grabbed the S'Cotar by the shoulders, ashen-cheeked.

The transmute smiled quizzically. "Bluffing?"

"Yes." He dropped his hands.

"I wasn't."

"She's not . . ."

"No. Your tough little hellcat's safe, Harrison. For now."

They resumed their slow walk, the lunchtime crowd flowing around them.

"I'm glad that's resolved," said the transmute. "I'll be taking you through the portal to Terra Two, tomorrow at noon."

"Why then?" asked John, wanting very much to kill Guan-Sharick.

"It's the only time for the next seven months that my loyalists will have charge of both sides of the portal. I could get you through now, but not without some commotion."

"Then what?"

"Then we slip you into Major Harrison's new posting—Boston. There you'll contact the resistance, and lead them against Shalan-Actal's outpost in Vermont, escaping just before they blow up the portal device."

"Either you're crazy," said John, "or you've set this all up very carefully."

They stopped at the corner of Fourteenth and H streets, waiting for the light.

"Major Harrison was a resistance sympathizer," said the transmute. "His assignment to Boston was arranged by certain elements of the CIA for the very purpose we want—disposal of Shalan's covert outpost on Terra Two."

"You had nothing to do with that, I suppose?"

"Me?" said the blonde, wide-eyed.

"Why aren't those killer machines trundling down the street, slaughtering away?" asked John as the traffic rolled past. "The portal works, the machines are on Terra Two."

"Not in great strength. And there's a problem with the linkage between Terra Two and the machines' universe. You have to close the portal from Terra Two to here before machine reinforcements reach Terra Two."

They didn't notice the light flashing. Pedestrians streamed around them. "Take an army through, seize the portal," said John.

"Shalan would disengage the portal device before even a platoon got through. My loyalists hold only a few key points on both sides—not enough to mask the hosts of humanity."

"We're going to miss the light." They hurried across as the warning blinked.

"Read the briefing book," said Guan-Sharick as they continued down H Street. "Know it. I'll be at your town house tomorrow morning, at eleven. Then we'll flick through the portal to Terra Two." The S'Cotar stopped in front of a junk electronics store, back to a doorway full of kids and the blare of punk rock. "Make sure you . . ."

Movement caught John's eye. From across the entrance's "Odds & Ends" table, a tall black kid with a Mohawk was aiming a shotgun mike at Guan-Sharick.

"Down!" shouted John. He tumbled the blonde to the pavement as an azure-blue blaster bolt snapped over their heads, exploding a flower delivery van in a great *Whump!* of pillaring flame.

Screaming. People scattering. Burning bits of roses, mums and driver rained down. Across the street, a car alarm hooted.

The gunman stepped around the table. John tried to untangle himself from Guan-Sharick, tugging at the pistol inside his parka. The transmute held him, pinioned, as the blank-faced killer aimed from five feet away.

The street was gone. John saw a room flash by: S'Cotar warriors, raising their rifles, more blue blaster bolts. A dark pool closed over him, cotton-soft and cold.

Another, bigger area: harsh, blinding light, blaster fire. Gone.

Guan-Sharick let him go. They were in a hotel room, all burnt umber and teak—twin beds, a desk, two chairs, double dresser, TV, curtained window. The transmute held Sutherland's attaché case.

Dropping the attaché case, Guan-Sharick sank onto a bed, hand to shoulder, crimson blood oozing through the fingers. John's parka was splotched the same red. "Shalan's killers?" asked Harrison.

"Shalan's killers," said the S'Cotar. "Seen with me, Harrison, you wouldn't have lived till morning. You're the only John Harrison I have left. So we went through the portal, hard and fast."

"Where are we?"

"The Toronto Hilton."

"And why are you bleeding red?"

"One projects either a whole illusion or none," said the transmute. A S'Cotar sat on the bed, a tentacle clamped over a torn thorax, green oozing through the exoskeleton.

John looked at his parka. It was daubed with green blood.

The blonde and the red blood reappeared. "This isn't clotting fast enough," said Guan-Sharick. "Cold compress, please."

Going into the small bathroom, John ran a white hand towel under the sink faucet. Returning to the bedroom, he tossed it to the S'Cotar.

"You're too kind," said the blonde, catching it.

"For you, anything. Now what?"

"Now you take off your jacket and do your homework," said the S'Cotar, applying the compress. "Terra Two, modern history. U.S., Western Europe and the Soviet Union, current history and relationship. Boston, demographics and current history. CIA, order of battle. CIA combat brigade, mission, current deployment and order of battle. Urban Command, Boston, table of organization. Biographies—Major Harrison, Colonel Aldridge, Captain MacKenzie, his sister, Dr. Heather MacKenzie, and Wehrmacht *Hauptmann* Erich zur Linde." The blonde lay back on the bed, eyes on the white-stippled ceiling. "There's also a précis of Major Harrison's doctoral dissertation in there. You might skim it—it's rather good.

"Wake me when you're ready for interrogation." Guan-Sharick's eyes closed.

"Hold it," said John. The blonde's eyes opened. "How long do I have?"

"Major Harrison's booked on tomorrow's eight p.m. flight to Boston—he's being met. There's a four-hour uptime difference between Terra One and Two. You have about twenty-two hours.

"The coffee shop's open all night, mezzanine level. Bill it to your room number. They make a nice Spanish omelet. Do take that bloody parka off first." Guan-Sharick's eyes closed again.

Dropping his coat on the desk chair, John went to the window and drew back the curtain. Their room was at least fifteen stories up. Cars moved along the boulevard below; lights shone from the buildings opposite. It could have been any downtown nightscape in any of a hundred cities.

Turning back to the room, he put the attaché case on the desk and opened it. Taking out the familiar blue-vinyl CIA briefing book, he settled into the armchair, opening with a sigh to the first of some two hundred pages.

"I feel like a centurion being sent across the Rhine," said John. He and the S'Cotar were walking down the Air Canada concourse. Harrison wore the black uniform of an Urban Command major, leather flight bag slung over his shoulder.

"More like Hadrian's Wall," said Guan-Sharick. "A positon of limited retreat." The S'Cotar seemed recovered from its wound, striding briskly beside John, cheeks ruddy with health, golden hair cascading over white cable-knit sweater. Faded jeans, docksiders and powder-blue down jacket completed the image.

"What if I can't take the portal?" asked John as they reached the boarding gate.

"Then you'll be staying on Terra Two—you won't like it. And don't look for help from above. There are no K'Ronarins in this reality—we checked. Where K'Ronar should be is an asteroid belt."

"Must have made you feel good."

"Luck, John." The blonde kissed him quickly on the lips, two lovers parting, then turned and disappeared into the crowd.

Choking back the bile that rose to his throat, John wiped his lips with his jacket cuff, glaring after the S'Cotar.

"Final call for Air Canada, Flight One-Seven to Boston," warned the public address system. "Now boarding, gate fourteen."

John's uniform didn't exempt him from the security check. Luggage and person electronically probed, he hurried across the lounge and down the carpeted ramp, making the plane just as the stewardess reached out to pull the door shut.

The aircraft's interior looked like any wide-bodied Lockheed or Boeing, but the blurb in the seat pocket described it as a Fokker-Hughes 803. About half the passengers were American military, most of them wearing the brown-wool class A's of the U.S. Army. Taking the aisle seat, John fastened the seat belt and closed his eyes, falling asleep as the big jet roared down the runway.

". . . pee." John opened his eyes. The obese young man in the next seat was shaking his arm. "I'm sorry, but could you get up? I've got to pee."

"Sure." Stepping into the aisle, he let the man out; a round, top-heavy form draped in gray Harris tweed that seemed almost to float, balloonlike, toward the lavatory.

A moment later, the uniformed stewardess appeared, pushing a coffee-and-pastry cart. Giving up on sleep, John took coffee and sweet rolls for himself and his absent neighbor.

Returning from the lavatory, the man introduced himself as he ate. "Walt Wenschel," he said, putting down the pastry and extending his hand.

"Harrison. John Harrison." Shaking the hand, John felt the honey frosting transfer from Wenschel's plump fingers to his. "You live in Boston, Walt?" he asked. Freeing his hand, he slid it under the tray table, rubbing his fingers on his napkin.

"Moving there." He smiled. "One-year, tax-free Urban Zone assignment. I'm a research chemist with Patch-Grumbacher. PG's got a small facility inside the Green Line. Pretty safe, great tax break for PG and me.

"You part of the UC garrison, John?" asked Wenschel.

"G2. Intelligence officer."

The chemist nodded absently. "Want your sugar?" He nodded to the two white packets.

"Please, take them."

John closed his eyes as Wenschel stirred four packets of sugar into his cup.

The chemist turned back to him a moment later, set to discourse on Urban Zone tax credits. John was asleep, breathing deeply, chair reclined.

Boston's Saltonstall Airport was a stark, white utilitarian box, all sharp right angles, high ceilings and fluorescents. Much smaller than the Montreal facility, it held few passengers, mostly male, all well-dressed, and soldiers—lots of soldiers—patrolling in pairs or flanking doorways, deadly little machinepistols slung over their shoulders. Walking from the Air Canada gate toward the waiting area, John counted eighteen of the black-uniformed troopers. None were over thirty, and all were white, with the shifting eyes and expressionless faces of professionals. He felt those eyes follow curiously as he crossed the room, black patent-leather boots clip-clopping on alabaster-white tile.

Have a good look, you bastards, he thought. I've come to save you from slimy green bugs and worse.

"Major Harrison."

A short, bald UC officer in black fatigues and combat boots was coming through the waiting area, a .45 holstered to the webbed belt around his waist, two troopers behind him. "Captain Grady, sir," said the older man, saluting. "Garrison adjutant. Welcome to Boston, Major."

"Thank you, Captain," said John, returning the salute. One of the troopers took his bag.

"We have transport waiting," said Grady. "The Hospital's ten minutes by chopper."

"The Hospital?" said John as Grady led the way toward a "Restricted Access" door.

The captain smiled—the thin smile John came to associate with Terra Two. "They built headquarters on a big hill, over in Roxbury. There was a hospital there once."

The chopper looked like a Vietnam-vintage Huey to John, a black-painted troop carrier complete with helmeted door gunner. Engines roaring, it swept them up and out over the harbor, skirting the brightly lit shore for a few minutes, then turning inland as the city lights vanished.

Holding a safety strap, John stood behind the gunner, ignoring the damp, chill wind knifing through the door cracks. Stars above, dark ground below—he saw little else through the closed plexiglass gunport. Once, far off, there was a glimmer of light, quickly gone.

He gripped the safety strap as the helicopter banked suddenly, dropping toward the brilliantly lit helipad that had flared to life below. The helipad topped an unlit, sprawling structure of uncertain shape, its outline twisting into surreal shadow beyond the landing lights. As they touched down, John saw other Huey-like choppers to one side, and smaller, deadly looking gunships to the other.

"The Hospital," said Grady as they touched down.

Outside, the lights went off, dying to a sullen glow for a few seconds, then vanishing. "Don't want to draw fire," explained the UC officer. The gunner swung the door wide as the rotors died.

"Here." Grady handed John a black helmet with an equally dark visor. "You use starhelms in CIB, Major?" he asked, pulling one on.

"Never used one," said John. Imitating Grady, he fastened the helmet and dropped the visor.

The Huey's dark interior resolved into the phosphorescent hues of infrared—Captain Grady and his squad were now a S'Cotarish green.

"Jungle maintenance would be a bitch," said Grady, making the small jump onto the concrete. "We have elevators. Follow me, please."

Troopers patrolled the roof, green-and-red from a distance, green closer up. The walls were sandbagged, topped with razor wire and interspaced by tarpaulined machine guns and mortars. At the far end of the roof, four sleek surface-to-air missiles pointed skyward.

Walking behind Grady, John saw a tier of circling radar dishes, set atop a square concrete mast above the elevators.

An elevator was waiting, dark inside except for the control panel. As the door shut, the light came on. The two men removed their starhelms.

"UC doesn't have any friends in the neighborhood, does it?" said John.

"About as many as CIB has in Mexico," said Grady as the elevator descended. "We're in a war here, too, whatever Frederick wants to call it." The elevator stopped, doors opening silently. "BOQ level," said the captain. "You'll be quartered here."

John squinted as they stepped into the long white hallway. The light was harsh—more fluorescents and latex-painted walls, he saw.

Grady led him along the deserted hallway to a tan door marked "Petersen" by a stenciled placard. "Here you are," said Grady, slipping the placard out of its holder.

"What about Petersen?" asked John as Grady turned on the lights. It was a small room, just a maple bed with matching dresser, black footlocker and a small armchair. The walls were white, the floor brown.

"Captain Petersen was our last G2," said Grady, setting Harrison's bag on the footlocker. "Against orders he went to parley with one of the ganger chiefs. Some of him came back in a poncho.

"Can I do anything else for you?"

"No, thank you."

"Colonel Aldridge expects you at oh-eight hundred tomorrow, Major—level five, turn right. Office with the flags out front. Officers' mess is level three—just follow the herd."

"I will. Thank you, Captain."

"Good night," said Grady, pulling the door shut. His foosteps receded down the hall.

On the whole, thought John, slipping into the too-hard bed, I'd rather be with Zahava, in that little villa near Caesarea.

He dreamed of reporting to the CO's office, where a long line of John Harrisons waited, each dressed as a UC major. An argument broke out as to who was the real John Harrison—an argument growing louder until the office flew open and Guan-Sharick-the-blonde stepped out, wearing a UC colonel's uniform. The S'Cotar looked at them, then threw back its head and laughed and laughed and laughed.

3

It might all have ended much sooner, differently, had Hitler survived Wolfsschanze. Stalin's refusal to ratify the Basel Accord and his subsequent catastrophic use of biological weapons, uniting Germany and the Allies against Russia, would not have occurred had von Stauffenberg's briefcase been less well placed. The war would have been fought to its bleak conclusion, surely no later than mid-1946.

—John Harrison

The Second World War: Key Variables and Consequences *(Unpublished doctoral dissertation, submitted to the Faculty of History, McGill University)*

" 'Reassigned Urban Command by order Lieutenant General Quentin Harwood, Director, Central Ingelligence.' " Colonel Aldridge unhooked his wire-rim bifocals, setting them down on John's file. "You must have stomped some big, hairy toes, Major. You were evidently very much in the general's favor, not long ago. The CIA did send you for your doctorate."

Tall, thin—gaunt, really, thought Harrison—Aldridge

was a man of strange contrasts. The boxy white office was too small for his awards and memorabilia: diplomas (B.A., M.A., Ph.D., all history, all Harvard); a lacquer-framed Chinese calligraphy (Lao-tzu, 6th century B.C.E.), and a faded black-and-white photograph of a mixed group of U.S. Army and Wehrmacht officers beside a blasted T-32 tank. This last was captioned "The Ukraine, Summer, 1949."

"The general didn't care for certain arguments in my dissertation, sir. I was ordered here the day after receiving my diploma. My phone calls to the Agency aren't—weren't returned." John was fairly certain, from the way Guan-Sharick had structured everything, that General Harwood had long been replaced by one of the Illusion Master's transmutes.

"You're in good company, Major," said Aldridge. "Urban Command has few volunteers. Everyone starts fresh here—killers, rapists, deserters, intellectuals. Do your four years well and you'll get a good posting.

"Sit, please."

John sat.

"You know, Major," said Aldridge, leaning back in his chair, "the longer I'm at this job, the more I flirt with Marxism."

Aldridge's face held John: a craggy, weathered New England patriarchal face, seemingly lifted from a John Singleton Copley canvas and set atop the long, black-uniformed body. Colonel's eagles, silver star with oak leaf cluster and the Wehrmacht liaison ribbon lent the final incongruities. James Lowell Munroe Aldridge, soldier, scholar, Yankee; gauleiter of Boston, military governor of what remained of the Athens of America. An iconoclastic Boston Brahmin, Guan-Sharick had said of Aldridge.

"How's that, sir?" asked John.

"I come more and more to believe in economic deter minism, Major," said the colonel. "Why do you think anarchy's triumphed in so many of our cities? Why do you think we're here, an encircled garrison defending the remnants of civilization in the urban enclaves?" Soft, cultured, a hint of steel beneath, his was a voice made for the Socratic method.

There'd been a chilling note in Guan-Sharick's briefing about the consequences of free speech. John answered carefully. "The War, Colonel. We've never recovered from the War."

"The German War, the Japanese War or the Soviet War, Major?" He smiled indulgently. "Or do you mean the endless war preparations, the alleged Armistice that saps our resources, fueling a huge force that may never fully engage?"

John held out a pack of Lucky Strike Greens—the late Major Harrison had done two packs a day.

Aldridge shook his head. "Enjoy."

"Why is a man of your attainments an Urban Corps commandant, Colonel?" asked John, lighting a cigarette. "Many Canadian schools would welcome you."

Aldridge looked into his coffee mug, index finger thoughtfully tapping the faded red coat-of-arms etched into the side. "A man needs more than the pap of intellectualism to hold his life together. Duty is my cement, Major." He looked up. "It keeps me here. That and a sense of place. My people signed the Mayflower Compact, stood at Lexington, broke Pickett's charge, fought at Château-Thierry. Boston bred and buried, the lot."

He reached out, pressing a button.

"Know anything about our situation here?"

"Very little, sir."

"We're essentially a Norman castle, protecting the few from the many."

A young Wehrmacht captain came in, carefully shutting the door. He snapped a brisk salute at Aldridge. "At ease, Erich," said the colonel, returning it sketchily.

"Major John Harrison, Hauptmann Erich zur Linde of the Fourth Reich's Civil Order Unit. Erich's an exchange officer, here for a year. His experience in Southwest Africa is proving most helpful with the gangers."

John took the German's hand, shaken a bit by the field gray uniform and the jackboots—the Fourth Reich had obviously kept the Third's military dress.

"Erich's father and I served under Speidel. We crossed the Malinkoff Line together in '49." Aldridge pointed his pen at the photograph. "He's third from the left." John glanced at the picture. The younger zur Linde might have been his father's twin: tall, broad-shouldered, with the same square jaw and disturbingly resolute expression. Harrison supposed they also shared the same blond hair and blue eyes.

"Erich, I'd like you to give Harrison the tour. He's our new G2, with CIB experience. Let's hope his insight's as useful as yours."

"My pleasure, Colonel," said the young German. His English bore only a trace of Central Europe.

"See you tomorrow, gentlemen. Staff meeting at 0830."

The two saluted and left, leaving Aldridge to his reports.

The tour began over ruins and ended over cocktails. Leading Harrison to the rooftop heliport, zur Linde signed out one of the small recon choppers. Sliding into the pilot's seat, he motioned John to the copilot's seat. They lifted off and swung east.

The Hospital by daylight was a squat rectangle as bleak

as its surroundings: windowless, gray concrete fronted and topped by the sandbags and razor wire. The rubble around it had been cleared from the hill on which it sat, providing a thousand-meter killzone. Landmine furrows puckered the slopes.

Away from headquarters, the ruins stretched for miles. Burnt and shattered tenements, stores, garages, factories, schools, all spilling into weed-choked streets. A forest of broken glass glinted in the noon sun. Once they flew over a rusting tank, its left tread gone, eighty-eight millimeter cannon cranked at an absurd angle. Nothing moved in the whole desolate landscape.

"Roxbury and North Dorchester are like this," said zur Linde, voice clear in John's headset. "Uninhabited since '68. South Boston, Jamaica Plain and Hyde Park are turf—ganger country. Not on our tour. They hit us in the enclaves, we hit them where they live. Otherwise, we stay clear."

Issued in August of '68, Executive Order 1016, the Soweto Order, had mandated photo IDs and travel documents for all residents of the proscribed areas. The day after 1016's promulgation, a fifteen-year-old Chicano in the Los Angeles barrio had Molotoved a UC registration point. Two days later, the cities were burning.

When it ended, air strikes, armor and rolling artillery barrages had laid waste much of urban America. Tens of thousands were dead, with most of the stunned survivors being herded aboard trains bound for resettlement camps in the Southwest. Those who'd hid, staying behind, learned to fight, turning their turf into death zones for the patrols.

Urban Corps had been formed in '70, mandated to restore order. Badly mauled by increasingly formidable gangs, UC had taken to merely patrolling turfs' perimeters, guarding the burbs and enclaves from ganger forays.

Reading it in a briefing book was one thing. Seeing the result was quite another. John sat numbly, watching the passing wasteland.

Coming to the shoreline, zur Linde turned north to the harbor. "Here we are," he said after a moment, bringing the chopper over the waterfront. John had a fleeting glimpse of a jammed marina, old warehouses upgraded to atrium-lobbied condos and chic market-stall boutiques, now filling with the lunch-hour crowd. Skillfully weaving between the tall office buildings, zur Linde set them down atop one of the twin Fed towers overlooking Government Plaza.

"Did you see the marina?" he asked later as they sat sipping Rob Roys in a Back Bay plaza dubbed Cinzano Bay. ("All these *tricolore* table umbrellas make it look like a red-white-and-blue bay.")

John nodded.

"I have a thirty-two foot Morganer moored there. If you'd like to go sailing, just let me know. I can fix you up with a date."

"Does everyone who works here live here?" John pointed his celery stalk at the passersby. Most were well-dressed, with the sleek, easy ways of early affluence. Except for a sharp-looking black woman sitting alone, the few minorities were waiting table.

"Many of the technos do." Zur Linde munched a handful of macadamia nuts. "Some come in from the burbs, but there's only one open road, an expressway with lots of checkpoints. Sometimes it's mortared."

"The gangers have mortars?"

"Not just mortars. Spandaus, claymores, bouncing jujus, TOWs." He eyed a leggy Japanese as she passed, blue silk dress slit almost to the waist, gaily colored boutique bag swinging from her left hand. A piece of war booty from occupied Japan.

The two sat silently, watching that dahlia-blue dress melt into Cinzano Bay.

"Why is UC headquartered between turfs?"

"Stupidity. Pride," said the German, signaling for another round. "They built HQ there years ago, just after '68, thinking all resistance was crushed. When the incoming rockets burst that myth, it was decided—by officers in Frederick, Maryland—to enlarge and harden all the regional headquarters, rather than pulling them back, losing face.

"You've seen the result—the Hospital." He polished off his drink, reaching for the next as it arrived.

"I have this recurring dream," he said, slouching down in the white wrought-iron chair. "The Hospital is being overrun by dusky hordes. It's night. I'm up on the roof, carnage all about me, machinepistol in one hand, knife in the other—Dietrich at the gates of Leningrad.

"Turning to Aldridge, I shout, 'It's hopeless, *Herr Oberst*! Permission to autodestruct?' "

Heads turned toward the two soldiers.

"He just stands there at the parapet, watching wave after wave of gangers surging up the hill in the glare of the arcflares. Finally he says, wonderingly, 'Now I know how Camus must have felt, seeing those ants swarming up from the graves in Algiers.' I always wake up then, soaked, stinking of sweat."

The German's breast pocket beeped. Annoyed, he pulled out a small paper, inserting the privacy jack. "Zur Linde," he said. The tiny crypto light glowed amber.

He nodded after a moment. "Understood. On my way."

Rising, he tucked the device away. "If you'll excuse me, I have to go.

"No, no," he waved John back down. "Finish your drink, have something to eat—the prime rib's very good—order an end cut. You might want to do some shopping over on Newbury. When you're ready, just go across to our Copley substation and requisition a ride back to HQ. They're always choppers on standby. Ciao."

"Ciao."

Zur Linde stepped past the planters walling the red-awninged café and was gone.

John ordered the prime rib and sat nursing his drink, wondering when the resistance would contact him.

"Hey, Major Harrison!" Walt Wenschel was rolling toward his table, clad in a great swath of three-piece pinstripe.

"Hey, Wenschel," said John as the chemist stopped by his table. "All settled in?"

"Sure am—big Beacon Hill town house for free, free maid, free car. God bless America."

"Amen."

"My lunch just came," said Wenschel, pointing three tables away, where a big plate of steaming clam linguine sat. "Care to join me?"

"Thanks, but no. I'm expecting someone." John smiled apologetically. "Take a rain check?"

"A what?"

"Another time?"

"Any time. Good to see you."

Sighing, John lifted his drink, draining the last of the vodka-and-tomato-juice.

A shadow fell across the table. Two UC troopers, corporal and sergeant, stood there, lean, pale kids with hard faces. The corporal had bad acne. John returned their salute.

"Sorry to bother the major, sir," said the sergeant. "May we see your ID?"

John looked around. A second set of troopers was checking the other side of the café. All carried those deadly little machinepistols he'd first seen at the airport. Schmeisser minimacs, he'd learned.

The diners presented their orange IDs with practiced boredom, hardly noticing the soldiers.

"Thank you, sir."

John put his green card away.

The troopers moved on to the next table as John's food arrived. Chewing, he watched the black woman at the corner table smile, open her lavender purse, take out a large-bore derringer and shoot both troopers in the face. The gunshots were still ringing as she leaped the low wall, turning to hurl back a small round something. It rolled clattering beneath a table.

"Grenade!" shouted Wenschel, trying to squeeze under the tiny table.

Taking two quick steps, John dived over the concrete planters as a minimac burped and the grenade exploded.

He rose to pandemonium—dead and dying littered the shattered café, moans and screams mingling with hoarse shouts. Eyes glazed, Walt Wenschel sat with his thick legs splayed in a growing pool of blood. Ignoring the intestines spilling over his cordovans, he daubed with crimson-soaked napkin at the clam sauce and blood ruining his suit.

Sirens rose, drawing near. The woman who'd thrown the grenade lay on the sidewalk, right leg shattered. The gathering crowd watched silently as she began crawling the pavement, blood trailing her, face twisted in agony.

One small, well-formed breast hung from her chic lavender evening dress.

On the crowd's edge, a dapper young man in khaki boating togs pointed to the girl, saying something to the slim, tanned brunette at his side. They chuckled.

Oblivious to all else, bleeding in a dozen places, the UC sergeant walked slowly, painfully to the woman. As he reached her, she sat up and spat, white spittle smearing his crotch.

John saw it before it happened. "Sergeant!" he snapped, voice ringing across the plaza. "Take her into custody!" He scooped up the dead corporal's minimac.

Gleaming black, the NCO's steel-toed boot broke the woman's jaw with a loud snap, slamming her head onto the paving. "Nigger whore," he said, the long burst from his minimac smearing the cobblestones with blood and brain.

John put three bursts into the sergeant, toppling his body across the woman's.

"God bless America," he said, letting the minimac slip to the ground.

Black uniforms filled the plaza. After a while, they took him away.

4

Surely one of history's great ironies: The same day Roosevelt heeded Einstein's admonition to scrap the atomic bomb proposal as "the beginning of the end of humanity," Hitler directed Heisenberg to "proceed with all dispatch on Prometheus."

—*Harrison*, ibid.,
p. 38

It was very hot in the small, white interrogation room. Stinking of sweat, eyes burning, John dropped his head, trying to avoid the burning track lights and the water carafe, just beyond reach on the table.

They'd searched him on the plaza. Taking his ID, a graying captain had put him aboard a helicopter, escorted by two senior NCOs. "You'll have to see the colonel," he said.

As the chopper lifted, John saw them zipping Wenschel into an olive drab body bag.

A silent lieutenant had escorted him from the heliport to Interrogation, deep within the Hospital. Shackling arms and legs to the metal chair, he'd mumbled "SOP" and left. A moment later, the lights had blazed high.

He waited a long time, counting slowly to five thousand and thirty-eight before Aldridge came, squinting through his bifocals in the blazing light. "Erich," he called. "Dim those lights, please."

In the subdued glow, Aldridge took out a key, unfastening the fetters. As John stretched and rubbed his limbs, the colonel poured him a glass of tepid water. He tossed it down. "Thank you, sir," he said hoarsely.

"Send you into town and you kill one of my men, Major." The colonel's voice was mild as he pulled up the other chair and sat facing John. "Why?"

"Because he disobeyed my direct order, sir."

"Not because he brutalized and killed a desperate, beautiful young woman, Major?" His tone was all gentle rebuke.

"She was a beautiful killer, sir. She murdered a whole lot . . ."

"Eleven."

"Eleven innocent people. She certainly wasn't deserving of mercy."

Aldridge nodded, smiling his wistful scholar's smile. "True. And I've found that summary execution has a soothing effect on the genteel classes, far beyond the value of the intelligence we usually extract—it's policy for such incidents."

He rose, pacing for a moment, then turned, big hands gripping the back of his chair. "Your action was ill-advised, Harrison, but I'll support it. Sergeant Hallam disobeyed a direct order. You were within your rights, especially not knowing my policies." He wagged a bony, admonitory finger. "Don't do it again."

"No, sir. Sorry for the trouble. Who was the terrorist, Colonel?"

"Some nameless ganger on courier run. They have friends among our technoaristocracy, Major. Revolution may be fueled by peasant hatred, but it's always directed by middle-class malcontents. Mao, Lenin, Trotsky, Marx, Engels, General Giap, all come to mind.

"Did you know that Giap was briefly a busboy here in Boston, at the old Parker House?"

"No, Colonel, I didn't," said John dully.

"Yes. Trained at Carlton House, London, as a *chef de cuisine*. Imagine eating a five-star French dinner prepared by the scourge of French colonialism."

He stood.

"I'm assigning you as patrol officer for the next week—good way to learn procedure. You'll be working with Erich's special troops. Better get some rest."

John rose, limping painfully as the blood surged back into his feet.

Aldridge helped him to the door, where a barrel-chested sergeant major waited impassively. "Erich's first-rate, Harrison. Watch him and learn."

John and the NCO gone, Aldridge spoke. "What do you think?"

"Maybe," replied zur Linde, voice hollow over the monitor. "Certainly he bears watching.

"His retina scan came back during your chat, sir."

"Positive, of course," said Aldridge.

"Of course."

"Keep on him, Erich, keep on him. If he's Opposition, we'll want to know everything before he's killed. *Klar*?"

"Klar, Herr Oberst."

Turning the field jacket collar against the biting wind, John adjusted his starhelm and stepped cautiously into what had been a street.

This part of the city was utterly destroyed, worked by howitzer fire into story-high mounds of masonry that choked the once broad avenues, ruins the starhelm showed in green-white-red phosphors.

Alone with the night and the northeast wind, John moved through the desolation like a wraith. Overhead, the stars shone cold and hard, undimmed by urban albedo. Here and there the rotting vestiges of shattered elms jutted through.

The gargoyle was an impish green through John's starhelm, grinning viciously atop a great tumble of hand-dressed granite. Further back, a mountain of broken stone towered—marble angels, gargoyles, saintly visages poking out of the wreckage. He halted by a half-buried brass cross and waited.

Sensing a presence, John whirled, finger curling around the minimac's trigger.

A boy stood there. A small, thin boy in worn corduroys, ragwool sweater, sneakers and a pair of nitespecs. John's weapon didn't waver. "You have something for me?" he asked softly.

The boy extended a torn piece of cloth. Fishing in his jacket pocket with his free hand, John withdrew an equally torn patch. Together they formed a compass rose with bayonet-fixed rifles, rampant. "OK," John nodded as each repocketed his half. "What's your name?" he asked, lowering the minimac.

Turning noiselessly, the boy disappeared behind the gargoyle-topped mound. Following, John saw the hole yawning amid the rubble, a great slab of stone looming to one side of it. Monkey-agile, the boy scuttled down metal rungs set in the shaft's concrete. With a wary glance at the thick slab, John followed.

The shaft dropped a hundred yards, opening onto a large

tunnel. The rungs ended in a tiled wall, just above one of a set of railway tracks. The only illumination was in infrared.

The boy did something to one of the cracked wall tiles. High above, the slab swung silently down, sealing the shaft with a faint hiss. Without a backward glance, John's guide set off down the tunnel.

They walked a long time, the crunch of their feet in the gravel sending the big sewer rats scampering, squealing in protest. Once they forded a rushing stream where it'd washed out the railbed, collapsing a section of wall. A graceful, frail gazelle, the boy leaped nimbly along a row of eroded, half-submerged cinder blocks, gaining the opposite bank with dry feet. Burdened by uniform, starhelm, equipment belt and weapon, John plowed through the cold, tugging water.

His guide led on through a final series of cross tunnels, then up a ladder identical to the first, emerging from behind a false bookcase into a library: deep burgundy carpet, mahogany paneling that reached up to the high ceiling, ornate kerosene lamps, red-leather sofa with matching armchairs and a crackling fire in the fieldstone hearth. A balcony with more books girdled the room, breached by a spiral metal staircase.

The ganger came from the other side of the fireplace, silken red hair cascading over the shoulders of her black UC battlejacket, a chunky, stainless-steel magnum holstered at her slender waist. Extending John a crisp, dry hand, she sized him up with cool, green eyes. "Welcome to Viper Command, Major Harrison. I'm Heather MacKenzie, Ian's sister."

The Heather MacKenzie in his briefing should have been in a physics lab on the West Coast.

"Heather," he smiled, taking her hand. His eyes flicked to her coiled-rattler shoulder badge. "Where's Ian?"

Ignoring his questions, she turned to the boy. ''Jorge, Tomas left your supper upstairs.'' She pointed to the balcony. ''We got some chocolate bars in today.''

Face brightening, Jorge bounded up the stairs.

Heather watched him go, then turned back to John. ''He hasn't spoken since his mother was killed in a skirmish, three years ago,'' she said quietly, shaking her head. ''If we only had somewhere decent to send him.

''Sit down, John, please,'' she said, indicating one of the chesterfield chairs flanking the hearth. They sat.

''Any trouble getting to St. Mark's?''

''No,'' he said. ''I found your note and half a CIB shoulderbadge yesterday, in my boot.'' The note, disintegrating after he'd read it, gave only a time and place. ''I checked out a recon chopper, landed it near St. Mark's and met Jorge.''

''And how are you going to explain all that to Aldridge?''

He shrugged. ''A G2 has to have some autonomy. Engine trouble forced me down near turf. I repaired it and returned. I've arranged for engine trouble if they look.''

''They'll look,'' she said.

''Where is Ian, Heather? And why aren't you back at Berkeley?''

''My brother's dead,'' she said.

John shook his head. ''How?''

''We were scouting Maximus, as requested. We landed in a small valley about a mile from its outer perimeter . . .''

They'd left their machines—salvaged UC choppers—and moved out on foot: Ian, Heather and a few Vipers. The gangers were in their late teens, early twenties, a mixed group of blacks, Hispanics, Orientals and white ethnics. All were platoon leaders, picked and trained by Ian over the past two years, bloodied in skirmishes with Aldridge's troopers. They were the nucleus of the guerrilla army Ian had molded from a thousand turf-seasoned gangers, part of the "dusky horde" troubling zur Linde's sleep.

Seen through binoculars from the brush, Maximus conveyed a seedy air of neglect: a weathered chain-link fence and a gate, the fence sagging away into the forest, rusty chain and padlock securing the gate. There was no guard, just a peeling sign: "U.S. GOVERNMENT PROPERTY—KEEP OUT." Rising from behind the gate, a narrow dirt road snaked up the mountain, twisting from sight around a bend. Weeds flourished between the road's shallow ruts.

Ian passed the big Zweiss 12x50s to his sister. She looked, shook her head and handed them back. "You're thinking of *attacking* that? Why not just wait for a storm to blow it over?"

Ian laughed, looking back at Maximus. He was a big, lantern-jawed man, with his sister's red hair and their mother's green eyes. "Watch," he said, pointing to a sparrow alighting on the fence. Zap! Heather gasped as the bird vanished in a blue flash. Gray smoke rose from a misshapen lump beneath the wire.

"Can't that be shorted?" she asked uncertainly.

"Sure," he nodded. "Once you get through the mines. Then there's the minefield on the other side. And the road's mined too, probably rigged for command detonation. Surviving all that—and we could, 'cause the Outfit's provided maps—at the top there's a battalion of rent-a-Brits: Scots Guards under a brigadier. They're in a heavily fortified position with light artillery. Only after getting past them would we reach the research facility, a brutish agglomeration of concrete and glass—all sharp edges—with staff quarters, labs, power plant, barracks, admin building."

"I see," she said. "But you still haven't told me the

reason for all this. Or why you dragged me all the way across the country to be here.''

''Two reasons. The people I work for asked for my evaluation of Maximus's defenses. As these same people also provide the Vipers with weapons, materials and training,'' he pointed to himself, ''I agreed.'' Leaning closer, he dropped his voice. ''I've never heard Angel, my controller, sound scared. But he's scared about Maximus. Something up there's frightened the bejesus out of him.''

''As for the other reason . . . Julio!''

The young platoon leader scampered over. ''Tell my sister what you told me, please.''

During the War, the government had brought levies of cane workers from Puerto Rico to man the vital mainland factories. With thousands of Americans dying every week on the Russian steppes, the draft had stripped the cities of all but the youngest, the oldest and the sickest. It was hoped that the Hispanics would prove docile, tolerating the substandard wages and deteriorating living conditions, the 108-hour work weeks. Many had. But their children, those who survived '68, hadn't.

''Until last year,'' said Julio in careful, faintly accented English, ''Maximus used laborers and cooks from fringe burbs near turf, rotating them every three months. My cousin Raoul was part of a construction crew. At least, that's what they told him when he was hired.'' The dead UC trooper's field jacket was too large for Julio's small frame. Rocking slightly on his heels, he hugged himself for warmth. ''He came home a month overdue. He was old. Old.'' He shook his head, awed by the memory. ''My age, but he looked eighty. Shaking, gnarled hands, wrinkled face. And his mind . . .''

''Senile?'' prompted Heather.

''He could barely sign the monthly disability check.''

"Disability check?" Social insurance in America had died young. Social security had been converted to war tax in the dark months of '48 and never restored after the fighting died in '53.

Julio nodded. "Two hundred a month. We moved to West Roxbury, bought a trailer." Cleared of rubble, West Roxbury had no gangers and enjoyed nominal social services. Trees and playgrounds dotted the miles of trailer "parks" —refurbished war surplus units sold and financed for a handsome profit by government licensed brokers to the minorities and ethnics working the industrialized inner burbs.

"How is Raoul?" asked Heather.

"Dead," he said flatly. "Heart failure, arteriosclerosis."

"If we could access UC's data base, we'd know what they're doing up there," said Ian.

"Angel told you nothing?" asked Heather.

"Indirectly he did," Ian smiled wryly. "He asked me if I thought the Berkeley physics department could spare you for a few months. I suggested someone from the Outfit. He said that was 'very tenuous ground,' and changed the subject."

"What sort of physics are they doing up there?" she wondered.

"If we go in, maybe you can tell us." He and Julio rose, giving her a hand up. "But Angel was very firm about wanting a theoretical physicist, not a bomb guy from Livermore."

"Odd," she said, half to herself. "Now what?"

"Julio and I are going to make a photorecon in the Bell. We did it two months ago, but Angel wants fresh pics." The Bell was the fastest of their choppers, the only one with cameras. "Coming up under their radar, we'll be gone before they can react. But the rest of you get clear first, just in case."

Hiking back to the valley, all but Ian and Julio headed

southeast in the big Hueys. After ten minutes, the two took the Bell over the fence at full throttle, following the road up the hill.

Their first pass held no surprises: the same cold architecture as before, no discernible movement anywhere. It was after their second pass, just turning for home, that the Messerschmitt dropped on them from the clouds. Ian tried for the treeline, but the ME's missiles were faster.

Heather didn't see the Bell go down—they were too far away. The orange blip disappearing from her radar told all. Tears streaming unnoticed down her face, she sent the Huey even lower, almost brushing the treetops. Winding out of the Green Mountains and into New Hampshire, she took them home.

It was a setup, John saw. A setup engineered by Guan-Sharick to attract attention to Shalan-Actal's base—to Maximus.

"When did this happen?"

"Yesterday. I sent you the note as soon as we got back."

"That year in CIB, we must have saved each other's lives a dozen times down in that green hell. We were closer than most brothers. He was very proud of you—his sister the scientist."

All true, in its way, thought John. Harrison and MacKenzie had been close.

"You'll have to assume they took either Ian or Julio alive and are interrogating them," he said, collecting his thoughts. "You'd better evacuate."

"We're finishing that up now," she said, matching his brisk tone. "I gave the order last night. The final group leaves within the hour."

"You're staying with the Vipers?"

"Someone has to be in charge, till the Outfit sends another officer. None of the kids are ready. I think I've earned their respect. I'm not as good as Ian, but I put in my four years as a Ranger captain."

"I see," he said, upping his estimate of her age.

"Why are you here?"

This is it, he thought. Fail now, you might as well have stayed home.

"It's been decided to take Maximus," he said. "I'm to extract the Maximus data base from UC's computer—it may be of use. And I'm to help in the attack."

"I see," she said, noncommittal. "Did you know Hochmeister's in the area?"

Hochmeister, Hochmeister. Grand master in German. There was something in the briefing book. He groped desperately for it. Gray. Feldgrau. Wehrmacht. Abwehr. Of course.

"The Gray Admiral? The former Abwehr head?"

"The same," she said, nodding. "Called in by Alliance Intelligence—Kassel's crew. Something to do with Maximus. Nothing firm—just something Ian heard from an old CIB buddy on the last weapons run."

"No one knows what he looks like, do they?"

"No. He's the man without a face. The last photo of him was taken in the forties. The day after *Wolfsschanze,* he somehow got past a brigade of Waffen SS and calmly put a bullet through Himmler's head."

"Thus ending effective resistance to the Putsch," he nodded. "He must be in his sixties."

"Easily. God!" She jumped up. "I almost forgot, and it sounds like you'll need it." Going to the big Governor Winthrop, she pulled open a drawer. Extracting an oblong black plastic case, she handed it to John. "Nixdorf-IBM

7000 series authenticator. Insert it into the authorizer port of UC's computer, and the machine will answer its own challenge."

"You're sure?" he asked dubiously, turning the small device over in his hands.

"No." She smiled for the first time. Thin, but still a smile. "Don't worry, though. They'll give the next poor bastard something better."

"Comforting." He pocketed the device. "OK, if you'll have someone lead me back to St. Mark's from here . . . Where, by the way, is here?"

"Can't do any harm now. This is the Barcroft Estate in Brookline, abandoned in '68, carefully unbooby-trapped and restored by the Vipers. You arrived via the old Green Line subway tunnel, which in turn accesses part of the Underground Railroad, circa 1855. We built the entrances and connectors."

"One more thing." He related the story of Cinzano Bay. "One of yours?"

She nodded, grim-faced. "Lotte. She was to meet someone with information on Maximus. Maybe she was set up, maybe she was just unlucky. We'll probably never know."

"But why the grenade?" John asked. "A lot of innocent people died." Neither saw the bookcase swing wide.

"Innocent?" she snapped, eyes blazing. "The technos get tax-free income, hazard pay, cheap servants and subsidized housing to live here as colonialists. They know the risks. The grenade's our answer to Aldridge's summary justice." Their eyes locked. "We don't go gentle into that good night, Major Harrison."

"But go you shall," came a low voice from behind. "Don't even think of it, Major," zur Linde said as Harrison's eyes went to the distant sofa and his weapon. Stepping into the library, minimac leveled, the German spoke into his starhelm. "Septime to Crispin.

"I couldn't, Colonel," he said to the voice complaining in his ear. "I was in a tunnel. Please respond the alert company on this vector, sir. I'm in a nest of Vipers."

Not for the first time, it struck Harrison how dehumanizing UC battledress was: black uniform, black gloves, black boots, black starhelm. Even the machinepistol was black. Hard to believe anything human existed within that darkness—certainly not a man with a weakness for Oriental women who'd invited him sailing. "May we put our hands down, *Herr Hauptmann*?" he asked.

"Red scum. Keep them up."

"Is that what you think we are, Erich?" John lowered his hands. "How can I convince you . . ."

"Hands back up, Major," said the German coldly, "or you lose a kneecap." John complied.

"Don't be a silly bitch," said zur Linde, centering the muzzle on Heather. Her hands went back up, away from the magnum.

"Put the cannon on the sofa, please. Thumb and forefinger." The big pistol bounced onto a cushion. "Thank you."

He turned his back to John. "We're of an age, Harrison, you and I. Your biography says your father died at Second Stalingrad. True?"

Captain Tristram Malory Harrison had been killed at Chosen Reservoir. "Not Stalingrad," said John. "A different battle."

"My father died at Second Stalingrad," said zur Linde, "when Das Reich's Division saved your Third Armored. How could you betray what both died for?" It bothered him, you could tell from his voice.

"I'm here to save, not to betray, Erich. You're counter-intelligence, aren't you? Abwehr?"

Zur Linde nodded curtly. "The best."

The great unabridged dictionary, largest made by the Merriam poeple, dropped like a stone from the balcony, its binding cracking as it struck zur Linde's starhelm, toppling him. Rolling to his feet in a blur of motion, his hand streaked for his pistol, only to freeze when he saw the minimac's unwavering muzzle.

"You know the drill, Erich," said Harrison. "Toss the PPK." Heather scooped up both weapons. "Now sit." Zur Linde sat.

"Well done, Jorge," Heather called, looking up at the small brown face bearing over the bannister. He bounded down the stairs to a warm hug from Heather.

Walking to the door she called, "Chin Lee! We have a prisoner!"

A squad of Vipers came at the run, led by a big, tough-looking Chinese with an old knife scar puckering the length of his right cheek.

"Starhelm, Erich," demanded Harrison, hand outstretched. When the Abwehr officer didn't move, Heather said, "Chin Lee."

Drawing a long-bladed ranger knife, the platoon leader stepped purposefully toward zur Linde. Fingers flying, the German unfastened the helmet and handed it to Harrison, scowling.

"Nice to see your pretty face again," said John. Chin Lee sighed and put the knife away.

Touching the starhelm's bottom rim, Harrison flipped the commswitch off.

"Think they had time to vector in?" asked Heather.

Harrison nodded.

"Chin, get everyone together," ordered Heather. "There's a strike force on the way." He ran from the room, shouting orders.

Walking to a bookcase, Heather removed a leather-bound copy of Robert Louis Stevenson's *Infernal Machine,* then threw a small, red switch behind it. She carefully returned the book to its niche. "In forty minutes, the house will blow up," she said. Pulling a big backpack from under the desk, she shrugged her way into it. "Five minutes later, land mines in the lawn will detonate—take out their second wave."

In a few minutes, Vipers laden with packs and weapons were filing through the library and into the tunnel.

"I'll show you to the cathedral, John." Heather picked up zur Linde's starhelm as Chin Lee took the German away.

"You're not going to . . ." Harrison said, staring after the Abwehr officer.

"No." She strapped on the starhelm. "Not that he doesn't deserve it. We'll give him a dose of memscrub—this day will vanish from his life.

"The trick," she added, voice muffled by the helmet, "is to defeat the enemy without becoming him."

"You can believe that, yet hit that reaction force?"

"It's not excessive," she said as he fastened on his own starhelm. "There's too much here we haven't had time to destroy. Also, the carnage will slow them, buy us time. We're going to be exposed for about two hours, relatively defenseless. This'll pull in every chopper UC has."

"Where are you going?" he asked as they stepped into the passageway.

"Warren's Island, in the inner harbor. There's an old

fort there.'' She swung the bookcase shut. ''Not quite what we've become used to, but habitable.''

They looked up at the roar of choppers coming in low and fast. ''UC's about to find out just how hot a hot LZ can be,'' said Heather coldly. ''Let's go.''

5

Most international opinion was won, and any support for a countercoup dissipated, by the General Staff's calculated "discovery" of the death camps four days after the Putsch. The footage of Guderian's panzers smashing through the gates of Dachau, the horrified reactions of the soldiers to the grisly scene inside, sold the world on "the return of the Germany of Goethe, Schiller and Beethoven." Only the Russians didn't buy it. The war in the East ground on.

—*Harrison,* ibid.,
p. 74

Operations was quiet when John arrived—a paunchy, graying warrant officer, four young techs and a few guards. Up on the big board, Boston was a green island, surrounded by a line of red. Inside the green, another line of red divided three-quarters of the city from the remainder—turf. The yellow blip of an occasional plane or ship was the only movement.

John waved the warrant officer back to his chair. "It's

OK, Mr. Blackstone, just familiarizing myself with Operations.

"The red is what?" he asked, pointing up at the board.

"Perimeter sensors, Major."

A solid crimson ribbon sat alone above the warrant officer's right pocket: the First Day Ribbon. John wondered what irony had let Blackstone survive the Japan Invasion only to end up in UC.

"We monitor all activity along that perimeter, sir. We respond on anything BOSCO flags suspicious."

"BOSCO?"

"Boston Base Operations Command and Control." His hand swept the wall and its color graphics. "BOSCO—actually, the whole 7117 series—was designed for UC by Nixdorf-IBM."

"And you watch for . . . ?"

"Gangers raiding, gangersymps bringing in supplies and weapons. Anything out of the ordinary. We weigh the threat and react intelligently—a strategy of selective response."

The cities are lost, Guan-Sharick had said. Everyone knows it, but no one may speak of it. Policy is that they're not lost. Policy brings in the technos, to tax-free government R&D enclaves. Policy maintains a garrison to protect them. It's all a fragile artifice. The cities are lost. Those garrisons are penal brigades, badly understrength, living on tactical myths and Benzedrine. Let the gangs attack as one, Urban Command and the techno enclaves would vanish, a bloody bit of bad policy.

"Selective response," said John. "Interesting."

"Ah! A situation." Blackstone's eyes focused on the wall. "Excuse me."

John saw it then, the flashing red cross moving across the red line, into the green.

Who says there's no God? he thought as Operations came to life, technicians busy, guards turning to watch. Forgotten, John slipped around into the deserted computer area. Shielded by gray equipment banks, he inserted the authenticator into the slot below the big red arrow.

The CRT came on, amber letters flashing across the screen. SELECT VOICE OR SCREEN, it said.

Typing SCREEN, he homed the cursor.

SELECT MODALITY preceded a menu of options.

32, he responded, keying for RESTRICTED ACCESS.

? asked BOSCO, giving no clue.

MAXIMUS, typed John.

DOPPLEGANGER, challenged the machine.

Palms sweating, John waited for the alarm klaxon. If Heather's gift didn't work, BOSCO would scream for help.

LILITH, BOSCO said, duped into answering its own challenge. SELECT PROJECT FILE.

He had it all in five minutes, neatly transferred to a microfiche, pocketing it as a smiling Blackstone found him.

"Major Harrison, you missed a neat intercept," he said happily. "We zapped a dozen gangers, maybe survivors of our raid on Viper HQ. We'll know more after a G2 workup."

"We were the ones with survivors in that action," said John as the warrant officer saw him to the door. "Second battalion had sixty-two percent casualties and lost ten choppers. There were no ganger casualties. Jack Grady says the LZ smelled like a crematorium on a warm August night."

"That rabble couldn't . . ."

"They're very well organized rabble." John stepped past the guards and into the white corridor. "They fight for their lives, their homes, their families. What are we fighting for, Blackstone? Our pensions?''

''We're fighting for America,'' said the warrant officer, puzzled.

''Of course,'' said John. ''Good night.''

Your hours here are numbered, boy, thought John. Shooting up the help, thinking out loud, stealing from the cookie jar. Aldridge's going to feed you to his larks.

Microfiche still warm in his pocket, he went up to his quarters.

Alone in the room, he switched the film to the hollow heel of his right boot, then searched his pockets for the authenticator.

He'd been reaching for the authenticator. Blackstone's footfalls had alerted him. Tucking the fiche into his shirt pocket, he'd turned . . .

The authenticator was still in BOSCO's port, bloody red arrow pointing to it like a finger of doom.

How long till someone found it, saw that it wasn't standard?

Grabbing minimac and starhelm, he ran from the room and up the stairs toward the heliport, fourteen levels above. Elevators could be stopped, riders gassed.

''We have a situation, sir,'' said zur Linde, unknowingly parroting Blackstone's remark of a few minutes ago.

''Let's have it.''

Despite the hour, the colonel was alert. He prided himself on his Napoleonic courage, that ability to respond agilely to a crisis at any hour.

''Harrison bypassed BOSCO's authentication system.'' Phone to his ear, the German watched as two of his specials led a trembling Blackstone from Operations. The warrant officer's only familiarity with Napoleonic courage was a cognac of like name.

"He outprinted the entire Site Y file onto microfiche, then cleverly left his authenticator in the computer." Zur Linde thoughtfully hefted the thin device. "It would help to know who made it."

Yesterday was a hole in zur Linde's life. Found unconscious on the red line, his last memory was of a winking blue light in the Bell's cockpit as he'd kept a delicate distance between himself and Harrison's recon chopper. Then nothing till he'd opened his eyes in Dispensary.

"Impotent, treasonous old men," said Aldridge. "Only with competent agents are they dangerous. From your condition yesterday, Erich, I suspect Major Harrison is such a prosthesis. Where is he now?"

Something cold in Aldridge's voice made zur Linde hesitate.

"Well?"

"We don't know, sir," he said carefully. "He hasn't used his ID to access any level since returning to the BOQ from Operations. And he's no longer on the BOQ level."

"Then he's using the stairs. Security condition red—full alert."

"Yes, sir."

"Take him alive if possible—I'd like him drained by Interrogation. But stop him. That file mustn't leave here."

Slipping his ID to open the stairtop door to the heliport, John knew he signaled his presence to BOSCO.

The nearest sentries saluted him as he quick-trotted to the first chopper, a deadly Bushmaster-Fokker gunship. "Emergency!" he shouted. "Colonel's orders!"

The alert klaxon only moved the guards out of his way

faster, until its purpose sounded over their radios. They came for him as he slid into the chopper.

Starting the engine was no problem, but it took him a long moment to puzzle out the ordnance control. The first sentries were less than ten yards away when he swiveled the port gatling guns, firing high.

Scattering, the troopers fired back, slugs pinging off the duraplast armor as reinforcements charged off the elevators. Firing low and continuously, John revved the engine, pulling the Bushmaster up at a sharp right angle, then swept back, rocketing the heliport with a full rack of red-tipped incendiaries.

"Impressive," said Aldridge, watching on an Operations monitor: choppers exploding, fuel from each triggering the next, their tracers and rockets tearing through the troopers trying to fight the flames.

The floor rumbled as shock waves ripped through the building. The monitors flickered and died.

"Can't we take that renegade's chopper out?" Zur Linde turned to the AirDef tech.

"Negative." The sergeant nodded at a small screen, dancing with green fuzz. "Fire's knocked out all the radar. Arm those SAMs and they'll blow—they're heat seekers."

"Jettison those Hauzahns, Erich," ordered Aldridge, "before they chew our top off."

"Do it," said zur Linde. The great building shook as missile after unarmed missile tore away, roaring blindly into the sky.

The watch officer turned to zur Linde. "Fire's out of control, sir. Captain Grady reports the napalm's about to go. He's ordered fireguard down two levels. And all radio communication's out."

"Why is there napalm in the heliport, Erich?" Aldridge

fixed the German with his iciest glare. More explosions shook the room.

"We were going to use it this afternoon, sir. I wanted to try a technique perfected against the Bantu. It . . ."

Aldridge turned to the watch officer. "Evacuation, Bravo Plan. Alert all sections. And phone Copley and Harbor substations—assuming the underground lines are intact. Advise our situation, order up choppers."

"Erich, get . . ." The door slid open, admitting a begrimed Captain Grady, uniform singed. "Useless, Colonel," he coughed. "Top two levels are gone. It'll be here in thirty, forty minutes."

"Nothing you could do, Jack," said Aldridge, laying a hand on Grady's shoulder. "Get your men down to motorpool level. We'll deploy into the killzone and await the choppers."

"Colonel." The watch officer set the securfone down. "Major Sardon reports a general assault across the red line. They started probing as soon as they saw our smoke. BOSCO's blind and the gangers know it.

"The major's thrown a defense perimeter around the techno enclaves. He thinks he can hold until dark—if he keeps all his choppers."

A pall settled over the room.

Aldridge slowly polished his bifocals, then wrapped them back around his long ears. "Then we'll have to march out and face the enemy, just like real soldiers."

"That's five miles through ganger turf, Colonel," said Grady.

"Thank you, Jack. You may recall that zur Linde and I are the only ones who have ever taken a foot patrol through any part of ganger turf."

A throat cleared.

"We have armor, gentlemen. The gangers don't."

"They've got good antitank weapons, Colonel. And the terrain favors them."

Aldridge shrugged. "You can fight beside me, like men, or die here like cattle. Your choice." He walked to the door, then turned.

"Erich, get everyone down to the motorpool. Full combat uniform. Get the armor ready to roll. Deactivate the minefields. I'll join you in fifteen minutes."

Fort Todd's five granite bastions commanded Boston's inner harbor. Her rusting cannon had been silent over a century when John's chopper passed the weathered parapet, setting down on the island's weed-choked parade ground.

Running from the durable stone headquarters, Heather reached the gunship as John cut the engine and jumped out, triumphantly waving the microfiche.

"Idiot!" she shrieked, delicate high-boned cheeks red with fury. "Did you start that?" She stabbed a finger toward the distant city.

Confused, John turned, looking to where a great column of thick, black smoke billowed out over the harbor. "Sure I did! If I hadn't hit their heliport, we wouldn't have this." He handed her the Maximus fiche.

"I'd sacrifice this to stop what you've set in motion." Calming, she led him back toward the headquarters building.

"And that is?"

"A sweep. A fully bloody air and armor sweep of turf." They stepped inside.

Decades of water had stained the walls mucous-yellow, dropping great chunks of moldy plaster down onto the warped, broad-beamed floor. Heather perched atop a battered gray-metal desk. "Tell me about it," she said, ankle-crossed legs swinging over the edge.

"OK," she said when he'd finished, "let's make the best of it. If we assault Maximus, we'll do it during the sweep. It'll pull both New England divisions into Boston."

"If?" asked John, raising an eyebrow. "You mean when, don't you, Heather?"

Leaving the desk, she rummaged through an equipment stack, extracting a compact metal case. "We work for you, John. You don't own us." She plugged the case into one of the generator leads snaking the floor. "Ian was a dedicated CIA officer. He saw the Outfit as a counterforce to a lot that's wrong with this society—endless warfare here and abroad, pervasive German influence. He thought maybe, just maybe, the Agency could help bring us back from the broken, soulless nation we've become."

Unfolded on the desktop, the case became a microfilm viewer. She turned it on, slipping in the film.

"What are you telling me, Heather?"

She looked up from the machine. "I'm telling you I'm not taking my kids up against that horror in the mountains just because I'm told to. Life is too short and hard here. I'm not making it any shorter or harder without damn good reason."

How about two universes? he wanted to say. Logic, he thought. Good old half-step, Aristotelian logic.

"What if the microfilm shows Maximus to be a clear and deadly danger to us all, Heather? Then will you support my mission?"

"Sure." She turned back to the viewer. "Let's see if there's 'clear and deadly danger.' "

Her slim fingers made a delicate adjustment to the viewer, transforming a blurred diagram into a sharp-featured map of Maximus. "You realize with BOSCO down, UC's sensor ring's gone. They'll have to deploy every chopper, every company to try and protect the technos. Aldridge and his thugs may have to fight their way through turf. God! I'd love to see that!"

"We can't stay here much longer, Colonel," said zur Linde, worriedly eyeing the smoke wafting into the cavernous motorpool.

Aldridge nodded, pacing slowly in front of the four assembled companies, drawn up at parade rest. He glanced at his watch. "We might have ten minutes before the roof drops on us, Erich. If I don't get a recon report from Copley in five minutes, we roll blind." He stopped pacing. "Best mount up."

Zur Linde saluted, then executed a textbook about-face. "Company commanders, move your men into the vehicles," he ordered. No one needed any encouragement, scrambling into the APCs and tanks.

Zur Linde turned back to Aldridge. "What about the detainees, Colonel?"

Two levels below were some three hundred prisoners, the unfortunate Mr. Blackstone among them. Most were being held for interrogation or pending transfer to work camps.

The colonel shrugged, hopefully jiggling his handset. Nothing. "Killed tragically in the fire."

He looked up. "On second thought, have someone get Blackstone out and give him a weapon. He can take his chances with the rest of us. Any man who survived that hell at Shimoda doesn't deserve to die like a smoked rat." He lifted the handset as the German gave the necessary orders.

"Copley. Aldridge. Get me Major Sardon." In a minute he was listening without expression to the Copley commander. "I see, Terry. No, no, I understand. Do what you can. We'll get out.

"Sardon's being forced back, Erich. Most of our choppers are down. It's *Der Tag*, my friend. Let's roll."

Grim faced, zur Linde ran for his own tank as Aldridge headed for the lead M80, scrambling spryly up its side and down into the turret. Thick, toxic smoke was pouring through the ceiling vents into the motorpool.

Over a hundred armored vehicles coughed to life as the great blast doors atop the ramp swung open. Burning debris showered the column as it gunned up and out, thundering over the dead mines.

Behind them, the roof and upper stories crashed down in slow, booming majesty, a story at a time. The prisoners heard the fiery avalanche coming an eternal moment before it struck. Some screamed, some prayed, some wet themselves—all died. The column snaked down the hill and into the morning.

Heather looked up from the microviewer. "They're mad. Stark, raving mad." She shook her head, still not believing.

"Know anything about quantum mechanics?"

"Black holes, alternate universes, stuff like that?"

She nodded.

John shook his head. "Just a dumb spook."

"Yeah, with a Ph.D. in history. Listen, Professor Spook, there's no law of physics mandating the singularity of time or space. And there's some evidence, for those who care to see it, of an infinite series of alternate universes, some alien beyond our comprehension, others possibly different from our own only by my not having said 'possibly.' And if these alternate realities exist, they can be reached, given the right technology."

John nodded. "Based on this," he tapped the viewer, "you think Maximus is a gateway from an alternate reality?"

"Maybe. It's not a natural manifestation. It just appeared,

two years ago. A research facility was promptly constructed around it. And judging from the file reports, the crew up there still have no idea what it is—this despite early use of human subjects to probe the phenomenon.

"I mean, really, look at these reports. Much initial excitement, everyone wanting a crack at it, then nothing."

"More. The reports are almost the same after the first year. Verbatim."

Checking, she saw he was right. Maximus's staff kept sending the same negative reports, with only superficial changes in text. "Something's very wrong up there," she said. "It's almost as though the phenomenon's manipulating the experiment."

Their eyes met. "Then the Vipers *will* support my mission, Dr. MacKenzie?"

"Yes, Major Harrison. Once the situation in the city becomes clear."

The UC battalion's route of march took it through the heart of Lord's turf. Bull watched from a tenement roof as the column wound through Roxbury's broken streets.

Midmorning usually found kids playing in the rusting junk cars, women trudging to and from water and food points. Not today. The delapidated three-decker houses were hushed, the streets empty. Nothing moved, no dogs barked. Even the rats were still, hiding from the rising throb of powerful engines, the crunch of broken glass under clanking treads.

"Shee-it. Only fifty tanks, rest APCs," said Bull's lieutenant, called Chop for his karate-calloused hands. "We can wipe those mothers." Hundreds of gangers paralleled the convoy, well-ordered platoons skillfully leapfrogging through alleys and over rubble.

Bull shook his head. A big man, rippling with muscle,

he'd come to Roxbury from Chicago's South Side three years before. His finely honed street smarts and instinctive grasp of infantry tactics had soon put him at the head of the Lords. Over the top of his flak vest, gold chains glinted against rich ebony skin.

"They got trouble." He nodded at the column, nearing their camouflaged bunker. "Hit 'em," his voice rumbled, "then two, maybe three days, gonna be a sweep—wipe a few more miles an' couple thousand niggers to make an ex-sam-ple.

"Pass 'em," he ordered.

Zur Linde radioed to Aldridge, "Ground sensors show hostiles all around us, Colonel. About five hundred, armed with TOWs and automatic weapons."

"If they haven't opened up yet, Erich, they probably won't," said Aldridge. "But we can't take that chance. All strategy's predicated on enemy capability, not perceived intent. Kill them."

"Acknowledged."

Zur Linde switched to the command channel. "Manatee Leader to Manatee Pack. Execute Golf Alpha Sierra."

"What they doin'?" asked Chop, suspiciously eyeing the tanks as they slowed, turrets swinging, cannon cranking too high to hit the gangers.

Bull grabbed the radio. "The tanks! Hit 'em!"

The first shells burst overhead with a dull *whump,* vomiting greasy, grayish-yellow clouds that drifted gently down.

Rocket volleys answered from all sides, some hitting just so, where turret met body. Twelve of the M80s went up, volatile chemical munitions flaming blue, melting metal and turning men to ash. There was no second volley.

Shrouded in the oily, yellow pall, the column rolled slowly through Roxbury, firing methodically, cloaking itself in the slimy mist.

Seeping into cellars, attics, rough-hewn bunkers, the gas brought ethereal calm to young and old, male and female, animal and human. There'd be no rat problem for a while.

Bull carried Chop well away from the death zone, blood from the smaller man's orifices trickling unnoticed down his flak jacket and clothes. "Hey, man," he said, gently lowering his friend to the floor of the old elementary school, now an impromptu mortuary-hospital. Chop tried to speak, but managed only a rasping, wet gurgle. Shouting for a medic, Bull stood, speaking into the radio. "This Bull. What's it like?"

It was bad. At least three hundred gangers dead, no one yet knew how many civilians. "Old folks, kids, dogs," reported a woman dully. "We're goin' in as it clears, doin' what we can.

"You gonna let 'em get 'way with this, Bull?" she demanded, tone suddenly vibrant with hate.

"No way," he said softly. "Put out a call on the Viper channel. Get me Heather Mac."

Moving at the same careful pace, the convoy reached a deserted Copley Square at twilight, halting before the Italianate masterpiece that was the Boston Public Library. The cobblestone square should have been aflow with the early evening theater crowd, the cafés crowded.

Not tonight. The rattle of machine-gun fire had sent many of the urban pioneers scurrying north over the expressway, until mortars atop Bunker Hill had mangled the evacuation, sealing the technos into their enclaves. Now they huddled in their town homes and condos, as much afraid of UC's shoot-to-kill curfew as of the approaching rage.

Aldridge mounted the worn granite steps of the library, turning to face the troopers forming up between the fountain and stairs. *Homo fascis,* he thought, watching the black-uniformed, starhelmed troopers dressdown, each indistinguishable from the next save by position. You were wrong, Plato. The best guardians of the State aren't like obedient watchdogs; they're automatons, as much a machine as the needs of the psyche allow.

"At ease." His dry voice cracked over them like a whip. "You've done well," he said, a wireless microphone carrying his voice into every helmet. "But it's not over yet. With the red line breached and the Army hours away, it's going to be a long night. You'll be assigned to this and the Harbor subgarrison, maintaining zonal integrity. I know you'll acquit yourselves as honorably as you did today. Good luck."

Returning Grady's salute, he and zur Linde entered the library, heading down into the basement command post. The distant gunfire faded as the elevator's blastdoors closed.

"Hardly Pompey's battle oration, was it, Erich?" the colonel said as the elevator sank.

"Adequate, sir, if not enduring," said the German. The doors opened. Stepping into the CP, his became a gray uniform in a sea of black. Colors shifted, swirled and reformed on the big situation board as reports came. Alarms competed for attention.

The two stopped as a hollow-eyed officer came up, saluting Aldridge. "How's it going, Sardon?" asked the colonel, sketching a salute.

"Not well, sir, as you can see." They turned toward the board. Tired as he was, the Copley CO's voice was crisp, efficient. "Three projected breakthroughs—Brookline, the South and North Ends." As he spoke, three red gashes moved deeper into the map's green.

"Any hint it's a coordinated attack?" asked zur Linde.

"None," said Sardon, absently running his fingers through

his thinning, close-cropped hair. "But that doesn't help much. That Brookline incursion's headed straight for here. My Charlie and Delta companies are fighting house-to-house less than a mile away. Fighting and losing. Those animals are born urban warriors."

"Any gunships at all?" asked Aldridge, turning from the board.

"None."

The lights and air wavered, died, came back up.

"Got the mains," someone called as the ground shook. "We're on no-break."

"Make that half a mile," said Sardon, stating the distance to the Edison plant.

"Get some napalm down on them, Erich," said Aldridge. "I'll authorize air strikes. Also, have Air Command hit all turfs. We may go down, but so will the gangers."

Zur Linde frowned. "Simultaneous napalming of so much of the city might trigger firestorms, sir. Remember Leningrad and the Japanese cities."

Aldridge shrugged. Raising his voice, he spoke to the small group of officers his presence had attracted. "Recall, gentlemen, that Urban Command is an instrument of both domestic and foreign policy. We're not merely suppressing insurrection. We're also sending a message to Moscow, a firm demonstration of our resolve. If ever the Kremlin is convinced that the Alliance will flinch when attacked, anywhere, anytime, by anyone, then the West and five hundred years of humanism dies.

"Our willingness to incinerate many of our best people, to destroy one of our great cultural centers, can only be seen as a stand against barbarism.

"Never forget, gentlemen," he concluded with quiet passion, "it is we few, we valiant few, who hold back the long night.

"Sardon, coordinate with Erich. Erich, call in those air strikes."

"No need to worry about a sweep now," said John, watching Boston burn.

"Napalm. Those bastards used napalm."

Heather hadn't believed it at first, none of them had, watching from the fort as the bombers roared in, dumped their loads, then veered inland—not until the hungry flames began licking skyward. Only well after midnight had the last wave winged homeward. By then the beaches were packed, aristocracy and outcasts all fleeing the wind-whipped walls of flame.

Heather had sent their too-few choppers to ferry out as many as possible, but after a dozen trips the heat and wild downdrafts had forced them back. The thousands left on the beaches now streamed across the sand of low tide, seeking the water's safety.

"Firestorm!" John pointed to where three great fires had now joined. Trebled, the flames lanced thousands of feet into the air, greedily sucking in oxygen. A small gale raced over the island, bringing fresh sea air to feed the flames. Even this far from the city they could feel the heat as the firestorm danced howling to the water's edge, snuffing out life, choking the outgoing tide with twisted open-mouthed bodies.

Jorge came running up with a note from the commwatch. Putting down her binoculars, Heather read it, passing it to John.

"Who's Bull?"

"Lords of Darkness," she said as they turned from Boston's pyre and walked down the stairs to the parade ground. "They're *the* black gang in the city. Tough. Basic command structure, good leadership, decent weapons. They're Cuban-backed, supplied by Quevara's DGI. It looks like Aldridge mauled them, falling back on Copley."

"Roxbury's a charnel house now," said John. "Where are they?"

"Well away from the fire. Blue Hills, maybe. They've got choppers."

"The man wants to talk. Let's talk."

Aldridge looked up at the board, then back to the G2 reports. "Something's wrong, Erich," he said, ignoring the ongoing bustle of evacuation: boxes of hastily gathered documents, computer disks, code books, small arms, all being hustled outside.

It was a classical Aldridge understatement. The napalm had burned off the ganger attacks, at the cost of two firestorms now converging on the enclaves.

The Army choppers had arrived as the bombers left, following a closing corridor between the flames. Evacuation was under way, with troops ordering residents to staging areas soon littered with forced castoffs: video recorders, leather luggage, miniature stereo-TVs, microcomputers.

General Wyvern, the Army commander, was half listening to Aldridge. He had a problem: there wasn't enough transport to move all the evacuees in time. His men would mutiny before giving up their spaces. Panic and friendly machine-gun fire would sweep the staging areas long before the flames. By dawn, many of the best and brightest would be ash.

"How can something be wrong, Colonel?" said Wyvern. "You gas and burn one of our principal cities, killing thousands. You lose most of your command. Why don't you just shoot yourself and save Frederick the trouble?"

"See, Erich," Aldridge continued, ignoring the general,

''no Vipers.'' He tapped the action reports. ''Not a sign of the largest, best-trained, best-led gang. Nor, within the past four hours, of the Lords. Where are they?'' He stared at the situation board, mind far from the noise and confusion of the CP.

''Site Y, Erich!'' He snapped a finger. ''It's Harrison and that renegade MacKenzie. They're after Maximus. Get us a chopper!'' he ordered, heading for the door.

''Hold it, Aldridge!'' General Wyvern's hand dropped to his .45. ''What the hell are you doing? Deserting in the face of the enemy?'' He made no effort to lower his voice.

Aldridge turned. ''I remind you, General, that I hold extralegal authority. I'm not subject to your orders. As for the enemy, I am rushing to meet him, while you, sir, remain to contend with mere chaos.

''Good day, General.''

Wyvern's glare followed him to the elevator.

6

To date, the invasion and occupation of Japan has cost America almost three million lives. The war with the Axis and then with the Soviet Union, another two million. The wealth of centuries, the lives of two generations squandered, all because Prometheus's gift went to the Old World instead of to the New.

—*Harrison,* ibid.,
pp. 143–4

The Lords came to Fort Todd by chopper, wounded filling three of the machines.

"That'll have to be it for evacuees," said John as the last of the wounded were carried to the Viper's dispensary.

"I got people there!" Bull stabbed a thick finger at the mainland.

"We need what fuel is left for a mission, Captain," said John.

Bull glanced around. Except for Heather, they were alone, huddled between the choppers. "Ten Tango?" he challenged.

"Bravo Romeo."

"Your show, old man." Gone was the ghetto patois, replaced by the clipped accent of an English public school.

"Good God!" said Heather. "The city's going up in flames, thousands are dying, and you two play spy.

"Who the hell are you?" she demanded.

"This is Captain Geoffrey Malusi, Southern African Peoples Liberation Army," said John. "Captain Malusi, Dr. Heather MacKenzie, University of California at Berkeley."

"Delighted, Dr. MacKenzie."

She ignored the big outstretched hand. "Level," she snapped at John. "The whole truth now. Or I take the Vipers and our choppers and do what I can for the refugees."

John looked at the burning sky before answering. "Did Ian tell you about the Committee?"

She shook her head.

"They're the people your brother, Malusi and I work for, through the Outfit. Very senior government officials who don't like what's happened to America. It's the Committee who got Harwood to organize the gangers, using officers like Ian. Malusi's here as . . ."

"As a statement of American race relations," said the African. "Your country has no black officers. So the Committee turned to us for help."

"In exchange for what?"

"In exchange for help, or at least neutrality, in our war against the Boers and their German allies."

She shook her head, not satisfied. "Why Maximus? The whole story."

"Shortly after Maximus started up, the Committee, its principal members anyway, began noticing certain . . . anomalies. Odd things not at first associated with Maximus. Key officials who'd visited the site invariably brought back glowing reports of insubstantial progress. These formerly vigorous, aggressive men became strangely complacent, going thrugh the motions of work. This malaise . . .''

A series of shock waves boomed over the island. From the mainland, a pillar of black smoke billowed out over the water. The fire had reached Logan Airport's fuel tanks.

''This malaise,'' he continued, ''seems confined to the second-secretary rank—the people who allegedly make government work. Our foreign strategy became more irrational and the economy grew worse, if that's conceivable.

''The Committee became worried—hell!—the Committee got scared. Half of them are second-secretary level. They needed Maximus destroyed, without risk to them. I'd been out of it for a while, living in Canada, teaching, writing. Harwood leaned on me and here I am. Malusi and Ian were already in place, part of the Committee's long-term commitment.''

And all true, thought John, with a few last-minute improvisations—like a new John Harrison. He was acquiring a grudging respect for Guan-Sharick's ability.

''Why didn't they just send in agents?'' asked Heather.

''Agents were sent in. They never reported back. And we couldn't just bomb the place—not on suspicion alone. It is an American installation.''

''So you explain this away as a ganger raid,'' said Heather. ''But why did you have to break into the UC data base if the information's all in Frederick?''

''It isn't,'' said John. ''Strangely, all references to Maximus were lost last month in an electrical fire. That was when the decision was made to act. Actually, it was to convince you to go, Heather. Boston's burning as a result. You better say yes.''

''Choppers!'' someone shouted from the wall. ''Army choppers! Headed this way.''

''Now or never, Heather.''

7

Germany has the bomb. Russia has the bomb. They guard it jealously and watch each other warily.

America has poverty, ignorance and class warfare. It is a mercantile fief of the Fourth Reich, with an economy based on the export of raw materials, the import of finished and semi-finished goods. American draftees—those who cannot afford to pay a stand in—fight for German foreign policy in a dozen countries. Coming home, they can join the Urban Corps, the gangs, or, if fortunate, win a service job in the burbs.

—*Harrison,* ibid.,
p. 169

Aldridge's chopper was barely down before he was out, heading for Maximus's one-story Admin building.

The sandbagged entrance was deserted save for two black-sweatered British soldiers. Inspecting his ID, they saluted, waving him past.

"Get Fwolkes up," Aldridge ordered, identifying himself to the sleepy-eyed OIC, a competent-looking brunette in her midtwenties, with captain's pips and parachutist's badge. Nodding curtly, she picked up the phone.

Brigadier Charles Wesley Fwolkes arrived in five minutes, every inch the British officer, despite the hour: olive tunic and red-striped pants neatly pressed, brown shoes gleaming under the fluorescents, swagger stick tucked under his left arm, red-banded cap at just the right angle. He might have been inspecting Parade at Sandhurst. Only his graying moustache betrayed concern, twitching as he returned Aldridge's salute. "Bloody hell, Colonel," he complained. "0330 on a Sunday? This better be good."

"Rather." Aldridge's mimicry of the other's accent was flawless. Bristling, Fwolkes opened his mouth, only to be ridden down by the UC officer. "In the past twenty-four hours, Brigadier," he said, sweating in the humid, overheated room, "I've seen my command decimated and my headquarters razed. I've been compelled to destroy one of our major cities in order to save it. Imagine how I feel about your beauty sleep."

Fwolkes tried to interject again, face flushed. Aldridge would have none of it. "Go to full alert, Brigadier. You're about to be attacked by a thousand well-armed, ably-led gangers."

"You have no authority here, Aldridge. And you could have radioed, as you normally do. Just what are your reasons for this extraordinary request? Do you know what a full alert costs the taxpayers?"

"Radio transmissions can be intercepted, Fwolkes. I am never wrong, given a bare minimum of data. And I don't care about the taxpayers. As to my authority . . ." Extracting a small leather case from his breast pocket, he passed it to the brigadier. "I am Grand Admiral Hans Christian Hochmeister, Reich Security Administrator and Chairman of Alliance Intelligence. This officer," he indicated zur Linde, just entering, "is Captain Erich zur Linde of the Abwehr.

"Now, sir, will you stand to." It wasn't a question.

Fwolkes swallowed hard. "I shall have to confirm, sir," he said hesitantly, returning the ID and touching swagger stick to hat visor, saluting a legend. "Until then, though . . ."

He turned to the OIC. "Captain Mathieson, stand to, if you will. And someone get me a message pad," he added, as the alert sirens wailed.

Maximus was ready in five minutes, battened down and waiting. Reviewing the status board and TV monitors, Hochmeister nodded approval. "Excellent, Brigadier, excellent."

"Why, thank you, sir," said Fwolkes.

"I'd like Hauptmann zur Linde and you to accompany me on an inspection of your defenses."

"Very good, sir," nodded Fwolkes. "We must stay inside the perimeter." He pointed at the ground radar screen on which red blips were spreading like a pox. "And my apologies, Admiral. You were right. Hostiles approaching. It's going to get hot out there."

Hochmeister smiled thinly. "Good to see the old master hasn't lost his touch." He led them through the double-guarded entrance and down the floodlit driveway. Hands clasped behind his back, the Gray Admiral walked slowly past the sandbagged bunkers and razor wire, the mortar and machine-gun emplacements, nodding approvingly. This part of Maximus was all Security and Admin, halfway between the perimeter and the compact installation uphill from it. It was toward the distant gate, though, the one scouted by the now-dead Ian, that the trio went, walking briskly down the road. Arcflares burst overhead, lighting the area brighter than a July noon.

Passing through the final line of bunkers, Hochmeister continued down hill. Zur Linde and Fwolkes slowed uncertainly.

It was unnaturally still, no sound from the bunkers, armored vehicles or the forest. Only the occasional dull plop of an arcflare broke the silence.

Fwolkes cleared his throat. "Where are we going, Admiral, if I may ask?"

Hochmeister never broke stride. "Out into the night, Brigadier," he said, not looking back. "Zur Linde and I are going to join the gangers." Peering ahead, he thought he saw movement along the distant fence.

The British officer halted. "Sir, with respect—are you crazy?"

Brushing past him, zur Linde caught up with Hochmeister.

Stopping, the admiral turned, facing the brigadier. "Cagey, yes, Charles. Crazy, no." Hands thrust deep into the pockets of his baggy, black fieldjacket, pants wrinkled, face in need of a shave and some sleep, Hochmeister looked every bit his age, there in the pitiless light from the flares. "I'm somewhat surprised, Charles," he said easily, "that you don't remember me. Not only did we serve together at the Armistice Conference, your cousin Reggie is married to my niece Gabriela. We had a grand time at the wedding, last June in Salzburg."

Fwolkes was silent, face expressionless. The intelligence chief continued in the same light tone. "Equally distressing, though, was your HQ.

"Erich, did you feel that steamy heat?"

Zur Linde nodded. "Like the reptile house at the zoo," he said, eyes on the brigadier.

"Thirty-five centigrade in there, Charles, at least. Those machines shouldn't work at that temperature. Yet all their lights were twinkling merrily, the equipment humming, everything the picture of brisk efficiency. Except, as Erich notes, the room had the climate of the reptile house. The smell of it, too.

"You can't smell, can you?"

"Obviously, the equipment isn't as sensitive as you believe, Hans," said Fwolkes.

"Christian, Charles. You always called me Christian."

"Please," Fwolkes implored, glancing nervously toward the gate, "we've got to get back . . ."

He broke off, starting as the gate blew up, briefly lighting the circling woods and the advancing gangers.

"Quick! If we run, we can . . ."

"Imagine my great joy, though, Charles," Hochmeister continued as first ganger squads passed the gate, "to find you alive and well. This after Gabriela wrote only last week of your death in a car wreck—ashes to follow.

"Doesn't Charles look remarkably well for a corpse, Erich?"

"Indeed," said zur Linde, pulling his pistol.

"And what do you make of all this?" Fwolkes asked, cold amusement in his voice.

"That you—whoever or whatever you are—have taken control of Maximus; a control we know you're busy extending into vital areas of the American government. That your origins are probably the same as the—phenomenon—the Trojan horse around which we built the Troy of Maximus. That you mean this weary world ill."

Fwolkes stood motionless as a sibilant whisper filled the admiral and zur Linde's minds.

We mean no harm. We merely seek sanctuary. In our universe, we are a hunted race. We lost a war—we would have been exterminated had we stayed.

"You are called . . . ?" asked Hochmeister after a moment.

Shalan-Actal, servant to the S'Cotar.

"That's not your true form, is it, Shalan-Actal of the S'Cotar?"

Rippling, the Fwolkes-form shimmered away, replaced by six feet of mantislike insect, erect on four of its six limbs, its two upper limbs ending in gently undulating tentacles. Bulbous red eyes shifted between the two men before it melted back into the brigadier.

"We could use an ally of your stature, Admiral," the Fwolkes-thing said, taking a step toward them. "Return with me to . . ." It stopped at the sight of the two slim 9mm Walthers pointed at its thorax.

"I gather you accessed Earth through the object here at Maximus," said the admiral. "A gate of some sort?" The other nodded.

"We will return to your steamy little nest, bug," said Hochmeister, "but not with you. With the gangers. Then we'll have a good look at your gate. Who knows? Maybe we can form an alliance with your enemies—assuming even that to be true."

"You don't believe me?"

"Produce the real Maximus staff as witnesses to your goodwill, Shalan-Actal, then I may believe you.

"No? Well, then, shall we?" The admiral pointed downhill with his free hand. "If you'd be so kind as to lead?

"Erich, if it even stumbles, shoot." Tight-lipped, zur Linde nodded.

Five more S'Cotar appeared, flicking into existence beside Shalan-Actal. These were sturdier, larger insectoids, whiplike tentacles holding strange rifles. It was their mandibles, though, that held Hochmeister's attention—long, serrated, they were clicking softly. Warriors.

Rather, I think you will accompany us back to the compound, Admiral, Captain.

"Telepathic, telekinetic," said Hochmeister, impressed. "You're dangerous, Shalan-Actal." He fired once, a shot that became a fusillade as a ganger squad charged from the brush, minimacs blazing.

Shalan-Actal vanished as his reinforcements died.

"Major, you heard that?" asked the admiral, turning from the heaped insects as John stepped into the road, a squad of wide-eyed Vipers behind him. The gangers stared wide-eyed at the dead S'Cotar.

"Enough of it, Admiral."

"There can't be too many of them or we'd be dead," said zur Linde.

"Do you concur with me, Major," asked Hochmeister, "that this place must be taken, now?"

The arcflares had stopped. The darkness brought with it the same strange quiet the two Germans had experienced walking down the road. Not even a cricket chirped.

"How long have you known what was wrong here, Admiral?" asked John, suspicious of the other's unruffled acceptance of a Vermont mountain aswarm with aliens.

"Everything? Only just now. But we've known something was very wrong up here for some time—as you evidently have. I need your help, Major."

"This is just reconnaissance in force," lied John. "Surely you don't expect *our* help, Admiral?"

Hochmeister nodded.

"Why should we help you?"

"Are you familiar with the classical concept of an

umphalos, Major?'' asked Hochmeister, reloading his pistol and slipping it away.

''The Greek notion of a world navel, a confluence of all the conflicting forces in the universe in one place at one time. Oedipus at Colonus. So?''

''Exactly,'' said the admiral. ''Are you the Committee's court Jew, Major?''

John gave no hint.

''Well, no matter. We are now at such a confluence, as you so well put it. Our world hangs in the balance. These creatures, these S'Cotar, may even now be swarming through their device up there. There's no time to call in regular forces. We must take them with what we have.''

''What's in it for us?'' demanded Heather. Arriving with a fresh contingent of gangers, she'd been silent till now, looking at the dead S'Cotar, listening to John and Hochmeister.

The admiral was shocked. ''I should think knowing you've saved humanity from these creatures would be reward enough.''

''It isn't,'' she assured him. ''Though it's interesting to hear a monster like you calmly invoke humanity.''

''I may be a monster by your simplistic standards,'' said Hochmeister, checking his watch, ''but at least I am your monster. Would you prefer the bugs?

''We are out of time. A counterattack now would catch us out here, bickering in the dark. Yes or no. Save this world or let it die. The choice is yours, MacKenzie, Harrison.''

''Full pardon for all urban gangers,'' said Heather. ''The abolition of Urban Command. The opening of a significant dialogue with our representatives in a neutral country.''

''I am an officer of the Reich,'' said Hochmeister, ''I

can't speak for your government. America's a sovereign nation."

"Crock," said Heather. "The Reich's made all our major policy decisions since the war. You have the bomb. We don't."

"I don't have the authority . . ."

" '*Keiner oder alle, alle oder nicht,*' Herr Admiral," she said, quoting Brecht.

"Very well," he sighed. "The Reich will back your demands."

"Could we have that in blood?" said John.

"You have my word."

"How comforting," said John.

"The admiral has never broken a promise," said zur Linde.

"He's right," said Heather. "Hochmeister has never broken his word—it's a legend in intelligence circles."

Using her radio, Heather called in the rest of the gangers.

As Malusi arrived with the Lords, zur Linde gathered up the dead aliens' weapons, passing them to John, Heather and Hochmeister.

Bringing the S'Cotar rifle to his shoulder, the admiral fired a brilliant blue bolt into the night. A tree exploded as the weapon shrilled. He nodded, impressed.

A hasty briefing, relayed through ganger company commanders and platoon leaders, then the attack force moved up the hill, a long assault line approaching the silent defenses. Hochmeister strode to the fore, catching up with John at the line's center.

"Leading the charge, Admiral?" said John. "Not your style, is it?"

Hochmeister's glasses reflected the cold starlight, hooding his eyes. "It's my birthday—October twenty-fifth,

Crispin's Day.'' The squat, dark outline of the blockhouses was about two hundred meters away, seemingly devoid of life. ''I saw my first action on this night, leading a platoon of the Kreigsmarine. This would be an almost poetic end.

''Besides,'' he said as the arcflares burst anew, ''what'll be my chances once your troops recover from the shock of all this and recall their debt to Colonel Aldridge?''

Before John could reply, fierce beams of indigo shot from the blockhouses, a stunning barrage of light and sound that ripped through the assault line, sending the gangers to earth.

Prone, John blasted back, riddling a blockhouse with the alien weapon. The bunker ammunition exploded, tracers shooting out like fireworks.

''They'll break.'' Hochmeister looked appraisingly over his shoulder. The gangers were wavering, some starting to slip away.

Heedless of the blaster and gunfire, the admiral scrambled to his feet. ''What's the matter?!'' he shouted at the gangers hugging the hard ground. ''You want to live forever?'' Blue lightning flashed by, never quite touching him.

The gangers didn't stir.

''Scum! I should have gassed the lot of you! Watch a man fight for his world!'' Turning, he charged the S'Cotar defenses, running zigzag, firing his blaster.

''Bloody bastard. See you in hell.'' Malusi rose. ''Come on!'' he shouted above the din. ''We go or he's right!'' Wheeling, he followed Hochmeister, hearing his answer as a roar swept the line. Vipers and Lords, blacks, whites, yellow, browns, all surged after him, charging uphill over their dead and dying.

Irresistible, the wave swept up John, Heather and zur Linde, carrying them along as it broke over the bunkers, smothering the blue flames, sweeping on into the compound, where a gaunt, cold man awaited, content for now.

8

The Christian Democrats and the General Staff are gentlemen: they never remind us that they have the bomb. They know that we know.
Knowledge is power.
—*Harrison*, ibid.,
p. 180

The wild charge surged into the compound, up the ramp to the closed double doors of the main building. There it halted, quivering under a murderous fire from windows, breaking as the gangers scrambled for cover.

"Nothing's touching those doors!" John shouted to Hochmeister. The admiral nodded as another antitank round exploded harmlessly against the dull gray metal.

"You! You! You!" He pointed to three blaster-toting Vipers. "Concentrate your fire centerpoint on the door."

It took twenty minutes, but a hole was forged, a hot, jagged opening the width of two men. Following up a grenade and missile volley, John and zur Linde took the first squad in. An hour later, the building was clear of the surprisingly few S'Cotar.

The insectoids fought desperately, materializing among their attackers, dying in point-blank firefights with the humans. Casualties soared.

John was the first into the amphitheater housing Maximus, blasting a warrior as it whirled to fire. Heather, Malusi, Hochmeister and a hundred gangers were seconds behind him.

The floor of the cavernous room sloped down to a round, still pool of unbroken black. To one side two transmutes stood beside a small console. They watched unmoving as John shot the sentry, then vanished as the rest of the humans entered. Guan-Sharick's loyalists? he wondered, advancing to the pool.

"This is it?" said Malusi, pointing his blaster at the pool.

"That's it," said Heather. "The Maximus gate. Just as it was discovered. This shrine," she waved her hand at the building, "was built around it."

The pool held their eyes, an unmoving, deep-hued blackness, a stillness emanating a sense of rippling, primordial energies somehow held in check and channeled by the slim console.

No biofab had built that device, John was sure. The S'Cotar were probably the most efficient killers the galaxy had seen in millennia. And they were competent engineers. But a work of genius such as this was beyond them. Another miracle of the old Empire?

"Area secured," zur Linde reported over the radio. "There were only about fifty of them."

Hochmeister shook his head. "Illusions. All those troops and lights—illusions." He looked down at the portal.

"They must have come through and wiped out everybody as they slept."

He looked up. "We've got to close this down, now. Imagine not fifty, but fifty thousand of those things loose on this world. As a species, we'd be extinct in a month."

"He's right," said John.

Heather frowned at the console. "How do we shut it down? I feel like a Neanderthal visiting Brookhaven."

"No time for experimentation," said Malusi. "Blow it up. They could come swarming through from wherever any second."

Don't blow it up yet! John wanted to scream. Wait till I'm gone. You got the last of the S'Cotar. There's just a handful on the other side. He stepped toward the pool.

Harrison!

John froze. Guan-Sharick?

Don't jump, Harrison. You'd be butchered.

What . . .

Shalan-Actal's allies have changed the portal's terminus. You'd come out in their underground nest, below Maximus. Shalan's regrouping. Hundreds of warriors and killer machines are about to counterattack.

Why from the portal? Why not just appear outside?

The machines can't teleport. And the logical German is busy positioning your gangers facing away from the complex. Shalan-Actal is a very competent Tactics Master.

John stepped back from the portal. "Malusi's right," he said. "But let's find a way to turn it off. Touch off plastique and we could wipe out New England."

"Unlikely," said the admiral. "Anything this sophisticated must be failsafe."

"Care to gamble a few hundred square miles, Admiral?" said John. "Or maybe a continent?"

"No."

Heather reached gingerly toward the console. An invisible something stayed her touch inches from the surface. The harder she pushed, the harder it became. "Force field," she said.

Imperial, thought John. The secret of miniaturized force fields had died with the Empire.

"I've got to get at it," said Heather, raising her blaster.

"No!" cried John.

She fired point blank at the console, holding the trigger back.

A pulsating golden aura encased the machine, its edge darkening to red as the weapon shrilled.

Heather was still firing when the blades came.

Flat, silver, keen-edged, perhaps four feet across, three of them soared from the pool, multiple blaster fire snapping as if by magic from their unbroken surfaces.

John ducked as the blades flashed by, knifing into the nearest gangers, severing heads from torsos with surgical precision, blasters firing at those further away. Each execution took half a second.

"Blasters!" shouted John, firing from behind the console. Bullets were ricocheting from the blades back into the humans.

Most of the alien weapons were held by zur Linde's group. They burst through the doors, firing, just as the machines rose to regroup. The machines crashed to the floor, exploding in eye-searing bursts of blue, scorching the concrete.

Half a hundred gangers lay dead. The few wounded were from the ricochets. Where the blades had touched, they'd killed.

"Good God," said Heather, rising from beside Chin Lee's body. A perfectly centered blaster hole pierced the ganger's forehead. "They didn't waste a shot." The air reeked of smoldering metal and charred flesh. Blood trickled in small streams over the portal's rim.

A flash of gold caught John's eye. Kneeling beside a shattered machine, he carefully retrieved the jagged square of metal.

"What's that?" asked Heather.

"Something that shouldn't be here," he said, slipping the warm piece of metal into his pocket.

He turned to Heather. "Get everyone out. I'm going to blow this before we're overrun." Even if I have spend the rest of my short life on this pisshole world, he thought, pulling flat gray packets of plastique from his fieldjacket.

"He's right," said Hochmeister. "Let's go."

No one moved. "Not your show, Admiral," said the Malusi, turning to Heather. "Well?"

"Pull everyone out. Get that defense line turned around, facing the building."

Malusi nodded curtly, issuing orders that sent the gangers running for the doors. He, Hochmeister and zur Linde followed. The Bantu turned at the door, waved and was gone.

Alone with their dead and the hiss of burning machines, Heather and John rimmed the console and its force field with plastique and set the detonators. Running best they could on the blasted, blood-slicked concrete, they were almost to the door when S'Cotar stormed from the portal, flicking ahead to block their retreat. Warriors intercepted them, dragging them back to the console, where a transmute waited, antennae weaving impatiently.

Disarm that, it ordered, dipping a tentacle toward the detonator. Wave after wave of warriors were pouring through, flicking almost as they appeared. Gun and blaster fire filtered in.

"Do it yourself, v'org slime."

Harrison, you will live long enough to curse the day you met the K'Ronarins or our traitorous Illusion Master. I am Shalan-Actal.

"You're the traitor," said Harrison. "You betrayed all sapient life in two universes."

Those baleful red eyes turned on him for a second, then to the console.

Obeying an unspoken order, a warrior stepped forward, tentacles reached for the detonator.

John pivoted, kicking his guard hard in the genital sac. As the warrior folded, he grabbed its blastrifle.

The warrior holding Heather shoved her toward John and raised its rifle. John sidestepped, firing. Arms flailing, face wild with fear, Heather lost her balance and fell backward into the portal. Leaping after her, rifle high, John took a blaster bolt in the back as the plastique exploded.

Pain, pain, falling, falling . . .

We have MacKenzie, Glorious. She arrived in the breeding vault an instant before the explosion.

What of Harrison?

No trace. He is probably just so many scattering atoms.

Probably?

Our knowledge of the machine is slight, Glorious. It might have a failsafe.

He may be alive?

And on Terra One, if the machine reverted to its last interspatial setting before shutdown. It was never designed for intraspatial transport. The Imperials had matter transporters.

Clean this mess up, see to the machine. I will be with allied commander. We must move quickly.

* * *

A delicate green-red fantasy copied from the Han dynasty, the dragon kite rose a few yards, trembled, then dove into the soft earth.

"Run faster, Jason!" the old man called to the boy. "Into the wind!"

The Mall in front of the Smithsonian was alive with tourists, bicyclists, joggers and kite flyers, all reveling in the sudden glory of Indian summer.

"Let Melaine try, Jason," said McShane, tugging his khaki shorts back up over his comfortable belly.

Pouting, the auburn-haired eight-year-old relinquished the string to his sister. Standing by his grandfather, he silently willed her to fail.

She almost made it, expertly holding the string between spread fingers, running toward the Capitol on fast, sturdy legs. Trailing up behind her, the dragon soared, dipped, soared, then barrel-rolled down out of sight into the Sculpture Garden's walled pit.

Melaine stomped her foot, saying something no nine-year-old of Bob's generation would have said.

McShane laughed and began winding in the string. "OK, gang, let's try again. Jason, would you kindly rescue Puff from the Rodin?"

The boy took off around the shrubs and down the stairs. He was back in a moment, empty-handed. "Grampa!" he said wide-eyed, pointing to where the string disappeared. "A man came out of the air! He's got a gun!"

McShane suppressed a sudden rush of fear. Finishing with the now-taut string, he set it down and searched his baggy pockets. "Maybe I'll talk with him while I get the kite. You two get something at the refreshment stand." He handed Jason a five-dollar bill. "Large lemonade for Gramps."

Bob gauged the line of tourists at the distant green-and-white kiosk—ten minutes. Long enough.

The kids ran off. Waiting till they were in line, McShane turned for the Sculpture Garden. Fool, he thought to himself. Why not just call a cop? Because you taught political philosophy most of your life, and know what Machiavelli meant by civic virtue. Besides, it might just be another of Jason's invisible friends, like the large talking toad that guarded the basement. Even if it was a S'Cotar, it was probably miles away by now.

Walking across the grass, he stumbled and fell. A jogger broke stride, helping him back to his feet. Clumsy old man, he thought, thanking the woman as she handed him his blackthorn Irish walker. Third time this week. Suddenly tired, he stepped carefully down the stairs and into the garden.

The man sat on a bench beside a Henry Moore, head buried in his hands, black uniform singed and torn. It was the weapon, though, that stopped Bob cold, heart pounding: a S'Cotar blastrifle, gleaming dully where it rested against the bench. There should be no S'Cotar weapons left on Earth, at least, not in human hands.

As Bob forced himself forward, the man staggered to his feet, raising the blaster. His were the wide, glazed eyes of someone in shock.

"John!"

"Bob!" The rifle dropped. "Home?"

"Home," said McShane. "But how?"

He moved quickly, catching John as the other fell. Only then did he see the blaster wound, a charred two-inch hole running from below the left shoulder and out the left side, where ribs had been.

"You!" he shouted at a young couple coming down the

stairs, baby asleep in a backpack. "Get an ambulance." They stared at him.

"Across the street, in the Smithsonian. Tell the guard to call an ambulance. Move!"

The woman turned and ran up the stairs as the man hurried over. "What can I do?"

"Help me treat for shock. Prop his feet up."

"He . . . he doesn't seem to be breathing."

Bob dropped to the ground, ear to John's chest. There was no heartbeat.

The baby started to cry.

Kneeling in the gravel, Bob moved through the measured cadence of CPR, not hearing the baby, not seeing his grandchildren. Until the medic gently shook his shoulder, there was nothing but his hands and lungs ministering to the dead.

9

D'Trelna looked up from his desk complink. "I really hate this, H'Nar," he said to L'Wrona, sitting in front of the desk. "Had I known when they gave me these"—he tapped the stylized, four-pointed silver star on each collar—"that I'd be confined to quarters half the watch, filling out moronic reports . . ."

Implacable's captain smiled. "You're only happy when the battle klaxon's banging away, J'Quel.

"How's Harrison doing?" he asked, changing the subject.

"Better." D'Trelna stared at the complink, not really seeing it. "Sick Bay says his new heart's holding. They'll be waking him up soon."

"When can we debrief him?"

"Two days, local."

L'Wrona rose, walking to the armor glass. He stood looking at the *V'Tran's Glory* for a moment, then turned to D'Trelna. "We don't know what happened on Terra Two yet. That bothers me, J'Quel."

"Guan-Sharick told Sutherland the portal's gone, H'Nar.

That'll have to do for now. Medical won't bring him out of it until regeneration's over."

"I hate taking that bug's word for anything."

"Only for now, H'Nar. Only for now.

"Computer, resume."

"Resuming," said the too-perfect voice. "State composition and current tactical deployment of task force and reason for such deployment."

"Computer, just copy the last entry under this category and change date to current."

"Illegal command."

D'Trelna's face flushed dangerously. "Computer, nothing has changed since the previous entry. Copy the previous entry."

"All entries of this nature must be original."

D'Trelna reached for the large crystal water carafe.

"Damaging a remote terminal will not injure main computer," said computer. It had lost five other screens beneath the same hairy hand before discovering that disingenuous sentence.

"Blood pressure, J'Quel," warned L'Wrona. "Blood pressure."

"Very well." The carafe returned to the desktop. "Composition of force: two vessels. The L'Aal-class battle cruiser *Implacable*, Captain Lord Captain H'Nar L'Wrona, Margrave of U'Tria, commanding. And the S'Rin-class destroyer *V'Tran's Glory*, Captain H'Tan S'Tur commanding. Both warships are in geosynchronous orbit one hundred and seventeen standard units above the planet Terra. Task force is awaiting Fleet reevaluation of original mission versus current situation, planet Terra. See previous reports. Terra Two, cross references Shalan-Actal, Guan-Sharick and John Harrison, file number . . .

"Computer, will you condescend to insert the reference number?"

"Of course, Commodore."

"Thank you. End and file."

"Filed." The screen blanked, quickly folding back into the comparative safety of the desktop.

D' Trelna shook his head. "I really hate that machine."

"It's only a machine, J'Quel—it's not malevolent."

"Maybe." D'Trelna sat up, opening the top drawer of his desk. "Let's talk about malevolent machinery." He held out the golden triangle. "Here."

L'Wrona took it, looking at the device set into the metal: silver starship against a gold sun, a blue eye in each corner of the triangle.

"Early Empire," said L'Wrona, holding it up to the light. "Fourth Dynasty at the most. And beautifully detailed—the eyes are uncanny." He set it on the desktop.

"Under magnification, those eyes have a retina pattern—the same retina pattern."

"Interesting. Where'd you get it?"

"Harrison brought it back from Terra Two."

L'Wrona's eyes widened. "How . . . ?"

"How, indeed?"

"T'ata?"

"No, thank you."

D'Trelna tapped out a command, then took a steaming cup of brown liquid from the desk beverager.

"Harrison was briefly conscious on the way to the hospital. He gave that triangle to McShane—taken from a destroyed killer machine." The commodore sipped his tea.

"You ran it?"

D'Trelna nodded, setting down the t'ata. "You were close, H'Nar. Third Dynasty—the House of D'Lan."

The captain sat down on the chair. "Gods. The Machine Wars."

"Correct. The Empire built self-replicating, self-improving helpers. Said helpers decided man was obsolete. Man thought otherwise. Empire tottered, Fleet reeled, Emperor and dynasty fell—but machines were wiped out."

"Then these aren't the machines Pocsym warned against—they can't be," said L'Wrona. "Those machines predated man by millennia."

"Insufficient data, as our tame computer would say." D'Trelna thoughtfully circled the cup rim with a thick finger. "I would like very much to get to Terra Two."

"You can't—not if Harrison destroyed the portal."

"There may be another way." He turned, staring through the armorglass at Earth and the Moon beyond.

A silver spacecraft drifted by, running on n-gravs for the hangar deck aft.

"Shuttle coming in." He glanced at the wall chronometer. "American, I believe. If it's more social scientists with those quaint recording machines and inane questions, I'm hiding."

"But they're so earnest, J'Quel," said L'Wrona.

The commodore raised an eyebrow. "You were certainly very earnest with that lovely young anthropologist—the one who shared your quarters, for what? two watches?"

L'Wrona blushed. "You're a voyeur, D'Trelna."

"Bored—merely bored."

A moment later, the alert klaxon brought them to their feet, startled.

"Battle stations. Battle stations." The view through the armorglass blurred as the shield went to battle force.

"This is no drill," warned the bridge. "This is no drill."

D'Trelna took an M11A from his desk.

"Command officers to the bridge. Command officers to the bridge."

Weapons in hand, the two rushed into the corridor. Officers and crew filled the passageways, running for their posts.

Captain and commodore burst onto the bridge, the battle klaxon still rattling through the long miles of the ship.

"Status," said L'Wrona to the XO, Commander T'Lei K'Raoda.

"Mr. Sutherland . . ." began the young officer.

"I requested T'Lei bring the ship to alert, H'Nar," said Bill Sutherland. The CIA Director stood to their right, by navigation.

"What is the nature of the emergency?" asked L'Wrona, eyes flicking to the tacscan up on the main board. Terran communications satellites, space junk and *V'Tran's Glory* standing five units off to port. All green plotted, all normal.

The battle klaxon stopped.

"As I was having breakfast this morning, Guan-Sharick appeared, au naturel, said four words and vanished. I left the granola scattered over the floor and grabbed the next shuttle from Andrews. I didn't dare use the commnet."

"What did the bug say?" asked D'Trelna.

The nearest bridge crew pretended not to listen.

"He said, 'The portal is back.' "

"Shit," said D'Trelna in English. He sank into the flag officer's chair, behind and above the captain's.

"High alert, Commander K'Raoda," ordered L'Wrona. "All S'Cotar countermeasures into effect."

"He also said to warn you—the machines need another star drive to punch through to their home universe. They'll be coming for one of yours."

"Sir, *V'Tran's'* shield has been down for half the watch," said K'Raoda.

L'Wrona and D'Trelna exchanged worried glances. "T'Lei, why didn't you report that?" asked the captain.

"It's only an anomaly during high alert, sir."

D'Trelna shook his head mumbling something. He punched into the commnet. "Commodore to *V'Tran's Glory*."

A woman's round face filled his commscreen. She was about D'Trelna's age, with close-cropped, graying hair. The bottom edge of the pickup just caught the gleam of the starship captain's silver insignia on her collar.

"How's that shield coming, H'Tan?" asked D'Trelna.

"Just about ready, Commodore," she said. "We'd have had it sooner, but I'm short three shield techs. Shore leave."

D'Trelna grunted. "Very well. Keep me posted." His finger paused over the cutoff.

"Oh, H'Tan. Just got a skipcomm from Fleet." He smiled knowingly. "Admiral T'Bul sends you his warmest compliments."

The destroyer captain's face brightened. "D'Trelna, you've made my watch."

"And you mine," said D'Trelna as her image disappeared. He swiveled the chair to face L'Wrona. "I think we should send *V'Tran's Glory* our warmest compliments, H'Nar."

"Agreed." Face a graven mask, he turned to K'Raoda. "*V'Tran's Glory* is taken, T'Lei. Blow her away."

K'Raoda had heard the exchange between D'Trelna and the destroyer. Calling up gunnery control, far amidships, he began speaking softly into the commnet, face pale and angry.

"Good God!" said Sutherland, aghast. "Are you sure?"

D'Trelna nodded wearily. "S'Tur would never let more than one shield tech go at a time. No competent captain would. And S'Tur is . . . was very competent."

"But . . ." protested the Terran.

"Admiral T'Bul's been dead for ten years, Bill," said L'Wrona. "He died in our first battle with the S'Cotar. He and S'Tur had a brief marriage contract. It didn't end pleasantly. She cheered his death posting."

"Gunnery will not fire without authenticated confirmation from both captain and commodore," reported K'Raoda.

"Target's shield just came up," reported T'Ral from the tactics console. "Battle force. I've implemented broad-spectrum countermeasures."

"Ahead flank," ordered L'Wrona. "Full evasive pattern. Prepare for hostile fire."

D'Trelna slammed down the commnet switch. "Gunnery! T'Laka! D'Trelna! Flanking Councilor seven to Archon two. You open fire or I'll kick your teeth in!"

Both ships fired as one, thick red fusion beams lashing from squat, gray weapons blisters, tearing at each other's shields—shields that turned red as the moments dragged by. Five minutes into the battle, and the destroyer's shield began sliding into umbra, the new color lapping out in concentric circles from the beam points.

"We outgun him ten to one," said D'Trelna to Sutherland. "He can't outrun us. Even if he made jump point, he'd have to drop his shield to jump. We'd vaporize him with a missile." They watched as the umbra blazed into scarlet, obscuring the other ship.

"Why isn't he favoring us with one of their famous suicide runs, H'Nar?" asked the commodore. "He can't last much longer."

As he spoke, *V'Tran's Glory* ceased firing, its shield slowly changing back to umbra.

"He's diverting weapons energy to shield," said the captain, punching into a tactics readout.

"Buying time," said D'Trelna. "For what?" He checked

his own instruments, then looked back at the screen, squinting.

"T'Lei, split screen. Give me base-plus-five magnification, grids one-seven by two-five. There's a color anomaly and he's headed right for it."

The screen split, the right still showing *V'Tran's Glory*, encased in the blazing cocoon of its shield, moving at flank, and a growing circle of something blacker than even the obsidian of space—something blotting out the stars as it expanded.

"Maximus," said Sutherland. "It's like the Maximus portal Guan-Sharick described, only bigger, spaceborne. That ship's headed for Terra Two."

"Gunnery," snapped L'Wrona. "Full missile salvo. Now!"

Missiles flashed from their launch blisters, long silver needles closing on *V'Tran's Glory* as she slipped through the portal.

Where the hole in space had been, stars shone again. The missiles continued on, straight for the Lesser Magellanic Clouds.

"Gone," said L'Wrona.

"Confirmed," said K'Raoda, checking the full battlescan.

"Gone to Terra Two." Sutherland sank into a vacant chair. "Why?"

D'Trelna shook his head, grim-faced. "Any number of unpleasant possibilities. With the excitement over, we'll have to . . ."

"Alert. Alert." It was computer. "Incoming ordnance. Incoming ordnance."

K'Raoda punched tacscan up on the big screen. Five arrows were converging on the central blip of *Implacable*. "Our missiles are coming home."

"Run for jump point, T'Lei," said L'Wrona. "Gunnery, destruct those missiles."

There was a brief pause. "They don't respond, sir."

"The shield will have to take it," said L'Wrona.

"They're queuing," said K'Raoda, looking up from a telltale. The five arrows were now in a straight line, chasing *Implacable* as she fled outsystem. The XO typed a rapid series of commands to the hull sensors. "And they're shielded," he said, looking to L'Wrona.

"Try for jump point, H'Nar," said D'Trelna. "T'Ral," he said to the tactics officer, "change shield frequency—random setting."

"What the hell's going on?" asked Sutherland.

"Sabotage," said D'Trelna. "Someone—something—has gotten to our missiles. Only a shield can penetrate another shield—if they have the same shield frequency. But shield frequencies are changed daily—randomly programmed, manually implemented by Weapons. So all missiles are unshielded. One counts on fusion fire to weaken the enemy's enough for simultaneous missile hits to punch through. Someone's gone to the trouble of shielding those missiles—someone on this ship—smart money says those missiles and our main shield are now on the same frequency."

"Which you're changing," said Sutherland.

D'Trelna looked back at K'Raoda. The XO was reentering the same data command again, scowling. "Smart money also says whoever could infiltrate our physical and programming security could imbed a frequency-lock command."

Gripping the bridge railing, Sutherland looked at the screen. *Implacable* was speeding toward the glowing blue circle of the jump point, but the missiles were closing even faster.

"Shield programming's dead-trapped," said T'Ral. "Change shield frequency now and the shield fails."

"I sense a master's tentacle in this, H'Nar," said D'Trelna. "Are we going to make it?"

"Computer says almost," said L'Wrona with a tight smile.

D'Trelna shook his head. "I will not be killed by my own weapons. It's embarrassing." The commodore sat silent, brooding as the gap between ship and missiles grew slim.

The bridge was very quiet, all eyes hypnotized by the five needles of death now only a few heartbeats away.

"H'Nar!" said D'Trelna, coming out of his chair. "If the compensator programming's not tied into those missile shields . . ."

L'Wrona swore—a rarity. "Gunnery, on my order, hit the lead missile."

"Acknowledged."

"T'Ral, advise me the instant their shields drop.

"T'Lei, drop our shield."

K'Raoda typed an authenticator, followed by a command. "Shield down, sir."

"Gunnery, fire!"

Touching the lead missile, the fusion beam triggered its warhead. A miniature sun blossomed where the missiles had been, vanishing as cheers swept the bridge.

"What happened?" asked Sutherland.

"Counter-programming in our missiles allows them to compensate for certain changes in target status," said D'Trelna. Sitting down again, he dialed up a cup of t'ata. "Target turns, missile turns, it speeds up, the missile speeds up, it jams, the missile counterjams. But shielding's not a category—those weapons aren't shield-bearing design. And, for complex but perfectly logical reasons, a shield would have to have been set through the counter-programming.

"We dropped our shield; the missiles dropped their shields." He sipped his t'ata. "And so, unlike the crew of *V'Tran's Glory*, we live."

10

"You're looking better," said Sutherland.

"How was I looking?" John did a final chinup, then dropped to the mat. It was mainwatch—the two had the officer's Rec Area almost to themselves.

"Very dead," said Sutherland. Grabbing a horizontal bar, he did two chinups. "Medtechs were wheeling you from GWU Emergency to a shuttle, life support gear stuck into every vein. You were the color of the deck." He scuffed the gray battlesteel with his shoe. "I was rehearsing a speech for your wife."

Taking a running start, John cartwheeled to the end of the mat, then backflipped to his feet. "Nothing like a new heart."

"Very nice."

They walked to the beverager. John punched up a cup of water, holding it out to Sutherland. The CIA Director shook his head.

"Any rejection problems?"

"None." He gulped down the water. "It's my own

tissue, vat grown and installed by Q'Nil and the med staff."

"Prime stuff. Remind me to check in here for my coronary.

"Heard from Zahava?"

"Just a postcard, shuttled up from the Embassy. I'll call her Saturday."

Sutherland frowned. "She doesn't know?"

"Her sister in the hospital, me with a nicked heart? She'd have freaked. I'll tell her when she gets home." He tossed the cup down a disposer.

"You must be getting restless, sitting up here, convalescing."

John's eyes narrowed in suspicion. "What do you want, Bill?"

"You," he smiled. "You're needed back on Terra Two. The K'Ronarins found the S'Cotar portal and we've confirmed it. Time to raise some hell."

"No way." He stepped back a pace. "I almost got killed! If the K'Ronarins weren't here, I'd be dead meat!"

Sutherland held up his hands. "Easy, boy. All I ask is that you come with me to our leader's briefing."

"Is this leader short and round?"

"He is."

"When and where?" he sighed.

"Fifteen minutes. Deck four."

"OK. Let me shower and change.

"Who's going to raise this hell?" he asked a few minutes later, as they rode the lift.

"L'Wrona and the commandos.

"Did they tell you about the decal you salvaged from that machine?"

John nodded. "The Empire again—where it shouldn't exist."

The lift stopped with a faint whine. Two brown-uniformed crewmen got on. "I have a theory about the Empire," said Bill as the decks flashed by. "More whimsy than theory. It never died. It's out there somewhere, manipulating us, the K'Ronarins, the S'Cotar, those killer machines—God only knows what else. All for some esoteric and probably rotten end. It's cold, malevolent, immortal and hopelessly mad. Evil, if you will."

The crewmen glanced at him as they exited. The lift started again.

"McShane would call that the delusion of an aging paranoid, I think."

"And you?"

John smiled, shrugging. "Where the Empire is concerned, I reserve judgment."

"Our situation is precarious," said D'Trelna, looking around the briefing room table. John, Sutherland, L'Wrona and K'Raoda, all appropriately grim. "Despite John's and his allies' valiant efforts, the S'Cotar and their portal are alive and well—witness the dramatic hijacking of our sister ship. Further, the bugs can evade our detectors. One dropped in for a chat, the other—one of Shalan's, we assume—was on board modifying our weapon programming. Should you all turn into transmutes now, I wouldn't be completely surprised."

No one laughed.

"They can only have a few detection-avoidance devices," said L'Wrona, "or we'd all be dead."

"If those machines come through, we're dead," said John. "Where the hell are your reinforcements?"

"On the way," said L'Wrona. "It takes time. Fleet's scattered, mopping up S'Cotar remnants, running recovery operations. And this system's far from anywhere."

"We've found what seems to be our end of the Terra Two portal," said Bill. "It's the biofabs' access to this world. The energy traces are unique. J'Quel's had everyone doing a universal terrestrial grid search for similar readings. Nada." With practiced ease, he punched up a hot cup of t'ata from the table. "Your turn, H'Nar."

"A select force will go through that portal to Terra Two," said L'Wrona, "and harry the S'Cotar—a small force to divert attention long enough for reinforcements to reach us."

"So a few of you go and hold the bugs off for a while," said John, "and your reinforcements arrive. Then what? How are you going to get a ship to Terra Two?"

"We're working on that," said D'Trelna.

"How?" asked John.

The commodore shook his head. "No. If you're captured, they'll steal your mind. The less you know, the better."

"And the S'Cotar infiltration of this ship?" asked John.

"Our visitor's gone," said L'Wrona, "and a gunner's missing. Shield's up and will remain up. No one on or off the ship, except the assault force."

"Research's working on new detectors," said D'Trelna. He rose. "Mission briefing, here, in"—he tapped something into the complink, read the result—"one hour and seventeen minutes, then back you go to Terra Two with the team."

"Did I agree to go?" John asked Bill as the others left the room.

"J'Quel always takes silence for the affirmative."

"I see." He seemed to reach a decision. "Fine. I'll go. I have to deliver someone a present, anyway."

* * *

"Commanding officer!"

Twenty commandos sprang from their chairs as L'Wrona walked down the aisle, striding briskly to the rostrum. The Terrans—John and Sutherland—kept their seats.

"Sit," said L'Wrona. Like the rest, he wore a black turtleneck sweater, matching pants and a pair of low-cut black boots. The polished t'raq-wood butt of an M11A blaster protruded from the black leather holster on his right hip. All wore the long-barreled Fleet sidearm, but only L'Wrona's bore the starship-and-sun of U'Tria, gleaming in silver below the grips.

"You've all read Mr. Harrison's debriefing," said the captain. "It's been three Terran weeks since he returned and since we lost *V'Tran's Glory*. The situation on Terra Two should be unchanged.

"Our principal mission is to find and destroy the breeding chambers. Harrison saw no sign of them, but they would logically be in the vicinity of the S'Cotar nest, the Maximus Project. According to Guan-Sharick, this Shalan-Actal's using an untested growth accelerant to breed tens of thousands of new S'Cotar. Of course, any incidental havoc we can wreak, we will.

"Questions?" His eyes swept the row of determined young faces.

"Warsuits, sir?" asked S'Til. Blonde, attractive—no one would have called her cute—M'Taen S'Til was *Implacable*'s commando officer. The best of a good lot, she'd led the point squad into the S'Cotar citadel at the Lake of Dreams. Had she been Fleet and Academy, she'd have commanded a starship.

"No warsuits, S'Til," said L'Wrona. "We're expendable, the warsuits aren't."

The warsuits were another legacy of Empire, silvery bits of formfitting memory foil, impervious to all but multiple blaster hits. The secret of their making long lost, a few hundred had been found toward the end of the biofab war, forgotten in an ancient warehouse in the oldest part of K'Ronar. Without the warsuits, the Fleet Commando wouldn't have returned from the Lake of Dreams.

"All of you know Harrison," said L'Wrona. "He's our tactical advisor. I'll be in command, Lieutenant S'Til second in command."

"Where's the portal, sir?" asked Corporal N'Trun.

"Bill," said L'Wrona, looking at Sutherland. "Your area."

Taking the rostrum, Sutherland called up the overhead screen.

Nighttime. Colored lights, calliope music, whirling carousel, the rumble of a roller coaster, ponies, shrieking kids, laughing adults. Barkers, games, cotton candy, caramel popcorn, ice cream, funhouse . . .

Sutherland held the last shot. "You've all had lots of groundside time here," he said. "Know what this is?"

"It's an amusement park," said N'Trun.

"Right," said Sutherland. "It's the old Glen Echo Amusement Park, on the Maryland-District of Columbia line. The funhouse you see is the Maximus terminus in our universe."

"How do you know?" asked John.

"The signal traces D'Trelna picked up on the grid search. Plus something else. You remember when the bugs had the Leurre Institute?"

"Sure."

"Recall the name of that little bistro, tucked on the end of the main Leurre building?"

Harrison frowned. "Chez . . . Chez something."

"Chez Nichee," said Bill. " 'Place of the Nest.' Of course, we only learned later what nests and S'Cotar were. Well, they got cheeky again."

He tapped a control. Now they were looking at the front of a red-and-blue barn of a building, perhaps fifty feet high, windowless. A dozen broad wooden stairs led up to the smoked-glass double doors of the entrance. A bright red torii gate flared above the doors. The doors were padlocked. A permanent-looking sign read "Closed for Renovation—Watch for Grand Opening Next Summer." Two kids, about twelve or so, sat on the top step, eating orange Popsicles. At the bottom and to their left was a white ice-cream pushcart, the paunchy, balding vendor doling out ice cream to a short line of kids.

"Watch." Sutherland shifted to the tall gilt lettering over the torii gate: XANADU.

"So?" said John. "Colorful, romantic, Gay Ninety-ish. Probably some Madame Tussaud rendition of Coleridge inside, complete with demon lover. What makes you think it leads to Terra Two?"

"Because it says it does," said the CIA Director. He zoomed in on the smaller lettering below the name:

Not only the way to Xanadu,
But also the way to terror too.

"Weird, but not compelling," said John. "So they left off a comma. You found this after *Implacable* picked up the energy trace?"

"Yes."

"H'Nar, your show."

"It's a small S'Cotar nest," said L'Wrona, taking the rostrum as Sutherland sat back down, "but with the same strange energy output we recorded at the time of John's dramatic return from Terra Two. Detector readings show the staff to all be biofabs. The two children on the stairs are sentries. The pushcart, vendor and line are probably a heavy weapon's position, flanking the doorway. We've made five recons in there. Pushcart and children are always there. The faces change, but never the positions. That red structure is the center of the signal.

"We're going in and through to Terra Two. Indigenous Terran forces will take out the S'Cotar as we're quietly taking that building. We'll make certain that no S'Cotar slip through to warn Shalan-Actal. It will be daytime, just before public hours, so they'll be only combatants there.

"Terra Two. You've all memorized the Maximus complex map. We'll come into the portal building, seize it, then break out and regroup.

"If separated, you must make first rendezvous within one Terran hour. Otherwise, we'll be gone.

"Any more questions

"Very well. Luck to you. To the boats."

John watched through the shuttle's window as *Implacable* shrank to just another unwinking light among billions. He lost it as the craft breached the atmosphere.

"What did L'Wrona mean by indigenous Terran forces?" he asked, turning to Sutherland.

The two sat together aft. At John's question, he began adjusting his chair monitor's flawless picture, transforming a perfect forward scan of North America to a brown-blue blur.

"Marines, mostly," he said. "Some armed by the K'Ronarins and disguised by us, some coming in high and slow to keep the S'Cotar busy."

"Mostly?"

Sutherland looked up from scan. "All but one very sick, brave man to distract gate security. A man with 'Big C' who insisted on one last performance, battling alien hordes."

"Bob," said John softly.

Sutherland nodded.

"He hasn't been feeling well . . ."

"Two, three months left at the most," said Sutherland. "Metastasized throughout his body. He had a brief remission, but it's fading."

"I've got to see him," said John desperately. "You know how many times I wanted to drop out of grad school? How many times he bullied and cajoled me into staying, into working harder?"

Sutherland shook his head. "His contingent's leaving from a different point than yours or mine. There's no time."

"But he's my oldest friend!"

"He asked me to give you this," said Sutherland, handing over a white envelope.

Opening it, John slipped out the piece of white notepaper and read aloud the message, firmly penned by a strong hand:

> Dear John,
>
> You know me—no romantic palliatives: no harps, no heaven, no gentle Jesus. Ask my daughter to have them carve the stone with this, from John Donne:
>
> Churches are best for prayer that have least light:
> To see God only, I go out of sight;
> And to 'scape stormy days, I choose
> An everlasting night.
>
> Your friend always,
> Robert J. McShane

11

Turning into the empty dirt parking lot, the big silver-and-green bus crunched over the acorns, stopping beneath a stand of oak. ''Fairfax Charters'' read the lettering above the trim. From across the high white-picket fence, a calliope played.

The silver door swung wide. Out trooped the seniors, some leaning on canes. None were under sixty. Chattering, laughing, they followed the big white-bearded man up to the candy-striped admissions booth.

''Group reservation,'' he said, handing the attendant their yellow federal retirees' pass. ''We're the Double Dippers.'' The attendant, a lean, tanned kid in Levis and an American U. T-shirt, smiled faintly, checking his clipboard. ''Mr. McShane?''

Bob nodded.

''Welcome to Glen Echo, sir. We open in ten minutes.''

McShane raised his blackthorn Irish walker, pointing past the kid to where the Ferris wheel turned against a cloudless blue sky. "Your equipment is operating. We've paid enough for an extra ten minutes."

Even as the kid opened his mouth, the seniors were filing past, scattering into the park.

Need an underground command post? It's easy, if you're a S'Cotar transmute. Just teleport a clean, modest-sized nuclear weapon down to where it can be triggered without punching through to either surface or magma. Once the chamber you've created stabilizes, send down atmosphere and power generators, command and control systems. Finally, having carefully checked the life-support sensors, you may flick down your own green self. You're now a mile underground, sheltered in bedrock, impervious to standard K'Ronarin detectors and accessible only by telekinesis.

The command center under Glen Echo was small, just a single station with one transmute. Sug-Atra had had the good fortune to be outstationed on Terra Two when Pocsym blew the S'Cotar citadel to glory and *T'Nil's Revenge* wiped the biofab fleet. That had been a year ago. Now he sat bored, watching the surface telltales and monitoring the portal's status.

Sug-Atra saw the reality of Glen Echo, not the illusion created by his transmutes on the surface. Elderly humans strolled the midway, playing imaginary games, buying invisible junk food. Seen only by each other, S'Cotar warriors patrolled in pairs. In a weed-choked lot, where intense humans ruefully lost quarters to nonexistent video games, three transmutes stood with antennae entwined, constantly refreshing the illusion of Glen Echo.

An alarm chirped. Flicking a tentacle, Sug-Atra brought up a tacscan of the nearby Potomac. Rotary-winged aircraft, thirty of them, were proceeding upriver toward West

Virginia. Not unusual. The last week had seen an increase in military air traffic.

In about a month, Sug-Atra knew, the Terrans and their quaint war machines would be ash.

He replaced the tacscan with a bootlegged recording of a double-tiered, three-patterned mating dance—warriors and transmutes. It was delightfully perverse and utterly explicit. Sug-Atra was totally engrossed when the alarm sounded again. Angrily, he snapped out a tentacle, bringing back the tacscan. The helicopters were coming in low and fast, a narrow phalanx charging straight at the nest.

Alert! Alert! Sug-Atra's thought went to every S'Cotar in the park. *Air assault from the river. Ground defenses stand by to fire. Warriors deploy. Portal sentries alert Terra Two.*

What about the humans in the nest? asked the next senior transmute, one of the three in the vacant lot.

Harmless, said Sug-Atra. *Kill them later. Direct all fire at those helicopters.*

I remind you all, he called, *we are a sacrifice to the glory of the Race. We must hold this nest until our brothers in Terra Two can negate the portal.*

As the two boys turned and bolted up the stairs, McShane raised his cane and fired. The narrow red beam knifed through the two, shattering the doorglass and vanishing into Xanadu.

Tumbling down the stairs, the bodies became those of S'Cotar warriors. They lay heaped on the ground, viscous green slime oozing from their wounds.

Glen Echo turned into a small corner of hell.

The infiltrators, K'Ronarin crew and Terran infantry, were blasting away at preselected targets, taking out S'Cotar weapons positions, warriors and the occasional innocent pushcart.

Stunned for an instant, the S'Cotar blasted back, azure beams crisscrossing with the red, turning the midway into a deadly net of energy beams.

Illusion faded as the transmutes fought for their lives. Shimmering, the bright red Ferris wheel with its gaily colored lights imploded into a ball of primary colors that burst outward, then contracted into a compact gray shape—a shape Sutherland recognized.

"Fusion cannon!" he cried, staring wide-eyed out the plexiglass cockpit of the third helicopter. Green figures scuttled around the weapon, its great ugly snout now only a few hundred yards away, locking onto the lead chopper.

"Colonel Griswold," Sutherland called over the radio, "get 'em down now! Don't try for your primary LZ!"

The bulky troop carriers were still eighty yards up, making for the parking lot, when the cannon shrilled. A thick cobalt-blue fusion beam shot out, turning the lead chopper into a fiery ochre ball that hurled blackened bits of men and machine to earth.

The explosion was still echoing out over the Potomac when a second beam detonated another chopper.

Fifty yards above the parking lot, Sutherland saw the cannon lock onto his chopper.

"Shit," said the pilot, pulling the aircraft hard right.

Swooping in and over, the two escorting Apache gunships rocketed the cannon. The salvo went wide, small geysers of flame and dirt bursting around the S'Cotar position.

The cannon shrilled again, dissolving the tail rotor of Sutherland's chopper, then tracked right, firing short blue bursts. The Apaches exploded almost together, two flaming spheres touching as they dissolved into a rain of molten debris.

The earth rushed toward Sutherland, slamming him against a bulkhead. Blackness.

* * *

What was left of the real Ferris wheel lay between the midway and the cannon—only the motor housing itself, the motor and superstructure long since sold for scrap. Crawling low, McShane reached it just as the gunships were hit. He threw himself flat, hands over his head as flaming metal showered the area. As it ended, he peered cautiously over the rusting metal.

Most of the S'Cotar were deployed at the park's other end. The fusion cannon had only its four warrior crew: one in the gun chair, swiveling with the weapon, the other three maintaining tracking and energy feeds from a gray, all-weather console. Their broad green backs were to McShane. There was no sentry.

Remarkably stupid, thought McShane.

It had taken him five hard minutes to break from the firefight. He was tired, so tired. Sleep, his body told him, sleep. You'll sleep soon enough, he reminded himself.

Crawling along the midway, he'd wanted to stop a thousand times—stop, hide behind some piece of wreckage and close his eyes.

The screams had kept him going, brought him here. The screams of kids hit by S'Cotar fire, the commandos he'd sat with at briefing, joked with on the bus from McLean. The screams of the marines trapped and burning in the choppers' wreckage—high-pitched, keening, inhuman screams that finally, mercifully, died. Kids, all kids.

McShane wanted that cannon. And there it was, no more than one hundred feet away.

Twisting his blaster-cane to self-destruct, he stepped from cover, walking quickly into the clearing between him and the cannon, blaster held loosely at his side, its rising shrill lost in the whine and crash of blaster fire, the explosion of another helicopter as the cannon spat again.

The smoke, bedlam and his own surreal calm reminded McShane of Tarawa, a long time ago, crawling toward that pillbox, a grenade in hand.

At twenty feet he stopped, still unseen. Gripping the weapon by its muzzle, he spun it three times over his head, releasing it to land clanging against the gun console.

McShane had seen S'Cotar warriors in combat before. Their speed still amazed him. Whirling, the nearest three were out of their chairs before the blaster had barely touched the gray-mesh decking.

As the cannon shrilled again, two of them dove after the blaster, now screaming in terminal overload. Pulling his weapon, the third shot an unmoving McShane through the chest. Bob crumpled as a warrior scooped up his blaster-cane, tentacle arching to hurl it away.

Wah-whoomp! The blaster atomized the warriors and triggered the cannon's chargepac, vaporizing the gun. The explosion lit the Potomac Basin, a searing white flash seen from West Virginia to the Maryland shore.

As the cannon went up, Sug-Atra flicked to the surface, blaster in tentacle. *Form on me!* he ordered, standing at the foot of Xanadu's stairs.

The ninety surviving biofabs rallied, the warriors taking cover along the midway, fronting Xanadu, their last transmute appearing behind them. Beside him stood Sug-Atra.

Why is that portal still functioning? he demanded as the biofabs opened fire on the marines spilling from their choppers.

The portal sentries were killed, said the other transmute. *I've sent two more. The one who remains will report when* . . . The M16-round ripped through his thorax, throwing his body across the stairs.

Cursing, Sug-Atra flicked to cover.

You have blasters to their slug throwers! he raged. *Cut them down!*

They are too many, said the senior warrior. *We have no cover. Their infiltrators have our flanks pinned.*

Blaster beams and bullets rent the air. Gunfire and blaster shrilling mingled with the screams of the wounded and dying.

The S'Cotar were keeping the infantry at bay, blaster fire raking the marines' position. The Terrans' forward area was a charnel house—the blasted bodies of the point squad lay twisted among the smoldering wreckage of a chopper.

Sutherland staggered from the chopper, pistol in hand, blood oozing from a deep gash in his forehead. Running low, he zigzagged twenty yards to a light machine-gun position. "Where's the CP?" he shouted at the lance corporal feeding the belt.

The kid pointed to a shallow concrete drainage ditch skirting the shattered picket fence. Riflemen were spread along the ditch, raking the S'Cotar line.

Sutherland dashed off, covering half the distance before a heavy fusion beam touched the machine gun, scattering it and its crew like torn paper.

The CIA Director dived into the muddy ditch, azure beams crackling over his head. He looked up into Colonel Griswold's flint-gray eyes. "We got our asses wiped enough for you yet, Mr. Sutherland?"

"What time is it, Colonel?" Sitting, he rested against the concrete wall, breathing hard, pistol across his knee.

Griswold glanced at his watch. "Twelve twenty-eight. We are twenty-eight minutes into this debacle."

"Two more minutes, Griswold," said Sutherland. "Then you can take them."

Four men away, a gunnery sergeant dropped his rifle

and fell backward, spasms jerking his body. His neck ended in a charred, smoldering stump.

The PFC to Griswold's right started screaming hysterically. The colonel brought the muzzle of his .45 down behind the kid's left ear. He crumpled into the ditch, unconscious. Griswold turned him over, getting his face out of the brackish water.

"Why?" demanded the colonel, turning back to Sutherland. "I've lost over two hundred men in this idiocy. Why?"

Sutherland touched his forehead, feeling the sticky clot. "Can't hurt now. That building the S'Cotar are massed in front of?"

"Yes?"

"There's a K'Ronarin commando unit infiltrating it, from the rear."

"Are they taking the bugs from behind?"

Sutherland shook his head. "No. We're going to take them from the front. Those commandos will prevent the S'Cotar from accessing something in that building. Then they have a vital mission elsewhere. They're not to be wasted in this operation."

"And we are?" said Griswold, face pale.

"It's necessary," said Sutherland. "Otherwise, Colonel, in a few months, maybe sooner, you'd be fighting swarms of S'Cotar for this planet. Fighting and losing." He checked his watch. "Time."

Expressionless, the colonel spoke into his handset. "Red Pack Leader to Red Pack Pitcher. Execute, execute. Tango one niner."

From behind them came the dull *kruump!* of mortars firing.

"Fix bayonets!" shouted Griswold, looking up and down the line. "Fix bayonets!" He cocked his .45.

"Bayonets . . . ! Bayonets . . . !" The command echoed down the line. Drawing his combat knife, Griswold stepped from the ditch, bracketed by blaster fire. "Follow me!" he cried, voice high above the din. "Forward!"

Kismet, thought Sutherland, as the line surged forward. I'm going to be killed fighting bugs in an amusement park.

Taking an M16 from the dead, he joined the charge.

The first mortar barrage fell short of the S'Cotar line, turning two concession stands to matchsticks.

The next six didn't, exploding among the warriors, halving their numbers, splattering Xanadu's red walls green.

Through his one remaining eye, Sug-Atra saw the marines coming, bayonets gleaming through the smoke and flames.

Assault! he ordered the warriors.

A ragged line, the S'Cotar charged, weapons blazing.

Bleeding in a dozen places, Sug-Atra tried to teleport inside. Nothing. A piece of shrapnel had done something profound to his special abilities. Turning, he limped painfully up Xanadu's stairs. As he reached the top stair, H'Nar L'Wrona stepped through the doors and shot him dead, tumbling his body back down the stairs.

The Margrave stood looking out over the carnage for a moment, watching the olive-drab wave roll over the S'Cotar, then went back inside.

Along the midway, marines with dripping combat knives stooped low, taking weregeld from the S'Cotar.

"You could have taken those bugs from the rear, Captain," said Griswold quietly. He looked too exhausted to be angry.

"We'd have been exposed to your fire, Colonel," said L'Wrona earnestly. "Worse, we'd have exposed this building to it. A single ember falling through to the wrong place, and every man who died today would have died in vain."

"You're a hard man, L'Wrona."

"I know."

The two stood on Xanadu's steps, backdropped by the amusement park's smoldering ruins. Firemen hosed the hot ash and twisted metal that had been weapons positions and kiddie rides, their lines snaking in from the yellow pumpers out on the MacArthur Boulevard. From the parking lot came the whirr of medevac choppers as triage teams hurried down the long rows of stretcher cases. Wounded with the best chance of survival if medevaced now would go first. The rest would either go later or in the fleet of ambulances clogging the far end of the parking lot. Many would die where they lay.

To the west, a blood-red sun shone through the smoke and haze.

The S'Cotar lay where they'd fallen.

"I lost over two hundred good men today, Captain," said Griswold, looking over the midway.

"We lost billions fighting those things," said L'Wrona. "Billions."

"I want to see that portal, Captain," said Griswold, turning back to La'Wrona. "I'm entitled."

"How did you know about the portal?" frowned L'Wrona.

"Sutherland."

"Ah. Well, you're right. You are entitled." He opened a door, motioning Griswold in. "We're leaving in a few minutes. You can see us off."

"This is bigger than the Maximus portal," said John, staring at the pit filling Xanadu.

"How much bigger?" asked Lieutenant S'Til.

"Twice, at least. They must have widened the other end."

Looking at that too-dark pool, John felt what he'd first sensed on the side of the portal—deep, rippling power, lurking just below the surface—a power somehow controlled by a slim machine a universe away.

The portal nearly filled Xanadu. The building itself was facade, a slice of Hollywood on the Potomac. The back could be rolled open, two great garage doors that trundled on rubber casters across a cement apron. First seeing that, John had had a vision of something huge, gray and monstrous coming up from the pit, abristle with fusion turrets, moving silently out into the night on n-gravs, force field shimmering faintly in the moonlight.

The stench of burning men and machines wafted through the ragged blaster hole in the left door.

Led by L'Wrona, the commandos and the three Terrans had slipped in from the woods between Glen Echo and MacArthur Boulevard, the battle along the midway covering them as they'd moved through the fence, under the roller coaster and up to the building's rear. Blasting a hole through the wall, they'd poured in—there were no S'Cotar. Taking up positions, they'd waited, silently killing the four S'Cotar who'd come in.

The biofabs lay in a thick pool of green beside the door, necks slit by broad-bladed assault knives. The commandos lined the side of the pit, blastrifles at port arms, every other man facing out. Pacing slowly behind them, Lieutenant S'Til impatiently tapped the M11A's long barrel against her hard, slender leg. John stood to one side, away from the door.

"What are we waiting for?" he asked.

"L'Wrona," said S'Til.

* * *

"Major Harkness," called Sutherland, spotting Griswold's XO. "Where's the colonel?"

Young, black, the untreated cut across his left cheek still bleeding, Harkness turned from the radio, eyes glazed with fatigue. "Behind those concessions stands," he said, waving toward a charred heap near the Ferris wheel.

Sutherland headed down the midway, treading carefully past the dead. Bodies often entwined, marines and warriors lay where they'd fallen, knives, bayonets and guns against knives, serrated mandibles and blasters.

Sutherland tried not to look at the faces. The assault had been bad enough, but it had been fast, a blur of motion: shoot, move, shoot, move. For the first time since Korea, he'd used a bayonet, performing a clumsy but tenable parry-and-long-thrust series. This was worse, he thought, stumbling over a helmet. Something out of Goya, those young, dead, tormented faces staring sightlessly, throats ripped out, necks broken, holes you could put your fist through. And everywhere the stench of burnt flesh, hanging in a low haze over the clouds of flies come to feast.

He found Griswold behind the concession stand, face down in the dirt, a neat round hole through each temple. There was no blood—just a dead man, his mind stolen.

Sutherland turned in time to see L'Wrona and Griswold enter Xanadu, a good hundred yards away. Communicator lost in the chopper wreckage, he cursed and began running.

The Terran colonel paused at his first sight of the portal, then advanced gingerly to the edge, peering down. Brushing past the commandos, L'Wrona followed.

"This is it?" asked Griswold, looking at L'Wrona.

The captain nodded. "A hole in the heart of the universe."

"Ever hear of George Bernard Shaw, Margrave?" asked the colonel.

L'Wrona shook his head.

"A brilliant, crusty man. He said, 'The devil has all the best lines.' It's true."

"I don't understand."

"I'll give you an example, L'Wrona." *Follow me and die.*

L'Wrona fired as the transmute leaped into the portal. Sutherland burst through the door. "Transmute!" he gasped. "Griswold!"

Pulling his knife, L'Wrona jumped after transmute.

"Go!" shouted S'Til.

John and the commandos plunged into the portal.

Sutherland stood alone in Xanadu, breathless, watching the ripples fade in the black pool.

He was still watching when the portal flicked off, leaving a deep raw gash in the red clay and sand.

12

"How's he doing, Q'Nil?"

The words drifted distantly, touching and slowly stirring his consciousness. K'Ronarin, he thought. Bluff, gruff.

D'Trelna.

McShane opened his eyes.

"He's coming around now, Commodore."

D'Trelna stood at the foot of the bed, round face concerned. Beside him, thin and detached, Medtech Q'Nil was checking life readings off the unit's medscan. The three were alone in a small, cheery room, walls done in warm earth tones with matching bed coverlet.

"I didn't die," said Bob hoarsely.

"Close," said Q'Nil. Stepping around the bed he poured water from a carafe into a disposable cup, handing it to McShane.

Nodding his thanks, the professor downed it in two loud gulps. "How long have I been out?"

"Two weeks," said D'Trelna as S'Nil took the cup,

tossing it into the disposer with an economical flip of his wrist.

"You took a blaster bolt through the chest," said Q'Nil. "Plus shock and some complications. Otherwise, you'd have been up sooner."

Bob pulled open the front of his green bed gown. A patch of curly gray chest hair was missing, but the skin was smooth and seamless. "What complications?"

"A nasty viral infection," said Q'Nil. "Surely you're aware of it?"

"I have cancer," said Bob evenly. "Is that what you mean?"

"Whatever you call it," said Q'Nil. "We flushed it—took a few days. Very elusive, very adept at hiding from the immuno system. Altering one of its proteins, though, strips its camouflage. We introduced an antigen that did that, then kept you under while your body cleaned up."

Barefeet slapping onto the cold gray deck, McShane was out of the bed, gripping a surprised Q'Nil. "My God, man! You can cure cancer?"

"If we couldn't, you wouldn't be bruising my arm, Professor."

"Sorry," he said, letting go. "It's just that I expected to wake up dead, as my granddaughter says."

"Nothing wrong with your right hand," said Q'Nil, rubbing his left tricep. "How's the rest of you feel?"

"Great. Wonderful!" Vibrant, his voice filled the room. "Better than I have in months." He threw his arms above his head, then bent to touch his toes. "I couldn't have done that a few weeks ago.

"Are there side effects?"

Q'Nil nodded somberly.

"What?" asked Bob, voice suddenly tight.

"You may experience some flatulence."

"That's it?"

"That's it," said Q'Nil. "Now, if you'll excuse me, others await my healing touch." He left, the door hissing shut after him.

Bob sat down on the edge of the bed—sat down hard and was silent for a moment. "I'm alive and others are not," he said finally, studying the backs of his hands. "Is it because we're friends, J'Quel?"

"You are alive. Others are alive," said D'Trelna. "Not because we're friends, but because the Fleet of the Republic has extended aid and comfort to all casualties of the battle of the portal."

McShane smiled ruefully. "Sorry, J'Quel. I'm a pious old coot."

"You're not that old."

"You are going to release this discovery to Terra?"

"Sent it down to Liaison in New York five days ago," said D'Trelna. "They've forwarded it to all accredited Terran legations."

Bob shook his head. "There's a bloated medical bureaucracy with a vested interest in not having this released. Unless pressure can be brought . . ."

D'Trelna smiled his Cheshire smile.

"What have you done, J'Quel?'

"I felt a senior officer should personally transmit this marvelous discovery to Liaison. In the absence of Captain L'Wrona, I undertook that duty. Unfortunately, I'm not familiar with some of the communications protocols. The transmission was in the clear, in all known Terran languages on every operable voice and data frequency."

"These things happen," said Bob, eyes sparkling.

D'Trelna nodded sadly. "True, true. I will no doubt be reprimanded, should anyone be stupid enough to complain."

"And the reaction?"

"Tumult. Jubilation. Crowds. Demands.

"Q'Nil says the antigen is easily made and will work on all viral variants. Clinics are being set up to supplement existing medical facilities. Three months"—he puffed his cheeks—"pouff. No more cancer."

"You're a good man, D'Trelna," said McShane.

"True," said the commodore. Turning to the wall locker, he tossed boots and brown duty uniform onto the bed. "Get dressed. Fresh Kansas steak awaits in my quarters."

Tugging the boots on, McShane was suddenly aware of a gnawing hunger in his belly.

"Wine, Bob?"

"Just a tad. I'd better not overdo it."

D'Trelna poured from the graceful, long-necked bottle, topping McShane's delicate crystal goblet. Dining alone, the two sat at the big t'raq-wood table in *Implacable*'s spacious flag quarters.

"Delightful," said McShane, savoring the wine's rich, tangy bouquet. "From what strange vineyard under what far, exotic sun?" he asked. Holding the goblet up to the armorglass wall, he watched the crimson liquid catch the starlight.

D'Trelna read the label. "Modesto, California."

"A passable burgundy," said McShane, setting the goblet down.

"So, they got through the portal and that's all we know?"

Nodding, D'Trelna sliced off another wedge of medium-rare porterhouse. "That's all we know. Portal's still down, Fleet reinforcements are due shortly." He frowned, steak halfway to his mouth. "I don't know how long I can hold that flotilla here. The Confederation's a mess. Liberated planets are in dire need of everything, S'Cotar ships still attack understrength convoys. We even have pirates.'' He chewed the steak.

''Pirates?'' said Bob, eyes widening. ''Honest-to-God space pirates?''

''Honest-to-God space pirates—corsairs. Units that escaped the S'Cotar, lived off badly needed supply convoys during the war and are now raiding the liberated quadrants. Most of them are pre-war Fleet—rotten before the shooting started.''

''Lovely. Will you be the senior-officer-present when your reinforcements arrive?''

''No.''

''So if there's no crisis, off they go?''

''Correct,'' said D'Trelna. Finishing the last piece of steak, the commodore leaned back in his chair, eyes half closed, hands clasped over his belly. He sighed contentedly.

''You're taking this all very well, D'Trelna,'' said McShane suspiciously.

''I think I know how we can get *Implacable* and any fresh ships to Terra Two.'' Pushing back his chair, he walked to the armorglass. Hands behind his back, he stood looking out into space. ''Or rather, I know who may know the way.'' He turned back to Bob. ''I'd like you to come. It may involve some risk.''

Bob sipped his wine. ''Tell me about it.''

Startled, K'Raoda looked up to see a warsuited D'Trelna at his elbow, belted M11A blaster at his waist, M32 blastrifle slung over his right shoulder. ''Commodore! What . . .'' he said, swiveling in the command chair.

''Should anyone ask, T'Lei,'' said D'Trelna, oblivious to the stares of the bridge crew, ''especially Ambassador Z'Sha or FleetOps, I am indisposed. A raging fever of unknown origin has left me a useless, gibbering mass. Sick Bay has logged the necessary entries. As acting captain you have, of course, quarantined *Implacable*. Oh, and Bob McShane,'' he jerked a thumb over his shoulder, to where McShane stood, armed and suited, ''Bob McShane is still deathly ill. Clear?''

''Quite. May I ask where you're going?''

''Ghost hunting on Terra's Moon. We hope to be back.''

''Luck,'' said K'Raoda as the two left. D'Trelna waved absently.

''There's only one thing left down there,'' said T'Ral as the bridge doors slid shut.

''I know,'' nodded K'Raoda.

''But it's dead. Dead and empty.''

K'Raoda smiled thinly. ''Empty of people, certainly. Dead . . .'' He shrugged. ''That's a lot of fire power to take into a tomb.''

He waited until the shuttle cleared hangar deck, a stubby silver craft flashing past the bridge.

''Computer. Senior officer designating medical emergency.''

''Nature of medical emergency?'' said the pleasant contralto.

''Crew member stricken by fever of undetermined origin.''

''Medical department corroborates,'' said computer after a second. ''Fever of undetermined origin. Advise general quarantine.''

''Agreed,'' said K'Raoda. ''Shipwide,'' he said. Computer switched him into *Implacable*'s general address net.

''Alert. Alert.'' K'Raoda's voice echoed through the great old ship. ''This is Commander K'Raoda, Acting-Captain. Medical quarantine is now in effect. Medical quarantine is now in effect. We have a minor contagion of Terran origin. Until it's diagnosed, there'll be no more shore leave." He could almost hear the groans sweeping the corridors. "Crew now on Terra will have to remain there. Weekly leave party having just left, we'll be on double watches until Medical gives the all clear. Out."

"Whatever D'Trelna's up to," said T'Ral, "better be worth it. This leaves half the crew on Terra, the rest of us up here on double watch. If anything happens . . ."

K'Raoda turned, blue eyes meeting T'Ral's gray ones. "Reinforcements will be here soon. Meanwhile, if anything—untoward—happens, we can always do a computer tie to weapons."

T'Ral frowned. "You know what Fleet Regs say on that." The Fourth Dynasty forward had avoided problems with intelligent machinery by carefully restricting AI to necessary uses. Computers processed data. And there were no robots. Period.

"The option exists," said K'Raoda, keeping his voice low. "This is an Imperial warship. If you can't get our programming overlay to selectively revert, Y'Tan, I can."

The tactics officer shrugged. "We're beating a corpse, T'Lei. It's not going to happen."

"Let's hope not. Meanwhile, you have the pleasure of telling Ambassador Z'Sha that we've a quarantine." He stifled the other's protest with upraised palm. "No, no. I've got to compose a message about this to Fleet."

"But, T'Lei . . . !"

"Just tell him that the two junior officers whom he called 'Filthy, revolting animals' during the UN victory reception . . ."

T'Ral closed his eyes, pained. "I swear, all I remember is our dancing naked. I can't recall the women, the fountain or the horse."

"Assure him that these same two junior officers have the defense of the planet well in hand."

T'Ral opened his eyes. "He's going to go crazy."

"I know," smiled K'Raoda, nodding.

13

Some wiseass NASA cartographer had named it the Vale of Kashmir.

Geologically and topographically, it resembled any one of a thousand valleys on the Moon's Earth side; a dusty stretch of ancient, scarred basalt, pockmarked by eons of meteor showers, flanked by the impossibly sharp slopes of the Taurus Mountains.

Another time, McShane would have delighted in the stark moonscape, the deep, twisted shadows thrown by pure sunlight across ageless boulders. Not now. His full attention was on the immensity filling the Vale of Kashmir.

"I'd forgotten how big it was," he said.

D'Trelna nodded, head bobbing inside the warsuit's helmet. "You need the contrast to appreciate its size," he said, voice crisp and clear in Bob's communicator.

The mindslaver filled the valley, hovering just above the surface on n-gravs, twenty lethal miles of gray battlesteel bristling with fusion turrets, missile batteries and instrument pods. Her upper hull was almost even with where the two men stood, high on a ridge beside their shuttle.

"How'd you get her down with the brainpods destroyed?" asked Bob, carefully, avoiding the issue of who had destroyed the brainpods. That was a question now in the hands of Fleet Security.

"Central computer," said D'Trelna. "She has one. A very formidable one."

McShane shook his head. "J'Quel, that's *T'Nil's Revenge*, greatest and last of the symbiotechnic dreadnoughts—a great, bloody mindslaver. Disembodied human brains ran her—living minds ripped from healthy bodies to run the Empire's war machines. A computer would have been superfluous."

"Backup," said D'Trelna. "For mundane tasks and in case the brainstrips failed." Taking a small black cylinder from his belt pouch, he pointed at their feet and twisted it.

The broad band of green light flashed from the ship, arching into the ground before them in a tall geyser of dust.

Startled, McShane had stepped back. The dust settling, he stepped forward, next to D'Trelna.

"I submit," said D'Trelna, "that the computer works."

"Don't tell me," said Bob. "It's a light bridge."

"How did you know?"

"It's a popular fictional device." Bob peered down the jagged cliff that fell thousands of feet to the valley floor, then looked up at the frail, shimmering ribbon of green that spanned the gap. "I'm not trusting my life to a fictional device."

"It is real," said D'Trelna. "It works—you don't even have to walk. Watch."

Stepping onto the light bridge, he moved across it, reaching the dreadnought in a few seconds, never lifting his feet. "Nothing to it," he said, turning to drape an arm over the protruding muzzle of a small fusion cannon.

"So say you, D'Trelna."

"Come on. Let's get inside."

McShane hesitantly stepped onto the thin beam of translucent light. Soft but firm, something enveloped him to the waist even as it slid him across the light bridge. Something that brought him safely to the dreadnought, releasing him as the light bridge vanished.

"I'll be damned," he said as D'Trelna tucked away the control rod. "How far from the ship will that work?"

D'Trelna shrugged. "Who knows? There's been no research team out here yet. What with war recovery and mop-up operations, everyone is busy elsewhere. They'll get back to her, though. The variety and degree of Imperial technology in this horror is impressive."

"That's a very small cannon for such a very big ship, J'Quel," said McShane, pointing to where D'Trelna's arm rested.

D'Trelna stepped back, looking at the weapon and the small turret housing it. "Anti-personnel," he said. "To repel boarders." He turned, sweeping his arm along the seemingly endless expanse of *Revenge*. "Look around. The hull's littered with them."

McShane looked. The turrets went on forever, spaced every hundred or so feet, nestled between larger weapons and instrument pods. "Good God! People stormed these monstrosities?"

"Unbelievable, isn't it? Flesh and blood against miles of battlesteel and flawless latticefire.

"Shall we go in?"

"How? Last time here, I came through the hangar deck."

"Hangar deck," said the commodore, taking the rod from his pouch, "is only a few yards above the surface, blanketed in an n-grav field that would turn your body to protoplasmic mush.

"As for the door . . ." he said, thumbing the rod. A broad circle of hull, pods and turrets vanished. A wide tunnel slopped gently into the ship, lit soft yellow by hexagonal wall cubes. A distant gray smudge marked the passageway's far end.

D'Trelna led, stepping onto the steel flooring. Following, Bob staggered as the ship's gravity field clamped down, then recovered, catching up with D'Trelna. "Isn't it dangerous, J'Quel, having that bloody great hole in the ship?"

The commodore's shrug was visible through the thin miracle of the warsuit. "The shield would stop any space crud."

"Yes, but if enemy boarders knew where these tunnels were . . ."

"Those gently glowing cubes on the wall," said D'Trelna, not breaking stride, "are disintegrator pods. We're in a giant ionization tube. A simple command to computer and . . . phhht!"

"Phhht, indeed," said Bob, glancing uneasily at their light source. "And where does this . . . tube lead?"

"Into a reception area. We'll pick up a shipcar there."

"This just goes through the hull?" He stopped, regauging the tunnel's length. "That's over a quarter mile of battlesteel!"

"Yes." D'Trelna twisted off the warsuit's bubble helmet. "Atmosphere curtain," he explained, jerking a thumb back at the entrance.

Removing his own helmet, Bob took a breath of chill, metallic air. "Even smells like battlesteel.

"So, tell me," he said as they walked, helmets under their arms, "how did blood and flesh take a mindslaver?"

"Penal brigades were used to sop up the hull fire, fight off counterassaults and plant charges. If any lived long enough to blow a hole in the hull, assault boats would come in and Imperial marines would storm into the ship."

"Casualties must have been awesome."

"Tens of thousands."

"Why didn't the defenders just blow the ship up?" asked Bob as they reached the end of the tunnel and the inner door.

"Cost money. 'A' starts blowing up his mindslavers, then 'B' is blowing up his. The only thing left then is to destroy each other's ships. And that, as you may guess . . ."

"Cost money." Bob shook his head. "Whole economies must have been based on this bloody swapping."

"Oh, they were," said D'Trelna, frowning at the gray battlesteel door. "One could build a certain number of them, at great expense. Keeping a war going at just the right pace provides industrial growth and a certain hollow prosperity."

"The trick was not to lose many ships?"

D'Trelna nodded. "That would have been mutually ruinous. Mindslavers fought it out only twice—when they were invented and fielded by the R'Actolian biofabs, and when the Empire was in its final agony. The rest of the time—a long, long time—those tacit rules of engagement were followed."

"And life was cheap."

"Never so cheap as then."

Another ten minutes brought them to the end of the tube and a thick gray slab of battlesteel.

"Why isn't this door opening?" said D'Trelna after a moment.

"Problem?"

"Yes." He nudged the door with his boot. "It's supposed to open when someone stands here."

The disintegrator pods began humming.

D'Trelna turned, looking back down the tube. The pods were oscillating from soft yellow to a fierce white. Each cycle was shorter than the last, more white than yellow. "It's going into destruct mode! Something's triggered it."

"How long?"

"Not long. When it slips into pure white, we're dead." The commodore slipped off his rifle. "Fire at the door." Aiming carefully, he pulled the trigger, sending a raw beam of energy splashing against the door. The thick battlesteel lapped it up, not even glowing.

"Hurry!" he shouted above the blaster's shrilling.

McShane stood unmoving, right hand on the rifle's brown duraplast sling, eyes fixed, unblinking.

Suddenly he moved to the right, six practiced, economical steps that brought him to the wall, hands pushing four widely separated blocks just so, each on a different edge.

Dimming, the cubes slipped back into yellow as the door slid noiselessly open. Three broad corridors ended in a wide circle before the tunnel. Small shipcars rimmed the circle, fronts tucked into power niches.

"Bob!" D'Trelna shook McShane by the shoulder.

"What . . ." He blinked, dazed. "The door's open!"

"You don't remember?"

"No. Except . . ." He shook his head.

"What?"

"I was back in that pit of a room . . ."

"The mindslave chamber, here on *Revenge*?"

"Yes. Back in that room, mindlinked with those things, hearing their frenzied buzzing, feeling them rip at my mind, when the whole thing froze, became a sort of mental tableau and a voice, very calm, very slow, said, 'We gave even as we tried to take. The pattern of the cubes, sally portal one-four-two.' "

He looked at the commodore. "You said we were here to consult the ship's computer. Not quite true, is it?"

"Let's take one of those cars. I'll explain as we go."

"Very well."

As they stepped into the ship, the door closed behind them. Reaching the nearest car, Bob sank into the front passenger's side, rifle between his knees, helmet on the floor. D'Trelna tossed rifle and helmet into the back seat, climbed in and backed the noiseless car from its berth.

"We're here to see the overmind," said D'Trelna. Bringing the car up to speed, he turned down the left corridor. Doorways and side corridors flashed by.

"I thought you'd killed all the mindslaves."

"The overmind's in a different part of *Revenge*. It spoke to me after I destroyed the central brainpod clusters."

"Did the overmind pull that stunt in the tunnel?"

"I don't know."

"What is an overmind?"

"A mindslaver's central processing unit. It delegates tasks to the various brainpods, coordinates them. It's the interface between brainpods and ship's computer."

McShane grabbed the rollbar as D'Trelna threw the car into a tight spiral, plunging down a ramp toward the lower decks. "You may be a helluva starship captain, D'Trelna," he said, "but you're the worst driver in the galaxy."

"You want to walk?"

"No. Why are we going to see the overmind?"

"It told me to return when the S'Cotar did. Poor, mad brain, I thought. All those years without a body, all those millennia in stasis. Death would be a mercy.

"Well, the S'Cotar are back. And so am I."

Deep within the mindslaver, they stopped before a small, unmarked door. Powering down, D'Trelna dismounted as the car settled to the floor. Taking out the rifles, he handed one to Bob.

"Does the overmind shoot, too?" asked McShane, taking the rifle uncertainly.

"As an Imperial, it probably prefers treachery," smiled the commodore. "No. These are in case of bugs. Can't run max n-gravs and shield together."

The door opened.

McShane had been expecting a deep shaft of a room, like the sterile gray well forward that had housed the rest of *Revenge*'s mindslaves. "Very nice," he said, following D'Trelna into the stylish little room.

The walls were hung with tapestries artfully woven in skillful geometric patterns that deceived the eye. The carpeting was rich and deep, altering hue or color with each change of perspective. Two armchairs and a sofa of the same material as the carpeting sat against the wall.

"Gentlemen," said a faint, dry voice. "Sit, if you wish."

"We'll stand," said D'Trelna.

"Thank you for coming."

"Could you speak up?" asked Bob.

"Most of my remaining energy is holding off central computer," said the voice, slightly louder. "When you destroyed the mindslaves, Commodore, you destroyed the delicate balance between organic and inorganic minds on this ship. Pity, too. Computer was good company. We shared a liking for prespace mythology. But now that large lump of spun titanium crystal is about to finish me."

"Why?" asked Bob.

"It's quite mad. It was in stasis a long time, with the rest of this vessel. Its particular series does—did—not take well to stasis. It was computer that tried to kill you in the sally portal.''

''And you who joggled my memory?''

''Yes. You know much about this ship, McShane, absorbed from the mindslaves when they tried to destroy you, your last time here.''

Bob started to ask another question.

''Please. Let me say what I have to, then I and this ship are of no further moment.

''You're here, D'Trelna, because the S'Cotar are back.''

''Yes.''

''From an alternate Terra, according to your skipcomms to Fleet.''

The commodore nodded.

''You were right, guessing it's not a S'Cotar device the biofabs are using.''

''They got to the Trel cache!'' exclaimed Bob.

''No,'' said the overmind. ''The Trel cache was discovered just as the Empire entered its final cataclysm. It's never been explored. The device the S'Cotar have is Imperial—a prototype ferreted from Pocsym's vaults by Guan-Sharick and used to establish a fallback point on Terra Two. It's limited to surface use. The spaceborne unit that was used to remove your destroyer must have been brought by the machines.''

The color drained from D'Trelna's face. ''The Empire had no spaceborne unit? How am I to get a ship to Terra Two?''

''There's a prototype of such a device hidden on this ship. You will need one other starship positioned here to send you through.''

''Reinforcements are on the way.''

''Don't count your ships before they arrive, Commodore. I did, once. It cost me my body.

"Also, finding the device, you still have to escape the ship with it."

The overmind spoke quickly, voice almost inaudible. "Computer's heating my brain casing. Finishing me, it will come after you."

"Where's the device?" said Bob.

"Deck forty-eight—Agro. Program your shipcar with that deck number and flag section red one-eight-four."

"Agro red-one-eight-four," repeated D'Trelna.

"Computer's made a green hell out of Agro, piled all the treasures and mysteries there that the Empire sent, at the end. You'll find what you need there, in the house of the dead.

"Go now. Luck."

As they left, a faint tendril of thought touched McShane. *Empty is the House of S'Kal. Empire and Destiny.*

"What?" he said, turning back as the door opened.

From somewhere nearby came the high, wrenching sound of flawed crystal cracking. As the door shut, the men heard something soft and wet smacking onto the deck.

"Skirmish one to computer," said D'Trelna as they reached the shipcar. He turned, hearing a noise. McShane had slumped into his seat, head in hand.

"Bob, what is it?" D'Trelna bent over the Terran.

"I have a terrible headache."

"We have to go on."

"I know." Raising his head, Bob swung around into the car, ashen-cheeked. "I'll be fine.

"This car isn't tied into the computer, is it?" he asked, resting his head against the seatback.

"No," said D'Trelna, tapping numbers into the modest control board. "We'd have been squashed like bugs against a bulkhead if it were." He grunted with satisfaction as the confirmation flashed across the small screen. "Ready."

"Don't you want to call for help?" asked Bob.

"No." He engaged autopilot. The shipcar rose, pivoting 180 degrees. "Not only is *Implacable* under-crewed, but if our visit here becomes an official mission, official questions will be asked. They'll find out I killed those mindslaves and disabled this monster." The car picked up speed. "Court-martialed, I'd be found guilty. We have few prisons. My personality would be altered—for my own good. I would become a simple, happy, thin man. Losing my drive, creativity and intellect, I'd spend the rest of my long, useless life watching the fruits of others' imagination parade by on the vidscreen."

"To Agro," said Bob, taking the blastrifle from the floor.

"I should check in," said the commodore as the car spiraled down a ramp.

"D'Trelna to *Implacable*," he said, touching the communicator at his throat. He waited a moment, then tried again. There was no response.

"Odd," he said, looking at McShane. "Never had this problem."

"Could *Revenge*'s computer be jamming?"

Reaching behind his thick neck, D'Trelna unsnapped the communicator. Stubby fingers moving with surprising dexterity, he popped open the back of the tiny oval. "D'Trelna to *Implacable*," he said carefully, watching the pattern of light that flashed along tiny crystalline veins.

"Was I right?" asked Bob as the car raced along an interminable stretch of gray corridor.

"Yes," said the commodore, snapping the communicator together and fastening it back around his neck. "Something's blocking our signal."

"Computer?"

"Probably." D'Trelna glanced behind them. "At least nothing deadly's streaking after us.

"We're almost there."

McShane sat up, headache forgotten. "Check your weapons," said D'Trelna as the shipcar rounded a bend, slowing. "And put on your helmet. We're here."

McShane looked ahead. Soaring overhead, a great slab of armorglass blocked the corridor. Strange flora blossomed on the other side, an explosion of green.

The car stopped, settling to the ground.

Dismounting, D'Trelna twisted on his helmet, then took a flat, oblong device from beneath the dashboard.

"Locator," said McShane, recognizing the machine from times past.

"Programmed with our exact destination, taken from the car's navsystem. Shall we?" said the commodore, pointing with blastrifle toward the greenery.

Helmets on, rifles at port arms, the two men approached the transparent barrier.

Parting along an invisible seam, the armorglass slid open—an opening just wide enough for two. From inside came sharp, feral cries worthy of a Jurassic swamp.

"Sounds like everything in there eats everything else," said McShane.

"I should prove a filling morsel," said the commodore. Snapping off the rifle's safety, he stepped over the threshold. Bob followed.

Behind them, the armorglass snicked quietly shut.

14

"How are you, my dear Christian?" asked Jesus.

Hochmeister looked up from walnut writing desk, blinking at the Raphaelite Christ standing in the late brigadier's living room: thorns crowning chestnut hair, stigmata piercing the delicate frame, tattered, soiled white linen robe; the Renaissance vision of The Levantine as granted a shabby, five-color immortality by millions of cheap reproductions and shoddy interpretations.

"Shalan-Actal," sighed the admiral. He leaned back in the overstuffed green-velvet Regency armchair. "You look more like a Hollywood pretty boy than an itinerant Galilean rabbi. And your compassionate visage needs improving."

"Still working on your memoirs?" The transmute pointed to the neat pile of yellow foolscap on the desk.

"Still," nodded Hochmeister, setting his pen back in the ink well. "Art, Goethe reminds us, is long, life short. I'm now at chapter thirty-two, mine and Canaris's chat with Rommel, convincing him to join the putsch."

"I met Rommel once," said Shalan-Actal.

The admiral's eyebrows rose. "You met Rommel? I thought you were out pillaging your galaxy."

"Don't forget, Admiral," said the Jesus-form, "we—biofabs—were created on Terra's moon. Our war with the K'Ronarins only lasted ten of your years. And although Pocsym didn't allow us to meddle in Terran affairs, there were training missions. Naturally, I met the alternate Rommel. It was early in his career."

"I met him early in my career, midpoint in his. What was your impression?"

"Talented and daring."

Hochmeister nodded. "A great soldier and a fine Chancellor."

"Only a soldier in my reality, Admiral."

"Why have you come?"

"Need I have a purpose, Admiral?" The brigadier replaced Jesus.

"All you do has purpose, Shalan-Actal. In that, we're much alike."

"Perhaps," said the brigadier-form. "Although my kind don't call me monster.

"We will soon need spokesmen, Admiral." The dead brigadier's pale blue eyes met Hochmeister's. "We remain undetected by authorities in this reality. Soon, we'll have seized your sister world. That done, we will subjugate this world, not as green insectoids, though. Rather, as humans from space—a sort of peacekeeping galactic league, out to bring order to the backward worlds."

"Very romantic. Why should I sell your pseudo Pax Galactica?"

"The alternatives are not pleasant, Admiral. Experience has shown that our casualties soar when thousands of xenophobes hurl explosives at us. It then becomes cheaper to neutron scrub the planet and breed workers. And it frees our warriors for duty elsewhere—some compensation for lost time and industrial output."

"Interesting," said the admiral. "But why not just kill me, steal my mind and imitate me?"

"Would you believe we dislike unnecessary bloodshed?"

"No." Pushing his chair back, Hochmeister rose, facing the S'Cotar across the table. "I've been here three weeks to the day, Shalan-Actal. You've given me the freedom of the post. For which I thank you."

"Colleagueal courtesy, Admiral."

"Perhaps you think me either blind or stupid."

The brigadier-form shook its head. "Not blind. Not stupid. Merely incapable of hurting us alone and unaided."

"I've made some observations."

"Yes?"

"You don't have sufficient force, even with your special powers, even with the replacements you're busy breeding, to hold both this world and its alternate. The war that brought you here, the war you lost, greatly reduced your numbers and your machines. You must be very short of transmutes if you're trying to enlist my aid." Walking past Shalan-Actal, the admiral went to the picture window. He stood looking out over the Green Mountains and the fading splendor of autumn. The S'Cotar turned, watching him.

"Yet, knowing this, you're planning to invade your point of origin. Attacking World One, shall we call it, leaves you vulnerable here. If detected and attacked, you'd be overwhelmed. Failing on World One, you'd have no safe haven to fall back on."

"We call it Terra One, Admiral. And the attack will not fail. Our enemies have but one ship insystem. They're expecting reinforcements. Something other than reinforcements are on their way.

"Oh, and, Admiral—you missed something."

Hochmeister turned, frowning. "What?"

"Our allies. We have allies. Nonhumans, like ourselves. With their help, nothing can stop us."

"I've seen no other life-forms here," said Hochmeister.

"But you have seen them, Admiral. You even fought them.

"You and your pickup army gave us a hard fight. That you didn't stop us was due to the Maximus device itself. The genius of the High K'Ronarins went into it. It seems to be self-healing."

Blood etched in Hochmeister's mind, the S'Cotar counterattack was the most vicious fighting he'd seen since Third Warsaw: The last fifty or so gangers rallied in a rough square around Malusi as the S'Cotar warriors and their guard spheres charged, breaking against them, wave after wave. Blasters shrilling, machinepistols rattling, grenades exploding, screams, orders, counterorders, the whole ghastly scene backdropped by a rising red sun.

He'd looked down to where zur Linde lay beside him in a ditch. The admiral could see right through the fist-sized blaster hole in the captain's stomach to the mud beneath. Cut off from the gangers, they'd shot their way through the S'Cotar, trying for the woods, when an azure bolt had found zur Linde.

"Odd, Admiral." His glazed eyes stared at the wispy, pink-streaked stratocumulae now catching the first light. "I remember dying this way. Before . . . dawn." Blood-frothed lips.

"Perhaps you have, Erich," said Hochmeister. "Maybe we're fated to live forever that which we first became." He would have said more, but zur Linde was dead.

Standing, blaster in hand, the admiral had seen the S'Cotar and their machines vanish.

Stunned, the gangers had stood for an uncomprehending

instant, then broken into a ragged cheer—a cheer dying with them in fierce white flare; a tiny nova gone almost before it came.

Blinded, thrown back into the ditch, Hochmeister had been picked up by the S'Cotar and locked in Detention. His sight returning, he could see through the small, thick glass window the black-scorched earth where the gangers had died; killed, Shalan-Actal had told him, by something called a photon mortar.

After a week, they'd moved him into the Maximus CO's quarters, letting him roam the base unguarded. Knowing he couldn't escape, he'd tried anyway, believing they'd expect it of him, wanting to seem predictable. They'd caught him trying to slip through the neatly restored defenses and shooed him back to his quarters.

"The machines," said Hochmeister. "Those horrible slicing things. Those are your allies?"

"Yes. From yet another reality."

"You'll bite off more than you can chew, bug. It's a tyrant's fate."

"One that's befallen you, Admiral?"

"I'm merely a servant of the State," he shrugged, "a nineteenth-century man with a seventeenth-century philosophy, trapped in this poor and bloody time." He turned back to the window.

"You have one day to consider my offer," said Shalan-Actal. "If you won't accept, I'll turn you over to our allies. They want a human specimen. Do I make myself clear?"

Hochmeister only half heard the biofab. He was watching the men and women running from the Maximus portal building, leaping over two dead warriors. They carried blasters, wore black uniforms, backpacks, bootsheathed knives and purposeful looks. The last one out turned to throw something small and round back in. Hochmeister stepped casually to one side of the window.

"I said, Admiral, do I make myself clear?"

Slipping his hands into his pockets, Hochmeister leaned against the cement wall. "I'm clear," he said. "But before you plan too far ahead, you might want to look out the window."

It was only five paces. Shalan-Actal walked it, reaching the window just as the explosion across the courtyard blew it in, spraying the room with razor-edged glass. Hochmeister pressed against the wall, arms across his face.

When he looked again, seconds later, Shalan-Actal was gone, a few drops of green blood marking his passing. Seeing it, Hochmeister smiled. Blaster fire and the hooting of the old British alert klaxon resounded through the complex.

Shaking the glass from his writings, the admiral locked them in the desk, then left the room, carefully shutting the door.

There were two S'Cotar warriors near the portal when L'Wrona stepped through. The transmute lay beside the portal, a blaster bolt through its thorax. Two warriors were bending over it.

Firing two quick bolts, L'Wrona killed both warriors, then shattered the transmute's head with a third bolt. The last shot was still echoing when the rest of his contingent arrived.

John looked around. "You got him."

"He was just a bit too sure of himself.

"Follow Harrison," he ordered. "Skirmish order."

The corridors were well lit and empty, blaster hits and bullet holes unrepaired from the ganger assault. "Where are they?'' asked S'Til, running the prescribed distance behind John.

''Near,'' he said.

Soft-soled boots moving silently across yellow linoleum, they reached the edge of the sun-filled lobby. John stopped, staring at the plate-glass windows and the sentries beyond, then motioned everyone back into the corridor, against the wall.

''Those windows are new,'' he whispered. ''Probably battle repairs. We really shot this place up.''

L'Wrona risked a quick look. Two warriors stood outside, backs to the double glass doors, rifles over their shoulders.

''S'Til,'' he said, drawing his knife. ''You and me.''

Nodding, the blonde commando officer pulled her own blade. The two dropped to the floor and began low crawling, hugging the wall.

''They can't see in, H'Nar,'' said John. ''The whole complex is mirror glass.''

Rising, the two K'Ronarins ran low across the lobby, burst through the doors and knifed the startled biofabs. The other humans charged after them.

''Do it,'' said L'Wrona to Harrison.

John already had the round demolition grenade out of his pack. Pressing the arming stud, he rolled across the lobby, back the way they'd come.

''Motorpool,'' said L'Wrona. Abandoning stealth, they ran, following Harrison from the courtyard, toward the rear of the compound. They were well clear when the grenade exploded, collapsing the building's roof, burying the portal beneath tons of steel and concrete.

Reverting to its basic programming, the Maximus device closed the portal, diverting full power to its shield.

Green blood oozing from dozens of deep wounds, Shalan-

Actal stood in the Maximus command center. Hochmeister wouldn't have recognized the room, stripped of illusion. The equipment was alien, not designed for hands with opposable digits. The chairs were flat-topped platforms, supported by fluted stems set into the floor. Transmutes squatted atop them on folded, double-jointed limbs. Tentacles moved with blurring speed, flicking over controls and telltales.

The portal, Glorious! The portal's been destroyed! The watch officer's mental wail of anguish swept through every mind in the room.

You are a fool, Bator-Akal. Shalan-Actal swayed, then steadied himself against a console. *Look.* He pointed to a telltale. *The machine is intact, to be dug out later. There is the real danger.* He pointed to a screen. The scan showed the raiders entering the rectangular motorpool building.

But Glorious, they are so few—probably a suicide squad.

The tall one is the Margrave of U'Tria. They will find a way to come for him.

Eight assault clusters ready to counterattack, Glorious, reported Bator-Akal. *Allied commander offers assistance.*

Shalan-Actal's antennae weaved a firm resolve-commitment pattern. *No. We need what warriors are left. Activate that building's self-destruct device,* he ordered, then slumped to the floor.

Bator-Akal glanced up just long enough to flick Shalan-Actal over to Medical, five buildings away, then returned to his board and the self-destruct programming.

They fanned out through the motorpool, Harrison and five commandos going through the maintenance bays on into the small helipad out back. L'Wrona and S'Til went into the office, weapons ready.

"Who are you?" said L'Wrona to the thin, gray-haired

man sitting at the motorpool officer's desk, polishing his wire rimmed glasses.

The stranger smiled at him blankly.

L'Wrona repeated the question in English.

"My name is Hochmeister," said the admiral, putting his glasses back on. "I thought you might come here."

John came in. "Just Hochmeister's chopper out back.

"Admiral!"

"Major," nodded the admiral. "You've brought help."

"Where's Heather MacKenzie?" asked Harrison.

The admiral shook his head. "I haven't seen her since you both went into the portal."

"Later," said L'Wrona. "Let's get out of here before they counterattack. Can we all fit aboard one aircraft?"

"Too small. We'll have to take one of the trucks."

Opening a drawer, Hochmeister took out a flat, oblong block of what looked like dull-red plastic. He handed it to L'Wrona. The Margrave's eyes widened. "It's a destruct pack—remotely keyed. If they trigger this now we're . . .

"The S'Cotar placed these inside the electrical junction box of every building," said the admiral. "Are these each assigned a different detonation frequency?" he asked.

"Yes. The command center just enters location and firing code," said L'Wrona.

"We've been here three minutes," said John. "Why are we still alive?"

"What do the S'Cotar do with their old?" asked the admiral.

L'Wrona frowned. "Their old? They eat them. Why?"

"I wondered why they had no respect for age. They gave me the freedom of the base. Harmless old coot, watching the big bugs.

"I took the liberty of gathering the destruct packs and

putting them in the unused dumpster behind the command center.'' He looked at his watch. ''I should think . . .''

''Drop!'' shouted L'Wrona.

Whump! The explosion rocked the motorpool, shattering the wire mesh window behind L'Wrona, tumbling the yellow field manuals from the gray utility shelves.

Hochmeister stood, unruffled.

L'Wrona rose, extending his hand. ''Captain H'Nar L'Wrona, commanding *Implacable*. Welcome to our war, Admiral.''

Admiral and Margrave shook hands. ''Welcome to our friendly little world, Captain L'Wrona.''

15

T'Ral looked at the time. Smiling evilly, he punched into the commnet. "Commander K'Raoda," he called softly. "Wake up. We have company."

Five decks below, K'Raoda mumbled, turned over on his stomach and pulled the pillow over his head.

"Computer," said T'Ral, keying the complink, "where is the alert klaxon nearest Commander K'Raoda's quarters?"

"In corridor seven blue one-five, directly above his door," said the machine.

"Klaxon designation?"

"Seven blue one-five-six-zero."

"Mr. N'Trol," said T'Ral, turning toward the bridge engineering station, "please test battle klaxon seven blue one-five-six-zero. Three long bursts."

The first *awoooka*! brought K'Raoda out of bed. The second found him ripping his M11A from a drawer. He was at the commpanel when the third ended, calling T'Ral.

"Disregard battle klaxon." T'Ral's voice carried the length of seven deck. "Disregard battle klaxon."

"V'org slime," hissed T'Ral's communicator. "Pig shit," it added in English.

"Better get up here, T'Lei," said T'Ral. "Scans picking up three ships just clearing jump. No ID yet, but probably our reinforcements. That gives us about one watch to prepare for visitors."

"On my way," said K'Raoda, reaching for his uniform.

"Two things," said T'Ral, relinquishing the captain's chair to K'Raoda, a few minutes later. "The skipcomm buoy's no longer putting out a mark. And Ambassador Z'Sha wants to be part of the reception for the new units."

"Skipcomm's out?" K'Raoda frowned.

"Just after those three ships arrived."

A ship could jump from any point. But the closer she jumped to strong gravitational fields—planets, stars, large moons—the greater the degree of error in the jump. All jump drives were therefore calibrated for jump at null point: that point far enough from a system's nearest large body for minimum jump error, but within reasonable distance from point of origin at sublight speeds. "Null point" was a telltale reading, not the total absence of either gravitational fields or jump error.

Employing the same principles as the jump drive, the skipcomm provided almost instant communication with any other system having a skipcomm, jumping or skipping a message to the designated receiver, treating all intervening space as a porous, two-dimensional surface. Deploying a skipcomm at null point upon entering a new system was standard procedure—*Implacable* had done it when first arriving in the Terran system, over a year before. The original skipcomm had been blasted by the S'Cotar, as had its replacement. The skipcomm in question was the third, and had operated flawlessly for over eight months.

"Computer," said K'Raoda, "incidence of failure of skipcomm buoys, current model."

"One one thousandth of a percent," said the machine, speaking from the chair arm.

"Amazing coincidence," said T'Ral.

"Have we challenged?" asked K'Raoda, looking at the analysis T'Ral had run on the new ships' ion trails: the usual conical spiral rotated on the small screen.

"No. You saw from the ion patterns—they're ours."

"K'Lana," said K'Raoda to comm officer, "ship-to-ship, fleet priority channel."

"All yours, Commander."

K'Raoda spoke into the commlink. "This is K'Ronarin Confederation cruiser *Implacable* to unknown ships. Identify, please."

K'Raoda grimaced at the high-pitched blast from the armchair. "K'Lana, what. . . ."

The noise ended as the young subcommander did something at his console. "Sorry. He's using old code." The comm officer looked at a telltale. "Very old—wartime code."

"Have him repeat in clear, using one-time battlecode."

"Why is he using old code, Y'Tan?" K'Raoda asked T'Ral.

"He may have been sent here direct from deep patrol, without putting into base. FleetOps has done that before."

"You'd think they'd have couriered him new code."

"There's a tendency to get sloppy with the war over."

"Ship IDs received, in clear," said K'Lana. "The S'Raq-class light cruiser *New Hope,* the escort frigates *G'Lar Seven* and *P'Dir Four.*"

T'Ral gripped the back of K'Raoda's chair, knuckles whitening. "Repeat first ship."

"The S'Raq-class light cruiser *New Hope,* Commander."

"Wasn't that . . ." said K'Raoda.

T'Ral nodded curtly. "My brother's ship," he said. "Captain P'Rin T'Ral, lost at the battle of D'Lan."

"Computer," said K'Raoda, "last known disposition of the escort frigates *G'Lar Seven* and *P'Dir Four*."

"Assigned eight squadron, Second Fleet. Lost, presumed destroyed at the battle of D'Lan."

"Three possibilities," said K'Raoda, fingers gently drumming the chair arm. "One, it's a S'Cotar ruse. Two, those three ships are who they say they are and did what other ships did, cut off by the S'Cotar advance—hit and ran through the S'Cotar sectors. And three"—he looked his friend in the eye—"they went bad."

"You dishonor my brother's memory," said T'Ral stiffly. "P'Rin would never turn corsair."

"Y'Tan," said K'Raoda gently, laying a hand on the other's arm. "He's probably dead. Others may have. . . ."

"Incoming task force commander calling," said K'Lana.

"I'll take it," said K'Raoda. "What's his name?"

"Captain T'Ral," he said, glancing at the Tactics Officer.

"Don't raise your hopes," said K'Raoda as T'Ral's face lit with joy. "Stay out of the pickup, monitor from your console and say nothing. Do you understand?"

"But. . . ."

"Do you understand, Commander?"

"Yes, sir," said T'Ral, expressionless. Turning, he went to his console.

Save a ship, lose a friend, thought K'Raoda. If this is command, they can keep it. Pressing a key, he took the feed from communications. "Commander K'Raoda here."

The man on the console screen bore no resemblance to T'Ral. He was older, square-jawed, with high cheekbones and receding hairline. K'Raoda noted the silver starship of a captain on his collar and the double hash marks of the Second Border Fleet above the right pocket of his tunic.

"Captain T'Ral, Task Force Eight-Three," said the officer. "Commodore D'Trelna, please."

"The commodore is indisposed, sir."

The captain frowned. "Captain L'Wrona, then."

"He's offship, sir. I command here."

"Very well, Commander K'Raoda. What is your command's status?"

"I will not tell you that, sir," said K'Raoda evenly, "until you authenticate."

The pickup was small but perfectly detailed. K'Raoda could see Captain T'Ral's face cloud with anger. "I am senior here, Commander. Report status."

"Sir, your codes are pathetically obsolete and your ships listed as missing in action."

"Check with FleetOps, Commander. You'll find we were sent here directly from U'Tria quadrant. We've been operating behind enemy lines since the S'Cotar wiped Second Fleet."

"Our skipcomm buoy is not operational, sir. You are closer to null point than we. Have you one you could deploy?"

"No. Sorry. Cannibalized ours years ago."

"Then, sir, I must ask you to remain outside the orbit of the fourth planet until I can deploy a new buoy at null point. We'll have that done in no more than two watches."

The captain shook his head. "No. My orders say I'm to assume orbit around the third planet 'with dispatch.' And I will do so. With dispatch."

"Sir, if you proceed insystem without my permission, I will consider you hostile and will open fire under the authority of Fleet Regulation seven-five-one, 'Authentication of Incoming Vessels.' "

The captain jabbed a finger at the pickup. "You fire a bolt at one of my ships, Commander, and your ass is mine. We're coming in." The scan swirled into a kaleidoscope of color, then went blank.

"Tell me that wasn't your brother," said K'Raoda, turning to T'Ral as the latter walked over from the tactics station.

"That wasn't my brother," said T'Ral with a ghost of a smile. "Sorry, T'Lei."

"For what?"

"For being such a child."

K'Raoda waved a hand. "It's not important.

"Who the hell was that, using your brother's name and rank?"

"His first officer, Commander K'Tran. P'Rin was about to bring K'Tran and the third officer up on charges of commercial misconduct when the war broke out."

"What were they doing, smuggling?"

T'Ral nodded. "Running heavy drugs through their patrol quadrant—orgjags, sensedeps."

"Nice." Orgjags put the user on an orgasmic high, the brain's pleasure center—creating sensations just as powerful as direct current, but with greater variety. Sensedeps deprived the user of all sensory input: sound, sight, touch, smell. About eighty percent of the drugs' users became addicts. Orgjag addicts invariably died of exhaustion and starvation. Sensedep addicts just as invariably became hopelessly catatonic.

"With the usual prewar scum crewing those ships, it was no problem for K'Tran to kill your brother and go corsair."

"What are we going to do, T'Lei?" asked K'Raoda.

"First, we're going to make absolutely sure those ships

are corsair. Somehow.'' He stared at the main screen. The Moon was just rising above Earth.

''Pocsym,'' said K'Raoda.

''Pocsym? He's dead.''

''But his observation satellites aren't,'' said K'Raoda, turning to his friend. ''This system's littered with Pocsym's scan-shielded observation satellites!''

He keyed the complink. ''Computer. Have we the grid interlock protocols for the satellite observation system deployed by Pocsym Six?''

''We have,'' said computer.

''Is there such a satellite near this system's null point?''

''There is.''

''Interlock with that satellite and give us visual scan of the last known position of our skipcomm buoy.''

''Implementing.''

It came up on the mainscreen in a moment, the image growing larger as the satellite moved closer.

''Interesting,'' said K'Raoda, stepping down from the command tier to walk with T'Ral to the base of the screen. Together they stared up at finely detailed image. Twisted, scorched chunks of metal were drifting slowly apart, moving out to all points of the galactic compass.

''Consistent with a Mark 88 hit, wouldn't you say, Y'Tan?'' The Mark 88 was Fleet's principal ship-to-ship energy weapon.

''Yes.''

''Computer, from drift pattern of onscreen fragments, calculate approximate time of skipcomm buoy destruction. Postulate instrument of destruction to have been a Mark 88 fusion beam at standard setting.''

''Time of destruction approximately two-point-four-one t'lars ago,'' said the machine.

"Computer," said K'Raoda. "How long ago did incoming task force arrive at null point?"

"Two-point-four t'lars ago."

They returned in silence to the command tier, K'Raoda carefully avoiding T'Ral's face.

"K'Lana," said K'Raoda, resuming the captain's chair, "quarantine is abolished. Send recall, priority one. Get as many crew back up from Terra as you can by watchend. Then get me the ambassador."

"The ambassador is calling in now, sir."

"Ambassador," said K'Raoda as comm screen came to life. "I was just about to call you, sir."

"Subcommander K'Raoda," said the ambassador. "Why did you not return my call?" Born of the old aristocracy, over forty years a diplomat, Z'Sha was a grandmaster of implied slight and cutting innuendo. K'Raoda had tolerated the old patrician's disdain in the past—he had no time for it now.

"Sir, I am a commander, not a subcommander."

Z'Sha waved a negligent hand. "Whatever. I always confuse military ranks.

"I wish to be part of the reception for the incoming reinforcements, Commander. With the commodore indisposed, I suppose I should address you on the subject. How many people can you comfortably entertain, if helped with food and refreshments?"

"Ambassador," said K'Raoda, "three corsairs have just passed null point. I doubt you want to be part of the reception we're planning."

Z'Sha's eyes narrowed at the word "corsairs." "How . . . ?"

"They'll be here in eight Terran hours. As you can imagine, I'm very busy." He touched the commkey.

"Wait!" The ambassador's voice rang with steel. Startled, K'Raoda stopped.

"Yes?"

"Can you stop them? Honestly."

"Not with fusion fire, sir. No."

"D'Trelna would stop them, Commander."

"I am not D'Trelna, Ambassador."

"Terra has no defenses against our weapons, K'Raoda. Those murderers will butcher millions, loot the planet. Our expedition to Terra Two will be lost. The S'Cotar and their allies will come through that portal, take what's left of this world and push on into the galaxy."

"I know."

"You've advised Fleet?"

"They blasted the skipcomm buoy the instant they came in."

"I must alert the Terrans. Keep me advised." Z'Sha disconnected.

K'Raoda stroked the soft leather of the chair arm with his right palm, staring at the view screen, eyes distant. The bridge was quiet, a few officers speaking softly, the occasional chirp of instruments. Hard to believe it would soon be part of a blasted, corpse-filled hulk.

"Y'Tan," said K'Raoda after a time. "There's a way to take them. But we'll need Z'Sha's help. And luck. Lots of it."

16

"Smells like a jungle. Looks like a jungle. Sounds like a jungle," said McShane, arm sweeping the surrounding greenery.

"Not a jungle," said D'Trelna, holding up the small, flat surveyor, amber readout toward McShane.

The Terran squinted at it. " 'Flora—none. Fauna—none.' So?" he shrugged. "If we'd believed all your nice little toys over the past year, we'd be dead.

"Good God, man! Use your senses! Feel that hot, fetid air, smell the rotting vegetation, and listen—listen to the nonexistent fauna!"

Sweat-drenched, the two stood on the trail they'd followed from the armorglass gate—a trail leading straight toward the point set in D'Trelna's locator. A thick mist hung low over the trail, obscuring all but the closest brush. Strange, fierce cries sounded in the distance. Once, thinking they heard something large moving through the undergrowth, they'd stopped, rifles ready, waiting. The sound hadn't resumed, so they'd moved on, D'Trelna finally calling a halt to recheck his readings.

"Fake," said D'Trelna, clipping the surveyor back onto his belt. "All machine-generated vegetation. And we haven't seen a single animal, swatted any bugs. We've just heard noises."

Carefully setting the blastrifle down on the trail, McShane pulled the commando knife from his bootsheath. Slicing off the end of a thick-vined creeper, he handed the dripping specimen to D'Trelna. The commodore held it gingerly between two thick fingers, avoiding the white sap oozing from the cut.

"Plant life," said McShane.

"Inorganic," said D'Trelna, dropping the cutting. "Rigid green polymer exterior, resinous white polymer interior. Probably generated from troughs under this brown plastic." He scuffed the jungle matting. "We have supper clubs like this back home."

"How pleasant."

"The scale is less sweeping, the air is conditioned, and a man can get a drink." He wiped a damp sleeve across his sweaty brow.

"Let's go."

"But why not a real jungle?" said Bob as they walked, D'Trelna leading along the narrow trail. "If this was the Agro section, why not real plants?"

"I'd guess—just a guess—that the demented computer has taken over from the secondary systems that maintained Agro."

"This whole grotesque ship was demented from her launch day. How much further?"

D'Trelna checked the locator. "Not far. We're over halfway."

Something made McShane look back. The trail was

quietly vanishing as a twelve-foot wall of jungle rolled down it, great thorn-studded vines waving along its front.

"Behind us, J'Quel!"

Turning, the commodore stared at the advancing green mass. "Run!"

McShane had never seen D'Trelna run, couldn't have visualized it. But there he was, a small tank plowing down the trail, even putting some space between him and the Terran. I'll be damned, thought McShane, wheezing. There's muscle under there.

The trail turned hard right after a few moments, ending before a wall of massive, unmortared stone. Great, mist-wreathed boulders vanished above and to sides, swallowed by the fog. A wall made by giants when the world was young, thought McShane.

"Blasters?" he asked, panting. From behind, drawing closer, came a serpentine slithering as hundreds of meters of green death slid down the trail.

"Blasters," said D'Trelna, unslinging his rifle and clicking off the safety. The two men faced about, back to the wall, waiting.

"How long will the chargepaks last?" asked McShane.

"As garden trimmers? Not long.

"This is classic," added the commodore, eyes on the turn in the trail. "Classical, really."

"How so?"

"Prespace mythology. Seeking Sanctuary, Prince A'Gan slips through Death's Forest. The Forest pursues. A'Gan reaches the Sanctuary wall, but can't enter without speaking the Word-of-One. A word he doesn't know. He faces about, back to the wall, sword in hand."

"Do you know the word?"

"Of course." D'Trelna frowned, half turning his head toward McShane. "Every child on S'Htar . . ."

"Use it, man!" snapped McShane. "Just like your Prince A'Gan! Hurry."

D'Trelna could take orders as well as give them. Turning, rifle held two-handed over his head, he cried, "L'Asorg!" High and lilting, the word rang from the wall.

Blaster to his shoulder, McShane fired at the first creepers as they rounded the trail, aiming where they grew close and thick.

Splashing against an invisible barrier, the stream of red blaster bolts dissipated.

"Shielded! D'Trelna, it's . . ."

A hand to his shoulder turned him. "Come on," snapped the commodore, pointing to the tunnel that now pierced the wall.

They ran the few meters, the creepers snapping so close McShane could feel the air stir.

A brief impression of darkness, a passageway, then they were through, grass beneath their feet, the mist thinner, the air pleasant and cool. Turning, they saw that the wall had closed behind them.

"How did you know?" asked the commodore.

"Key words," said McShane, leaning on his blastrifle. "Demented. Club. Classical. We're performers in a psychodrama, J'Quel. Only it's the producer who's mad—a producer with some knowledge of the classics."

"Main computer, of course," sighed D'Trelna. "I should have seen it."

"We both should . . ."

"Thee hath found uncertain sanctuary, A'Gan," boomed a voice.

The big golden egg floated toward them out of the mist,

a purple cape fastened just below its top by twin metallic strands.

Stopping a few meters from the two men, it hovered noiselessly.

"What the hell is that?" said McShane. "A Nibelung?"

"It would appear to be a large talking egg," said the commodore, watching the egg. "One wearing a cape with some knowledge of prespace mythology."

"D'Trelna!"

"It's main computer, Professor."

"Why isn't it bolted down somewhere, computing?"

"It was designed as a mobile unit. If the battle went against the defenders, they could still control the ship's basic systems." The machine sat unmoving.

"We never did look for it, you know," said D'Trelna, watching the computer. "We were busy, and it did what we wanted, so why look for it?" He sounded apologetic.

"It's not armed, is it?" asked McShane uneasily.

"Not even the Imperials would be crazy enough to arm a computer."

"Why not? They were crazy enough to build mindslavers."

"Time to take charge here, Bob."

D'Trelna cleared his throat. "Computer," he said in his best command voice, "I am Commodore J'Quel D'Trelna. As senior K'Ronarin officer insystem, I direct you to turn over to me . . ."

The golden bolt struck midway between the computer and the men, blasting a hole through the fake turf, scarring the battlesteel below. "Silence, A'Gan!"

"It's cracked," said McShane.

"Certainly is." D'Trelna looked shaken.

"No, there," McShane pointed, "just to the left of the cape. See?"

D'Trelna saw it then—a jagged hairline crack running diagonally from beneath the garment.

"Know, A'Gan, that thee hath fled to thy death, for I am K'Lyta, thy father's brother. Much wrong hath thee done me, slaying my children."

"What's the rest of the legend, J'Quel?" asked McShane, his grip on the rifle suddenly sweaty.

D'Trelna spoke low and fast. "A'Gan is rightful heir to the throne of a small city-state. Returning from the wars, he finds his nephews have usurped him. He kills them, but flees when their father calls upon the Darkness to avenge his seed. A'Gan reaches Sanctuary only to find it false and his uncle waiting for him. They battle. A'Gan wins, though badly wounded. He returns home to rule a few sad years, then dies of his wounds."

"Inspiring."

"Now, A'Gan, I shall take your child as wergeld," said computer. McShane wondered how it spoke—it had no visible orifice.

"I am not A'Gan and I have no children, my lord of the fractured carapace," said D'Trelna.

Wreathed in a faint, shimmering indigo, a small transparent bubble rose from beneath the grass, stopping at eye level between men and computer. About a meter in diameter, it had two small holes at the top, two at the bottom.

As they watched, the bubble split in half and separated, the halves hovering beside each other, open ends up.

"Isn't that . . ." said McShane, feeling the bile rise in his throat.

"A brainpod," said D'Trelna. "The blue's a stasis field, the rims are distance-controlled surgical lasers. One half performs a craniotomy; the second half detaches and removes the brain, placing it in the first half. The halves rejoin. Stasis remains on till the brainpod's housed, with stem-absorbent nutrients flowing through those small holes."

The brainpod half to their right began moving slowly toward D'Trelna.

"On three, Bob," said the commodore in English. "You shoot the computer, I'll shoot the brainpod. Aim for the crack."

McShane nodded, not yet daring to move the rifle.

D'Trelna counted as the brainpod neared the muzzle of his rifle. "One. Two. Three."

The commodore's bolt took the moving brainpod half dead center, shattering it as McShane fired from the hip, holding the trigger back, raking the fracture.

"Die, A'Gan!" shrieked computer. It whirled, a golden blur spitting golden blaster bolts at the men. Blue-and-red energies rippling over their warsuits, they blasted back, beams concentrated at the machine's center.

Wobbling, the egg slowed, tilted, then crashed to the floor, splitting neatly in half. The end without the cape tottered for a moment, then fell on its side.

Approaching warily, the two men watched computer die, the light fading along the delicate crystalline network of its innards.

McShane shook his head. "Poor monster."

"Save your sympathy for our friends on Terra Two," said D'Trelna. "That mad thing was the only one who knew where the portal device is."

"What's this?" said McShane, walking to where the other half of the machine lay. Bending down, he picked something from the grass, then stood, holding out his palm to D'Trelna.

"Self-replicating computer," said the commodore, looking at the tiny golden egg, almost lost in McShane's big hand. "You're holding the key to a lost science light years ahead of our own, Bob. You could trade that little nugget for more wealth or power than you can imagine."

"Surely not more than *I* can imagine," smiled McShane. Placing the egg in D'Trelna's hand, he closed the other's fingers over it. "Here you are, senior K'Ronarin officer. Wealth and power beyond imagining."

"Such things are best earned," said D'Trelna, dropping the egg into a pouch on his utility belt. "Let's hope it doesn't grow before we get it back to K'Ronar." Running a finger along the seam, he sealed the pouch. "At least it's not wearing a purple cape.

"I believe the mist is clearing, Professor."

McShane looked up. "You're right. I can see the wall." His eyes widened. "It's shrinking!"

What had been massive before was minuscule now, no more than a few meters tall and collapsing in on itself with a sigh. As they watched, the wall melted into a flat gray smear.

Where the jungle had been was now all flat and green—a green rapidly fading to gray as the deck reappeared. There were no more cries, feral or otherwise. The air was cool and smelled faintly metallic. In the distance, they could see their shipcar, just the other side of the armorglass.

"Tertiary systems are taking Argo down to basic parameters," said D'Trelna. "Machines will soon be harvesting crops here, putting them in storage for no one to eat.

"Let's check the rest of the area, then go."

Turning back, they saw the building. White and square, it sat alone on the great empty plain of Agro, its size impossible to gauge without a reference point.

They reached it after a brisk five-minute walk. It was small, one-level, made of stone—real stone, McShane thought, touching the cool, marblelike surface—with no windows, just a doorway, barred by the shimmering blue of a force field.

"Could this be Terran?" asked McShane. "It looks almost Roman—perhaps a roadside temple to Diana."

"Our history, not yours," said D'Trelna. "That hypothetical ship that seeded Terra hadn't been built when structures like this were old. The House of the Dead, said the overmind—a tomb. See the inscription over the door?"

McShane looked up at the flowing script carved into the stone. "Very graceful—looks like Arabic. What is it?"

"There's a theory that humanity didn't evolve on K'Ronar," said the commodore. "That K'Ronar was a colony of some great and ancient people and that that script was their language."

"Can you read it?"

"No one can read it. Many have spent their lives trying."

"And the tomb? How old?"

D'Trelna shrugged. "Prehistory. Guesses start at about two hundred and fifty thousand years—Terran years."

"Surely the contents can be dated?"

"Maybe. Except that no one's ever penetrated one of those tombs and survived. Try to force your way in and whatever powers it goes critical—leaves a perfectly symmetrical crater."

"I don't believe it," said McShane, looking at the commodore. "Compared to you, I know we're technological primitives, squatting in the dust. But not intellectually. And my intellect tells me no power source could survive half a million years."

"Compared with whomever built those," said D'Trelna, nodding at the tomb, "we're all dust squatters.

"Structures like that dot hillsides on K'Ronar, S'Htar, U'Tria—all of our planets. All have force fields, none have ever gone dark. They'll tolerate a child's stick or a rock, but bring machinery or energy gear into play''—he threw his hands over his head—''boom!''

They stood silently for a moment, looking at the tomb. ''These tombs and their nature are common knowledge, aren't they, J'Quel?'' asked McShane.

''Since forever, Bob.''

''And none of our people would ever tamper with such a structure, would they?''

''Never.''

''Do we agree that what we want is probably in there?''

''We do.''

''I see. Now tell me, if since forever no one has successfully tampered with one of these structures, how did the Imperials get it here? And if there are Imperial artifacts inside, how did they get in there?''

D'Trelna slapped his leg. ''Fake! Of course—it would be perfect security! No one in his right mind would touch one of those tombs. As you've just seen, the sight of one tends to banish logic.

''Back to *Implacable*,'' he said, turning to McShane, eyes gleaming in triumph. ''We'll get a work party and crack that force field.''

McShane held up a hand. ''That may not be necessary.''

''Why not?''

''Can you deactivate a force field with the right verbal authenticator?''

''Of course.''

''Well, the overmind gave me a password and a countersign.''

''Try it!''

McShane faced the tomb. ''Barren is the house of S'Kal,'' he called.

The force field blinked twice.

''Some things never change,'' said the commodore. ''You've been challenged. Give the countersign.''

''Empire and Destiny.''

The force field winked off.

''Not bad for a dust-squatting primitive, Bob,'' said D'Trelna.

The small white room was empty except for a t'raq-wood table and the three boxes on it. The boxes were wrapped in a blue stasis halo—a halo that vanished as D'Trelna reached for the first box. The commodore hesitated, then raised the lid with both hands. A plain silver bracelet lay on black velveteen. Inside the lid was the familiar unical lettering of High K'Ronarin: ''Relic of the Nameless Emperor.''

D'Trelna carefully closed the box.

''Not going to take it out?''

''No,'' said the commodore, stepping along the table to the next box. ''First of the House of S'Kal, founder of the Empire, he's the Legend-Without-a-Name—perhaps the last of those who built these houses of eternity. That bracelet's undoubtedly a thing of power. I wouldn't touch it if it lay on the deck.''

The second box held a fist-size red jewel, set on a silver chain. As D'Trelna lifted it out, the jewel flared with an unnatural brilliance, all but blinding the two men. D'Trelna dropped the jewel back onto its cushion and slammed the box shut.

''Did you see an inscription?'' asked Bob, rubbing his eyes.

''Yes.'' D'Trelna opened his eyes as the red spots faded. ''It's the Star of T'Ilar. Worn by every emperor of the First Dynasty—the House of S'Kal. Supposedly, it'll kill any who wear it who aren't descended from that House.''

''I believe it,'' said Bob, eyes still watering.

"One box left, J'Quel," he said, nodding to the last one. "Want me to open it?"

"My job," he said, opening the box.

A yellow commwand lay beside a featureless black cube. The inside cover of the box read: Prototype two of two. Alternate Reality Linkage (spaceborne).

"Congratulations, Commodore," said McShane.

"Couldn't have done it without you, Bob," said D'Trelna. He tucked the box under his arm.

"Back to *Implacable*. Food, sleep. Listen to this commwand, brief Fleet, install the device . . ." He frowned. "We'll need another ship."

"Aren't your reinforcements due?" asked Bob as they stepped back onto the Agro deck. Behind them, the tomb's shield snapped back on.

"You heard the overmind," said D'Trelna. "Don't count your reinforcements before they arrive. The universe is full of nasty surprises."

17

K'Raoda turned from the tacscan to Ambassador Z'Sha. "They're here."

"Can we have visual, Commander?" Wearing the light blue uniform of a senior diplomat, Z'Sha stood beside the command chair, smelling of expensive Terran cologne, three rows of medals on his tunic and a great gold crimson-ribboned one around his neck. His v'arx leather boots would have cost K'Raoda a month's pay.

"Certainly, sir." He tapped out a command on the complink. At least the man was being polite. There'd been no mention of their previous encounter, at the victory celebration.

Above and to the front of the bridge, the big screen came alive, dividing in three. Two seemingly identical ships occupied its left and right segments: short, stubby craft, each with five weapons turrets facing *Implacable*.

The center image was of a very different sort of warship: long, sleek, about two-thirds the length of *Implacable*, with twelve visible weapons turrets.

All three ships bore Fleet ID markers, with the correct maintenance access indicators visible on closeup. They sat in standard Fleet geosynchronous orbit formation, the smaller ships flanking the larger ship, one above, one below, at precisely the same distance.

"You are absolutely certain those are corsairs, Commander?" said Z'Sha, turning to K'Raoda.

"Yes, sir."

Z'Sha shook his head. "They're good enough to be in a Fleet recruiting vid."

"Those were Fleet units, Ambassador."

"What is that data readout under each ship?"

"Their course, range, shield and our weapons status relative to target."

"What is their shield status, Commander?"

"Down."

"And if we blasted them now?"

"We're too close for missiles—the blowback would wipe us. They're too many to take out with a single cannon salvo—their shields would snap up at the first beam hit. We'd then be blasting away at each other, well within Terra's gravity. At this range, if one ship went up, we'd all go up. Poisonous debris would rain down on the planet, be absorbed into the food, air and water chains. Millions would die. We might even kill the oceans." He leaned toward the complink. "Indeed, computer projects . . ."

"Enough," said Z'Sha, running a hand through his perfectly set white hair. "I'm convinced. Get me commlink to that cruiser. I'll do my part."

". . . promise you a memorable reception, Captain."

"We're looking forward to it, Ambassador," said K'Tran.

"You're sure so many personnel won't strain *Implacable*'s facilities?"

"Her commander assures me they will not, Captain."

"Is this the same commander who was going to fire on us as we came in?" smiled K'Tran.

"Forgive him, Captain. He's very young."

"Fine. Consider us there, Ambassador. And thank you."

Z'Sha's image vanished from the desk screen. K'Tran turned to his executive officer. "What do you think, Number One?"

"Could be a trap." A'Tir was younger than he, but just as tough, a thin kid from a grimy industrial planet who'd risen through the ranks of the prewar Fleet, becoming third officer of a light cruiser—and a successful drug runner. When the S'Cotar had annihilated most of the Second Fleet, she and K'Tran had been quick to take advantage of the chaos, going corsair.

"Could be a trap, but is it?" said K'Tran, looking up from his desk. "Why should they suspect anything? We're what they want—reinforcements."

"The skipcomm buoy?"

K'Tran shrugged. "Even the best machines sometimes fail."

"Still . . ."

He waved a hand, the silver Academy ring catching the light. "You worry too much. This is our chance to add a heavy cruiser to our little squadron. We can start raiding closer in—hit primary shipping points. And that world down there—Terra—is open for some leisurely looting."

"You're so greedy, Y'Dan," she said.

"Of course I'm greedy," he laughed. "I'm a corsair!"

"Listen to me," she said intensely. "I say we blast *Implacable* now, while her shield's down, divide up our money and disperse. With the war over, Fleet's going to hunt us down and kill us."

"They'll try. We weren't expecting the Valor Medal."

She stood behind him, long tanned fingers massaging his muscular shoulders. "There's this grade-seven planet, Y'Dan, that's been offchart since the Fall. No people. I know a stretch of coast where the mountains tumble into the sea—lush, tropical, fruit growing wild. Warm night breezes under triple moons. We could . . ."

He stood, shaking her hand off. "We could what?" he said. "Eat fruit, live naked, love in the sand?"

A'Tir's face reddened.

"You sound like a travel broker, Number One.

"We have two commissions to execute," he continued, voice clipped. "For our primary client, remove *Implacable*. For our secondary client, fill those forty-one brainpods we're carrying. Seizing *Implacable* accomplishes both tasks and gives us a L'Aal-class heavy cruiser. And perhaps a side foray to Terra—nothing like a little rape and pillage to perk up the crew.

"We'll take all but a skeleton crew to the reception. How many shuttle craft is that?"

"Twelve," she said, emotions tucked back behind her usual diffidence. "Three hundred and twenty-one crew, dressed and armed as Fleet personnel."

"Eleven boats to land," K'Tran said. "I want you to command number twelve—thirty of your best fighters. Once inside *Implacable*'s shield, have your pilot turn back for *New Hope,* reporting engine trouble. Proceed parallel to the top hull . . ." He touched the complink. An engineering schematic of *Implacable*'s forward outside hull appeared. "Here." An access pod just behind the bridge began glowing orange. "That's the lift. Free drop as near to it as you can. Reaching it, just push the call tab and take it down to the bridge entrance.''

''Fine,'' she said, looking at the screen. ''We get to the bridge doors. They're armored and locked. A blastpak strong enough to take them out will destroy part of the bridge.''

''Use this.'' He handed her a small black wedge.

''What is it?'' she asked, turning it over in her hand.

''Shaped charge—pre-production model from K'Ronar via our primary client. See those rills along the bottom edge? That side is magnetized. Put it on the bridge doors and count to ten. It'll punch through them with no blowback.''

''Cute,'' she said, carefully pocketing it, the magnetized side toward her body. ''What about detection?''

''You'll be well inside the perimeter scan. Just avoid the hull-sensor clusters. If computer picks up an input anomaly, it's going to alert the bridge. Get to the lift and you're in.''

''It may work,'' she said grudgingly.

''Of course it will work. I planned it.''

''So, we take the bridge while you're shooting up the crew. Then what?''

''Seal compartments—coordinate with me on that. Cut life support to weapons batteries, engineering and armories. I don't want some heroes shooting up our ships, scuttling equipment, booby trapping the corridors. We'll let the survivors surrender, brainstrip the ones we need and space the rest.''

''And what are we going to crew *Implacable* with?'' she asked. ''Don't you want to try for converts?''

''No. I'd rather run her short. That's L'Wrona's ship—D'Trelna's before that. Trying for converts would be a waste of time.''

He looked at the time readout. "Operation launch minus fifty. Brief your assault team, meet me on the hangar deck at minus ten."

"Very well."

"Oh, and S'Hlo?"

"Yes?"

"When this is over, we're going to need a new base. Plan on a two-man scouting trip to your grade-seven planet. Just you and me. Agreed?"

"Agreed." She smiled faintly then left the room, mind on the assault.

"Farewell, my unlovely," said McShane, watching the dreadnought and its valley shrink in the rear screen.

"Home in time for lunch," said D'Trelna happily, switching the view scan forward. Earth filled the screen's center, growing larger as the shuttle raced away from the Moon.

The commodore keyed into the commnet. "Shuttle one-nine-seven to *Implacable*."

"*Implacable* flight control," said a hurried voice. "One-nine-seven, go ahead."

"Permission to land."

"One-nine-seven, hold."

D'Trelna frowned. "Odd."

"What?" asked McShane.

"Odd that I'm holding. Odd that flight control sounds harried—it shouldn't. We carry a lot of shuttles, but only three are scheduled out now—this and the daily Terran runs."

"One-nine-seven. Other traffic is ahead of you. Enter shield at point three-five and assume station forward."

"One-nine-seven confirming. Enter point three-five, assume station forward. Out.

"We're to stand by off the forward part of the ship," said D'Trelna, anticipating Bob's question. He pointed to a telltale. "Tactical summary. We've gained a light cruiser and two frigates."

"Reinforcements?"

"Finally. They must be shuttling their complements over to *Implacable* for a reception. No doubt Z'Sha will be there."

Five minutes brought them within sight of the four warships. A long line of shuttlecraft were leaving the light cruiser, making for *Implacable*.

"Oh, no," said D'Trelna as they closed on the flotilla.

"Problem?" asked McShane.

D'Trelna nodded, dropping their speed. "Big problem. Those shuttles are going to a formal reception—it's customary. There's only one place on *Implacable* that'll hold that many—hangar deck. Hangar deck is now teaming with officers and crew, among whom is Ambassador Z'Sha. After the ceremony, Z'Sha, my officers and the new officers are all going to troop down to Sick Bay to look in on the ailing commodore."

"I forgot about that," said Bob. "Can't you land and sneak in? Hangar deck's huge."

"Yes, but all the lifts are at the back. Z'Sha will be between me and the lifts. I am not a small man."

They were gliding past the light cruiser, close beneath her engines. The shuttle would have been lost in any of those three great tubes.

"I suppose I could steal in through the lift-access pod, hullside aft of the bridge," continued the commodore, "and send you and the shuttle in on auto . . . No." He shook his head. "It would look like you were piloting a shuttle. They'd really go crazy then. We'll just have to land and brazen through it—somehow."

"What about . . ."

D'Trelna stopped him with an upraised finger, staring at *New Hope*'s engines, sliding out of forward scan range.

He split the screen, putting the rear scan of the engines on the left half, shrinking the forward scan of *Implacable* and the other shuttles to the right half. Their shuttle was now in line behind the rest.

"Quick lesson in starship architecture, Bob," said D'Trelna, suddenly tense. "Those oval engine tubes are unique—the only set ever made for a line vessel. They didn't perform up to the expectation, so only the test ship, a light cruiser, ever had them. That cruiser was assigned to the Second Fleet. The Second Fleet was destroyed at the start of the war—all but that one cruiser. For years, Intelligence listed it as missing, possible corsair. With war's end, they downgraded it to missing, presumed destroyed. Prematurely, it seems."

"Those are pirates?" McShane stared at the shuttles.

"More than even money says so. And about to take over *Implacable*."

"Don't just sit there, D'Trelna! Sound the alarm, alert the bridge!"

"No."

Their speed dropped further as they passed through the opening in the shield, just behind the twelfth shuttle craft. The shield reformed behind them, a faint shimmer in their rear scan.

"A shootout this close to Terra could wipe your planet, Bob. These ships brim with poison—drive components, sublight engines, n-gravs, fusion cannon. Those particles get into your environment and you'll have a corpse-heaped world."

"You think we'd fare any better with those thugs?" said McShane. "Or the S'Cotar?"

The shuttle in front of them suddenly broke away, climbing to disappear over the top of *Implacable*.

"He's up to something," said D'Trelna. He dropped the shuttle to fly beneath the ship, flying along the bottom hull. "Let's see what."

The commodore slammed the shuttle forward. McShane pressed back in the flight chair, sure they'd collide with one of the turrets or pods flashing by, meters away.

"Number twelve shuttle reports engine malfunction and is returning to *New Hope*," reported flight control.

"Acknowledged," said K'Raoda. He stood beside Z'Sha in the great cavern of hangar deck, watching as the last of the shuttles landed with a faint whine of n-gravs.

The corsairs' shuttles were parked in a long line just inside the atmosphere curtain, spanning hangar deck from maintenance bays to berths. Outside, Terra was visible, a blue-and-white sphere just above the shuttles.

"Would one of your shuttles leaving now come to grief, Commander?" asked Z'Sha, watching the corsairs form ranks in front of their craft.

"Without a doubt, sir," said K'Raoda, noting the Mark 44 cannon turret atop the center shuttle. He couldn't see if there was a gunner—the turret was a black pod, sheathed in one-way armorglass.

Wearing Fleet uniforms, almost three hundred corsairs were drawn up in four ranks of eleven units, M32s at order arms.

K'Tran walked down the ramp from the last shuttle, turning right past the flank of the last unit, then right again. As he stepped in front of the first corsair, the entire formation came to present arms, two hundred and ninety gloved hands slapping *one-two* against the polished M32 stocks.

"That man is very dangerous," said Z'Sha as K'Tran executed a right-face at the front of the formation, smartly returning the salute, hand-to-head at just the right angle for just long enough. The rifles crashed back down to order arms, butts clanging to the deck as one, the echo ringing through the hangar. "He's molded that rabble into a crack unit. Imagine what he could do with two cruisers and those frigates."

"Only the inner quadrants would be safe," said K'Raoda. "For a while, Commander. For a while."

"Formation!" called K'Tran, eyes sweeping the ranks, "Port . . . Arms!" The rifles came off the deck, held at a forty-five-degree angle in front of the body. Heel and toe perfectly aligned, K'Tran executed an about-face. "Formation . . . Forward, march!"

"A mistake," said K'Raoda as the corsairs advanced with flawless precision, a column of eights with K'Tran at their head. "They should be at right-shoulder arms. To be at port arms displays either ignorance or hostile intent." The one-two cadence of five hundred and eighty-four battle boots striking battlesteel boomed along the deck.

The corsairs entered the long, narrow corridor formed by twin rows of commando assault craft parked nose-to-engine half the length of the hangar, their march resounding through the hangar.

"Tactical three," said K'Raoda into his communicator. "Remember," he said softly, his voice heard only by the thirty-man honor guard a few meters behind him, "when it starts, fall back to the lift access corridor and take out any who get through."

Z'Sha was watching K'Tran, now about two hundred meters away. "There's a Fourth Dynasty painting, Commander, in the museum ring on K'Ronar. It's done in old style—paint on spun plant fiber. The artist's name doesn't survive, but it's a brilliant work, 'The Assessor comes to T'Gan.' Do you know it?''

''No, sir,'' said K'Raoda, hoping K'Tran wouldn't notice the unfastened safety strap on his holster.

''It depicts a man at the head of a column of Imperial Marines, striding down the street of this squalid Agro town—you can all but taste the dust and smell the manure. The few people about are scurrying fearfully away. The artist's perspective is from the end of the street, watching the Assessor come. The Assessor is well dressed, handsome, with an assured, intelligent look. There is something cold and ruthless about the man's face, Commander, that holds one. It's the sort of face that comes toward us now.''

The deadly parade halted, grounding arms with a crash that rattled off the distant ceiling. K'Tran covered the twenty meters to K'Raoda and the Ambassador in a few seconds, halting before Z'Sha and snapping a brisk salute. ''Captain T'Ral, Task Force One-Seven-Five attending, Excellency.''

''Welcome, Captain.''

K'Tran turned to K'Raoda. ''I await your salute, Commander.''

K'Raoda nodded, looking into the other's pale blue eyes. ''You're fronted and flanked on two sides, K'Tran,'' he said. ''Surrender or die.''

A brief flicker of surprise crossed the corsair's face. ''Point one to you, Commander,'' he said, smiling faintly. ''Point two to me.'' His hand a blur of motion, he drew his blaster and fired point blank at K'Raoda.

''He's going for the bridge,'' said D'Trelna, bringing the shuttle out from under *Implacable*, racing toward her top hull.

"The lift access?" asked McShane.

"Yes." Reaching the top hull, they leveled off, D'Trelna keeping the shuttle so low that it barely skimmed the top of the highest turrets.

"What are you going to do?" asked McShane.

"Kill them," said the commodore, "before they kill us."

"Push that red button to your top right. Yes, that one," he nodded as McShane reached out.

A targeting overlay appeared on the screen, five concentric phosphor circles surrounding the familiar cross hairs.

"There!" cried McShane.

A line of space-suited figures were moving carefully toward the bullet-shaped pod lift housing, magnetized boots keeping them on the hull.

D'Trelna fingered a touch pad, sending a stream of tracking data across the bottom of the scan.

As the shuttle swooped toward them, all but the corsair nearest the bullet-shaped lift pod stopped and opened fire.

Oblivious to the red blaster bolts, D'Trelna waited till most of the corsairs were within the two smallest rings of the targeting overlay, then pushed the firing stud, twice.

Two small silver missiles shot out from the shuttle, flashing along the hull to explode silently among the corsairs, twin bursts of blue sending thousands of suit-and-flesh-rending flechettes into the corsairs.

The shuttle slowed, drifting over the carnage. McShane shook his head at the sight of torn bodies, severed heads, limbs and perfect spheres of blood slowly scattering into space. "What were those?"

"Anti-personnel missiles," said D'Trelna. "Crude but effective." He frowned at the screen readout. "Almost effective."

"What's wrong?"

"The pieces down there equal twenty-nine corsairs. One got on board." He punched into the tactical network. "Bridge. D'Trelna. 'Ware boarders, top forward lift access."

K'Tran whirled as a pneumatic hissing filled the hangar. The sides of the assault boats had dropped—three hundred warsuited crew stared down their M32s at the corsairs.

"Lay down your arms!" The command boomed across the deck. "Lay down your arms!"

Orders filled the air as the corsair column split down the center, forming two double lines facing each row of assault boats.

"You can't win against warsuits," said K'Raoda, picking himself up from the deck, the silver gleam of a warsuit visible through the blaster holes in his tunic.

K'Tran glanced at K'Raoda, coolly surveyed the long lines of grim-faced crew, then turned back to K'Raoda. "Commander, I can do anything.

"S'Halir," he said, his voice carrying over the commnet to one of the shuttles, "fire!"

The red fusion beam snapped from the center shuttle's turret, tearing into the ceiling. Sparks showered the deck as the hangar's primary power nexus shattered.

"Fire!" shouted K'Raoda as the lights died.

Over six hundred blasters opened up, turning hangar deck into a battleground lit red by millisecond bursts of massed blaster fire.

"Engineering!" shouted K'Raoda over the din. "Light!"

"Hold on," grumbled N'Trol over the commnet. "There's a glitch in the nobreak."

"Identify and authenticate," said the bridge security station.

Ignoring computer's challenge, A'Tir slapped the black

wedge onto the nearly invisible seam dividing the armored doors. She waited directly in front of the explosive, pistol in each hand, knowing if there was any blowback they'd have to scrape her off the bulkhead.

With a loud *whoomp!* the shaped charge punched a man-size hole through the doors. It was still sounding as A'Tir plunged through the smoldering opening, blaster in each hand.

"Hangar deck's gone black," said D'Trelna, bringing the shuttle in toward the dark rectangle. Gone were the green-and-orange guidelights rimming the opening, gone too the warm wash of yellow that greeted incoming shuttles. Red lightning flickered from within.

"Blaster fire," said McShane.

"Lots of it," said D'Trelna. "Flight control doesn't respond. Have to go in on manual."

"You're not taking us into that?"

"Of course I am."

Straddling K'Raoda's chest, the corsair squeezed harder, teeth bared, basking in the pleasure of another life throbbing desperately between his fingers.

Vision blurring, lungs bursting, K'Raoda felt his grip slipping from the killer's thick, hairy wrists.

The blaster bolt sheared off the top of the corsair's head, tumbling his body to the deck, teeth still bared, eyes wide with amazement.

Z'Sha appeared, M11A in his right hand. "Are you all right, Commander?" he asked, bending over K'Raoda.

Nodding, K'Raoda caught his breath for a moment, then took the hand the ambassador extended, climbing to his feet. "Thank you," he said hoarsely, rubbing his larynx.

The blaster fire ended as the lights flared on. K'Raoda

pulled himself up the side ladder of the shuttle. "Hangar deck," he said into his communicator. "General address.

"You can't win, v'org slime!" His voice boomed across the deck. "Down arms!"

Able to see again, the turret gunner in the corsair shuttle swung her twin-barreled cannon right, raking a packed commando boat with a double stream of red bolts that found the power cells.

Exploding in a pillar of orange-red flame, the boat became a pyre for forty-two crew. High, inhuman screams filled the tactical band as the cannon tracked left, locking on the next boat. Crewmen leaped for their lives as the turret fired again.

Using the confusion, the surviving corsairs broke for their shuttles.

The hangar rocked as the second commando boat and a corsair shuttle detonated, a double explosion tumbling corsairs and crew to the deck. The destruction continued as the remaining corsair craft exploded in quick succession.

"What . . . ?" said K'Raoda, trying to see through the smoke and flames obscuring the shuttles.

Silent on its n-gravs, a single shuttle flew out of the smoke, firing warning bolts near surviving corsairs. Dropping their weapons, the corsairs surrendered, fingers locked behind their heads.

The shuttle landed middeck, between the corsairs and the burning commando boats. As crewmen rushed by to take prisoners, the ramp lowered. D'Trelna and McShane stepped onto the deck, rifles in hand.

"N'Trol," said K'Raoda, hurrying toward D'Trelna, Z'Sha by his side, "move the atmosphere curtain in past those shuttles."

Barely perceptible, the shimmering air curtain advanced slowly past the inferno of burning spacecraft, stopping a few meters forward of the shuttles. Behind it, the flames winked out.

Where eleven silver ships had sat gleaming, eleven charred durasteel frames lay broken and buckled on the scarred decking.

Z'Sha looked at the air curtain. Shocked, he turned to K'Raoda. "Why didn't you do that to the corsairs, Commander? You could have spaced them all when they were marching along the deck. We'd have been spared all this." His hand swept the carnage.

"My uncle K'Zor served in the A'Rem Action," said K'Raoda as they walked toward newly landed shuttle. "He was aide to a planetary guard general. This general went to parley with F'Sal and his rebels, suspecting a trap. It was. The rebels wiped his guard, held him and my uncle prisoner for the rest of the war. Even F'Sal was surprised. 'Why'd you come, knowing it was a trap?' he asked. 'Why didn't you lure us with a hologram, then strafe us?' "

Z'Sha smiled faintly. "I looked into that clever thug's dope-widened eyes and I said, 'Because then there'd be no difference between you and us.'

"The older one gets, Commander, the greater the risk of being dosed with one's own words. A good man in a tight spot, K'Zor. How is he?"

D'Trelna and McShane stood watching as the crewmen foamed down the two burning commando boats, knocking down the fires. They turned as K'Raoda and Z'Sha arrived.

"Somehow, Commodore, I'm not surprised to see you," said Z'Sha. "You seem quite recovered."

"Thank you. I am."

He turned to K'Raoda. "Casualties?"

"One hundred and eight as of now, sir."

"You look like hell."

"Thank you, sir."

"Send a force to the bridge. They were trying to put an assault force in there through the forward section-four lift access. We wiped most of them, but . . ."

"We thought they might try for the bridge, sir." K'Raoda rubbed his throat. "That contingency's covered."

"No sign of K'Tran," said a voice over K'Raoda's communicator.

The commander looked at the line of prisoners being marched past. Stepping over the corsair bodies littering the deck, he stopped a large, bearded prisoner with commander's pips on his collar.

"Where's K'Tran?"

The corsair made an autoerotic suggestion.

"He's heading for the bridge, isn't he?"

Recognition flicked across the corsair's face, replaced by impassivity. It was enough. Waving prisoner and escort on, K'Raoda turned back to D'Trelna. "There's probably a very surprised corsair commander on our bridge right now."

"You can kill Captain K'Tran, Commander," said Ambassador Z'Sha, handing his pistol, butt first, to K'Raoda, "but I don't think you can really surprise him."

K'Tran and his last seven corsairs stepped from the lift. Leaving four men in the corridor, he led the others through the ragged hole in the bridge doors.

The bridge was empty, except for A'Tir, who sat at the engineering station. Seeing who it was, she lowered her pistol and turned back to the complink. "You didn't take the ship," she said, watching a readout.

"The ship took us," he said with a faint smile. Waving his men out, he sank into the adjacent comm officer's chair, pistol in his lap. "You found the bridge abandoned, of course."

"Of course." Frowning, she typed in a long series of numbers.

"They've switched control to Engineering, tied up the complink with all sorts of authenticators."

"Right."

"You're now trying to break through to computer and restore control to the bridge," he said. "Knowing you won't make it, that they're on their way."

"One must try."

Blaster fire sounded from outside. "Coming from both access corridors and the lift!" said a hurried voice over K'Tran's communicator. "Too many of them."

"Give it up, J'Lar," said K'Tran, standing. "We've had it."

The firing stopped.

"Weapons through the door, now, or we'll gas you!" K'Raoda's voice came from the corridor.

"A good run, friend." K'Tran smiled as A'Tir rose from the console. "But no paradise world for us, now."

"It was a good run," she said, returning his smile. "Friend."

Together, they walked to the door and pitched their weapons into the corridor.

"Your ships are taken," said D'Trelna. "Of the three hundred and eighty-four raiders who followed you here, all but sixty-two are dead." He sat behind his desk, looking up at K'Tran and A'Tir, duraplast security bond around their ankles and wrists.

"Commodore . . ." began K'Tran.

D'Trelna's fist slamed the desk. "Silence! You are slime! You betrayed humanity to serve the S'Cotar. You still serve the S'Cotar. And you serve something else." Reaching down, he picked up the brainpod, slamming it onto the desk. It rolled over the edge, stopping at K'Tran's gleaming black boots.

"A mindslaver," said D'Trelna. "There's a great bloody mindslaver out there—where?—one of the lost Imperial quadrants? And it's hired you to keep it supplied. Correct?"

"We don't betray confidences, Fats," said A'Tir.

"You're aware of the Fleet Regulations regarding corsairs?" said the commodore coldly.

"Quite liberal," said K'Tran. "The condemned have a choice of death by blaster, poison, disintegration, spacing or hanging."

"We'll be giving you and your lot a fair trial next watch. You'll be found guilty, condemned to death and executed immediately after the trial. You might want to consider your death preference."

He reached for the door button, then paused. "Do you remember me, K'Tran, from before the war?"

The corsair nodded. "You were a smuggler—blue seven sector. I was senior patrol officer, commanding four frigates. You wouldn't pay protection, so I came after you. Almost got you—twice."

"Three times. You were good—one of the best, in fact. Why'd you turn?"

K'Tran shrugged—an unnatural action with his hands shackled behind him. "When the S'Cotar wiped Second Fleet, we were cut off from any known jump path home. We raided loyally for a long time—shot up S'Cotar supply convoys, hit their occupation garrisons. Captain T'Ral was killed. We fought on. Finally we annoyed them enough to bring a whole sector fleet down on us. It was a very clever trap, well-baited. All they had to do was open fire and we were history. Instead, they had a talk with us—with me.

Guan-Sharick himself. He pointed out that humanity was doomed. I could save myself and my command, he said, if I served the S'Cotar. After they won the war, we'd be given our own star system, plus whatever booty we'd taken."

"Ridiculous. They'd have killed you the instant they were through with you."

"Easy for you to say, D'Trelna. The choice was either to die nobly, uselessly, or to go on living for a while. I'm a pragmatist. I chose life."

"Life," said D'Trelna thoughtfully. "And your crews—what did they chose?"

"Second Fleet were prewar conscripts—the street scum of a dozen worlds. Good soldiers, properly led and disciplined, but no fanatics. None of us were fanatics."

"So you made a stand for life and against fanaticism, by raping and pillaging in the service of genocidal biofabs. Is that your defense?"

They said nothing.

"Then, after the S'Cotar were defeated, you kept on raiding."

"We were hunted men," said K'Tran. "Though doing quite well, raiding commerce and outworlds. We have bases on the edge of civilization—places where money buys respectful silence."

"And the mindslaver?"

"We never met," said K'Tran. "The S'Cotar provided us with the brainpods and an advance against collections."

"Who's crewing the mindslaver?"

"I wasn't told. My impression was that it was—autonomous."

D'Trelna grunted, then sat staring at the two for a moment, rocking slightly in his chair. "You're not bad—

you're utterly amoral. Is there a single scruple between you?''

''Can we get on with this?'' said A'Tir.

''Let's not be hasty,'' said K'Tran.

''D'Trelna, you need us for something or we'd be dead by now. What?''

''I have a deal for you, Mr. Businessman,'' he said, clasping his hands over his belly. ''You and your killers will go free in exchange for your help.''

''What sort of help?'' said K'Tran.

''Nothing hazardous, unfortunately. I have something that must be done, now. And it can only be done with two starships. I have just one, and need every crewman I've got.''

''You'll let us go with our ships?'' asked A'Tir.

''One frigate, disarmed.''

''The cruiser, armed,'' said K'Tran.

''The cruiser, with one missile and one fusion battery.''

The corsairs exchanged glances.

''Deal,'' said K'Tran.

''Deal,'' said D'Trelna. ''Happily, I can't shake your hand.''

18

"That's it," said John, turning off the truck's engine. It died with backfire. Tune-up time on Terra Two, he thought.

"What do you mean?" asked L'Wrona. He sat between Hochmeister and John in the truck cab.

"We can't go any farther, H'Nar. The road's impassable."

The K'Ronarin stared at the stout saplings growing in the road. "There're only little trees. Just roll over them."

"They're enough to stop this truck," said John. "Internal combustion engine—not one of your spiffy floaters."

They'd turned off the Maximus access road half a mile from the complex, following the overgrown ruts of the old logging trail, branches scraping the sides of the truck.

"It's not much farther," said Hochmeister. Opening the door, he hopped from the cab into the brush, working his way around to the front.

"Everyone out," said L'Wrona over the commnet. Two by two, the commandos leaped the tailgate, tramping through the scrub to join the other three.

Leading with long, ground-devouring strides, Hochmeister set off down the road into the gray winter twilight. As they followed, snow started falling, dry flakes rustling through barren birch and oak.

"Looks like home," said L'Wrona.

"U'Tria?" sad John, walking beside him.

The captain nodded. "A world of short summers and long winters. But spring—spring's a green miracle."

"And the S'Cotar occupation?" asked John, regretting it at once.

"Left little." Squinting, L'Wrona turned his head from a sudden sharp gust. "It's going to be a howler."

The snow was thickening, the wind whipping it into a classic northeast blizzard.

Hochmeister stopped and turned, waving them to him. They huddled around him, a small circle of warmth. "The road turns right at the base of the hill," he said, "then runs to the river's edge—perhaps a hundred meters. The drainage tunnel's set in concrete, halfway down the embankment."

"We can climb down it?" asked S'Til.

"Easily. Thirty-five, forty-degree slope, no more."

"You're sure about the sentries?" said L'Wrona.

"None when I was there."

"Luck, then," said L'Wrona. "Maintain skirmish order. Follow me."

K'Tran's face appeared in D'Trelna's monitor. "Your engines are now destruct-tied, K'Tran," said the commodore. "Both frigates and all escape pods are disabled. Betray us, try to run, your drives will explode."

"You'd grieve, of course."

"Repeat orders."

"I'm not a cadet, D'Trelna," he snapped.

"K'Tran, I don't want to, but if necessary, I will crew your cruiser from *Implacable* and take my chances understrength.

"Repeat orders."

The corsair sighed. "Commanding the light cruiser, I am to take station at designated coordinates. Upon your order, I'm to activate the Imperial device installed in our drive. I'm to keep the portal so created open for *Implacable* to pass through and return.

"And if you don't return?"

D'Trelna smiled unpleasantly. "Then in five Terran days, you'll change from organic to inorganic garbage, wafting through the universe. The solar winds out here blow toward T'Kyar's Galaxy. There'll be a bad smell there in a few billion years.

"Assume station now. Advise when completed." He switched off.

"If anyone can slip your trap, Commodore," said Z'Sha, "K'Tran will." The ambassador stood beside D'Trelna's station, his pre-battle demeanor and attire restored.

"A clever slime, but he can't walk home." He punched up a drink. "T'ata, Ambassador?"

"No, thank you."

"Will that drive device work, Commodore?" he asked, as D'Trelna slipped the steaming cup from the beverager.

"We'll soon know," said D'Trelna, sipping carefully. "If it fails dramatically, then the surviving corsairs will be killed, not my people."

"Installation was no problem?"

"We put the cube into the cruiser's drive interfeed port, as specified. Jump drive mechanics have changed little over the centuries. Accessing the drive core, that cube should do whatever it's supposed to."

"Is that all the commwand had to tell you?"

"Directly, yes. Just a few simple instructions, no explanations." He set the cup down. "Indirectly, though . . . Voice analysis of the message shows it was recorded by machine. As far as I could tell, it was just a slightly pedantic baritone. Machine-generated phonemes, according to computer."

"Corsair moving on station, Commodore," reported T'Ral.

"Very well."

"Machines." Z'Sha sat at the captain's station. "Machines on Terra Two—with Imperial markings. Machine-generated commwand. And the Trel Expedition, held in abeyance by this madness"—he waved vaguely toward Terra—"was prompted by a warning of a machine invasion from another reality. How are these three related?"

D'Trelna shrugged. "We'll probably find out at great cost, as we do everything. I have one crisis to deal with, here and now. Actually, there and now. I'm dealing with it."

"These are all extensions of the same phenomenon, though, D'Trelna—they must be. And knowing the phenomenon, we can control for the variants."

"With respect sir, your logic is far exceeding your facts."

"Perhaps," smiled Z'Sha. "I'll tell you what, D'Trelna. You take this battle cruiser to Terra Two and bring us back some facts. An intact enemy machine would be marvelous."

"I'll do what I can." He glanced at the time readout. "You have little time to make your shuttle."

Z'Sha stood. "Mr. McShane will be riding down with me?"

"Yes." D'Trelna rose, seeing him to the doors.

"An interesting man. We land in New York. Perhaps

he'll have dinner with me." He held out his hand. "Luck to you, Commodore. From an old soldier to a younger one."

D'Trelna shook the firm, dry hand. "Thank you, sir."

He turned to the sentries flanking the doors. "Escort the ambassador to shuttle embarkation."

The commlink beeped as D'Trelna resumed his station. "Cleaned up?" he asked at the sight of K'Raoda's tired face in the pickup. Behind the commander, the hangar deck swarmed with repair crews.

"Reasonably," said K'Raoda. "Bodies and debris have been hauled off. It'll take two, maybe three more watches to tidy up."

"Very good, T'Lei. Get up here."

K'Tran's face replaced K'Raoda's. "We're in position."

"Activate your drive."

K'Tran turned from the pick up. "S'Kal, engage drive."

"Full forward visual on the screen, please," ordered D'Trelna.

Pale gray, a thin beam lanced up from the cruiser's blunt bow. Halting high above and ahead of the corsair, the beampoint became a gray rim that rotated slowly wider, banishing all light within its boundaries.

"Readout on that?" asked D'Trelna.

"Nothing coherent," said T'Ral, monitoring three telltales. "Wild energy fluxes. Peak, drop, peak, drop."

The dark within the circle rippled, growing even darker. After a moment, the rippling subsided. "Fascinating," said T'Ral.

"What?" said D'Trelna as K'Raoda came onto the bridge.

"There's a coherent signal now. It's the inverse of the readout we got when they snatched *V'Tran's Glory*. And the inverse of the readout from the Maximus portal."

"Any fluctuation in the signal?" asked K'Raoda.

"None."

D'Trelna nodded. "Ship's status, Commander K'Raoda?"

"All sections at battlestations."

"K'Lana, did our shuttle launch?"

"Yes, sir."

"Let's do it, then. Forward, point three, T'Lei."

Seen from *New Hope*, *Implacable* slipped away down a black hole.

"A'Tir," said K'Tran into the commnet, "they're gone.
Any luck?"

"None." She was wearing a white radiation suit. Removing the helmet, she handed it to an Engineering tech. "*Implacable*'s Engineer is too good to be Fleet."

"He isn't," said K'Tran. "Chief Engineer of the R'Tar Line. They drafted his ass. What did he do?"

"Tied a tickle line from the engines to the destruct programming. We try to move . . ."

K'Tran's eyes narrowed. "But we can jump?"

"There is no barrier to our jumping," she said wearily. "Only to disengaging that magic black cube."

"But we can't jump with it in the drive."

"Correct."

"I'll disengage the destruct programming," he said, reaching for the complink.

"Don't!" she said sharply. "He's looped the destruct programming back into the tickle line. Try to change destruct programming from current parameters and you'll trigger it."

K'Tran took his hands from the terminal. "I see."

"There's another problem. We've needed a good port overhaul for a long time."

"The better ports would not have us, Number One."

"We've got measurable power-core leakage. Nothing biologically hazardous, but enough to maybe spark a backsurge. If that surge were near the tickle line . . ."

"Got us by the shorts, hasn't he?" said K'Tran, running a hand through his hair. "What can we do?"

"Cut power down to emergency levels. Vital equipment only. Cold concentrates, cold showers, minimal life support."

He gave the necessary orders, turning back to A'Tir as the lights dimmed. "I'm going to get Commodore Fats and his friends, Number One. It would almost be worth dying to strand them in an alternate reality."

"Nothing's worth dying for."

"Yes, well, I'll find a way."

"You do that," she said, stripping off the radiation suit. The brown Fleet-duty uniform beneath was rumpled, the underarms dark with sweat. "I'll be showering with the last of the hot water."

K'Tran sat a long while in the command chair, his thoughts growing even darker and colder than his ship.

"Clean," said S'Til, pocketing her detector.

L'Wrona leading, the commandos, Hochmeister and Harrison swept into the tunnel, a long black line moving warily, rifles ready, wind screaming ahead of them down the dark tunnel.

Should have kept my starhelm, thought John, flashing his light ahead. Oblong-shaped, a good twenty feet across, the tunnel rose at an easy angle, disappearing beyond the range of the slim utility lights.

"No sediment," said L'Wrona, flicking his light along the pipe bottom's pristine concrete. "Admiral, isn't this used?"

"No," said Hochmeister, walking to the captain's left.

"It was dug for an atomic reactor—prematurely. The reactor was never approved for construction by the Reich. The pipe doesn't breach the complex, so it's unguarded."

"How many reactors has the Reich allowed outside of Germany, Admiral?" asked John.

"I've read your dissertation, Major Harrison," said Hochmeister, eyes and light sweeping the wall to his left. "You had an entire section on that issue—over thirty pages." He looked at John. "You're the alternate Harrison, aren't you?"

"Assuming we get out of this, Admiral," said L'Wrona, "I'm sure Fleet Intelligence could find a post for you."

"Everyone's offering me jobs I don't want, Captain," said Hochmeister. "First the bugs, now you. I'm needed here—civilization's roving proconsul."

"You call what I've seen civilization?" said John.

"Germany, all of Europe, is quite civilized, Mr. Harrison," said the admiral. "We've recovered from fascism, rebuilt from the war, aided less fortunate allies, kept the bear at bay. I shudder to think what this world would be like had we—or the Soviets—let the atomic genie out of its bottle."

"Equality, perhaps."

"Ah! Here we are." Hochmeister's light picked out a seemingly random scattering of feldspar along the left wall. "As best I could tell, this is the portion nearest the breeding vault. From here," he shifted his light to the right, along the tunnel, "the pipe runs up and away from the vault."

"Your guesses seem very close, Admiral," said L'Wrona. "We'll go with this one."

"Set your blastpak, S'Til."

"N'Tron," called the commando officer. "Blastpak."

The corporal hurried forward, shrugging the flat orange

pack from his shoulders. Taking it, S'Til knelt and set it against the wall. Unfastened, the top revealed a miniaturized console, complete with screen. The screen glowed green as S'Til pressed a button: ENTER TARGETING INSTRUCTIONS, it responded.

"Narrow focus, S'Til," said L'Wrona. "Edge down the blowback—we haven't got much cover."

"You wouldn't know how thick the wall is, would you, Admiral?" asked S'Til, looking up at Hochmeister.

"No idea," he said. "They weren't about to show me blueprints."

"The wall is four-meters thick, Lieutenant," said a voice from beyond the small circle of light.

L'Wrona swung his utility light around. Twenty-four blasters followed the beam.

"Beyond the wall," said Guan-Sharick, stepping forward as the light found him, "is eight meters of granite, honeycombed with breeding chambers." The transmute's eyes glowed red in the beam.

"Admiral Hochmeister," said John, rising from the prone firing position, "Guan-Sharick. Guan-Sharick, Admiral Hochmeister."

"You look just like Shalan-Actal, Guan-Sharick," said the admiral.

"Appearances can be deceiving, can't they, Admiral? Or should I say Colonel?"

"You're well-informed, Guan-Sharick."

"True."

"One more thing, L'Wrona." The transmute looked at the Margrave. "The growth accelerant Shalan-Actal's using in the nutrient cell walls—it's highly volatile. A few well-placed shots and the cavern will torch."

The S'Cotar was gone.

Everyone looked at L'Wrona. "Use the bug's figures,

S'Til,'' he said after a few seconds. ''The rest of you, back off and take cover.''

Outside, the blizzard roared higher.

''Well, what have we here?'' said K'Tran, his breath fogging the tactics scan.

''Incoming ship,'' said A'Tir, looking over his shoulder. She rubbed her hands, red from the cold, then reached over, making a careful adjustment. More data flowed into the readout. ''R'Dal-class dreadnought—latest thing out of the yards.''

''He's signaling, Captain,'' said S'Kal. Still wearing a commander's uniform, the big red-bearded corsair was the only other person on the bridge.

K'Tran stepped to the Engineering station, turning on the bridge lights and bringing the heat up. ''Get your jackets off,'' he ordered, stripping down to his tunic.

''There,'' he said, sitting back in the command chair, as warm air flowed from the floor vents. ''Put him on, S'Kal.''

''Commodore D'Trelna?'' asked the young captain whose face appeared in the monitor. K'Tran noted the double row of battle ribbons on her tunic.

''No, Captain,'' he said. ''I'm Captain T'Ral. You're our reinforcements?''

''The first part of them. Another dreadnought and two cruisers were jump-scheduled a watch after us.''

''And you are?''

''Captain G'Ryn, commanding the R'Dal-class dreadnought *Victory Day*.''

''Welcome to the Terran system, Captain,'' smiled K'Tran. ''My first officer says you're authenticated and cleared for insystem.''

G'Ryn frowned, touching a finger to her ear. ''Captain

J'Tan,'' she said, ''Your authentication failed. And we read you as a light cruiser and two frigates, not a L'Aal-class cruiser and a destroyer.''

''Oh?'' K'Tran looked perturbed. ''Now I'm confused, Captain. Didn't FleetOps advise you? *Implacable* and *V'Tran's Glory* have been lost—max casualties.''

''D'Trelna, dead?'' she asked, disbelieving.

K'Tran nodded. ''And L'Wrona, too. There was a S'Cotar attack from that parallel reality—wiped both ships just as we came insystem. The S'Cotar fell back through their portal as we approached.''

''And your codes?''

''We're a pickup force—been on deep-space patrol for the last three years. Our codes are obsolete. We've no skipcomm buoy. And the attack that wiped D'Trelna's force also took out their skipcomm buoy.''

''I can't believe D'Trelna's dead.'' G'Ryn shook her head. ''I served under him for a year—a harrier squadron inside S'Cotar space. He brought us home with only forty-percent casualties.''

''Believe me,'' said K'Tran, ''he's gone.''

''I'll deploy a skipcomm buoy, Captain.''

K'Tran held up a hand. ''Don't—not until we've met.''

''Why . . .''

''I don't want to explain over the commnet. I'll brief you when we rendezvous.''

''Very well,'' she said. ''I'll shuttle over as soon as we arrive.''

K'Tran smiled. ''Please, bring your crew over, too. It's been a long time since we've seen new faces.''

''Can you accommodate several hundred?'' she asked.

''Not only accommodate them, Captain—I think we can promise you a memorable reception.''

* * *

"Certainly looks like Terra One," said D'Trelna. He sat at the flag officer's station, watching Australia and New Zealand roll by on the main screen.

"The population centers are smaller," said K'Raoda, reading a comparison scan. "Sydney and Melbourne are about a third the size of their alternates."

"We'll be coming up on the Maximus site in a moment," said T'Ral. "No ship traces . . . wait.

"Scanning a Probe class scout, mark one-three, two-one-four."

"Gunnery," said D'Trelna, "standby. Target coming up."

T'Ral read a new scan. "Negative life support. Negative drive core flow to hull jump nodules." He looked up, surprised. "She's a derelict."

"Abandoned," said K'Raoda, reading his own telltales. "Why?"

"Maybe to augment *V'Tran's'* drive," said D'Trelna. "If the machines' universe isn't on the next plane to this one, like Terra Two, they may need more power to punch through."

"How'd they get that scout here?" said K'Raoda.

"Piece by piece through the Maximus portal," said T'Ral.

"He's right," said D'Trelna. "That scout's no larger than one of our shuttles.

"If we haven't picked up traces of our destroyer by the time we reach Maximus, deploy scanning satellites."

"Got them," said T'Ral a few moments later, as they passed over California. Computer recorded without comment a coastline radically different than that of Terra One.

"Mark one-seven, five-two-nine—just above . . ." He frowned. "They're creating a portal. Same general parameters as Maximus and the space portals—some minor energy anomalies.''

''Scan to screen,'' said D'Trelna. His eyes narrowed as the scan graphics came up: two green points of light equidistant from a single circle—a circle that grew larger as they watched. Targeting data began threading across the board.

''No shield,'' said K'Raoda. ''They're diverting all energy to the portal.''

''That's *V'Tran's Glory*, all right,'' said D'Trelna, reading the data.

''Coming within their scan range,'' said T'Ral.

''Sitting up here bare-assed.'' The commodore punched into the commnet. ''Gunnery. D'Trelna. Imperiad one-seven to Archon five. Take targeting feed and blow that ship away.''

''Acknowledged,'' said B'Tul. ''Destroy target.''

''Attention. Attention.'' It was computer—calm but very loud. ''The portal has closed. The portal has closed.''

They all looked up at the screen. The two green lights and the black were still there, the black continuing to expand.

''Computer—verify,'' said D'Trelna, annoyed.

''Our portal, Commodore,'' said T'Ral, checking a permanent rearward scan. ''Our portal is gone!''

''Verified,'' said computer. ''Portal to Terra One is gone.''

''K'Tran!'' D'Trelna lunged for the commlink. ''Gunnery. Redoubt one to flanking commander two. Abort that kill order!''

''Order aborted, Commodore,'' said B'Tul. ''Just.''

''Machine failure?'' suggested K'Raoda.

''K'Tran,'' repeated D'Trelna.

''Gunnery. Take out *V'Tran's'* shield nexus.''

Far amidships, in gunnery control, B'Tul called up a projection of *V'Tran's Glory*. Marking the forward shield nexus in flashing amber, he fed in the targeting data and pushed "Execute."

A stylus-thin red beam flicked from the number seven fusion battery, spanned two and half thousand miles of space and disintegrated a hull relay pod the size of a geode.

"Shield nexus destroyed, Commodore," reported the gunner.

"Very well."

"Something unwholesome is coming through the portal very soon," said D'Trelna as they continued to close on the two ships, "or they'd have run."

He turned toward Engineering. "Lock a tractor beam on that ship, N'Trol. Pull it away from the portal," he said. "Carefully. It's our only way home."

Shalan-Actal flicked from the auxiliary command post, deep in the Vermont granite beneath Maximus, to the bridge of *V'Tran's Glory*. Four transmutes worked the instruments, teleporting between twenty-four bridge stations. At the twenty-fifth station a bubble hovered above the command chair. About five feet in diameter, its interior swirled with a sullen red haze.

You and we haven't much time, said the Tactics Master.

We have enough time, replied a chill thought. *We are within the prescribed area. When this flashes*, a blue beam sprang from the top of the bubble, touching a telltale, *our portals are joined. Reinforcements will pour through. Nothing can stop us.*

You were stopped twice before—banished from this reality, said Shalan-Actal. *By the Empire and by the Trel of prehistory.*

The crimson mist swirled darker. *The Empire is dust. The Trel less than that.*

You are about to be tractor-towed and boarded. The K'Ronarins need that portal device. They are many, we and you are few. They will retake this ship.

Not before the Armada of the One is here. Our ships carry many such portal devices. We will retake the Home Universe. We will find the Betrayer.

The telltale flashed blue.

Victory, said bubble.

K'Ronarin commandos have penetrated the breeding vaults! came the distant alert. *They're firing the chambers!*

I will not save you at our expense, said the transmute, antennae weaving in agitation. *You are on your own, Forward Commander of the One.*

Shalan-Actal flicked back to Maximus, taking the handful of S'Cotar from the ship with him.

The last hundred warriors of the once Infinite Hosts of the Magnificent huddled in the old British barracks, sheltering around propane heaters from the blizzard howling under the eaves. Hatched and raised in dry, warm caverns beneath Terra's Moon, serving mostly aboard starships, this was their first exposure to a planet's wilder elements. They stood in small, uncertain groups, feet shuffling uneasily in the flickering light from the emergency generator.

Take arms! ordered the Tactics Master. *The K'Ronarins are torching the last hope of the Race!*

The blast was still echoing when L'Wrona ducked into the hole. Following, John saw a dark blur of himself, mirrored in the fused black surface of the blasthole; then he was through, standing on a gray granite floor.

"Good God!" He looked up and around. "It's huge."

Ringed by catwalks, the breeding vault soared fifteen

levels—thousands of small hexagonal chambers, all a misty jade-green. Gray equipment banks filled the half mile of floor, red-white light pulsing along scan and control feeds up to the chambers. Half a dozen unarmed S'Cotar techs lay dead, cut down by the K'Ronarins.

L'Wrona twisted his blaster muzzle right, two soft clicks. "First squad, set weapons on diffused beam," he ordered as the last of the commandos entered the cavern. "Fire those cells. The rest of you, high alert." Aiming two-handed at the top tier of cells, he pulled the trigger, sweeping the broad beam slowly along the cell walls.

"It certainly is 'volatile,' " said Hochmeister, standing beside John. The two shielded their eyes as fierce green-tinged flames leaped toward the ceiling.

Fire raced along the catwalks as the commandos emptied their chargepaks into the walls. Thick, pungent smoke drifted down.

"S'Cotar!" shouted a commando.

Shalan-Actal and his force materialized in the vault's center. Blasters shrilled, blue-and-red bolts knifing through the smoke.

Choking, tears streaming down his face, John held his fire again and again as uncertain targets drifted through the smoke.

Something shoved him, hard. Caught off balance, he sprawled to the floor as a burning section of fused wall fell, exploding where he'd stood, showering him with molten fragments.

A thin hand reached down. John took it, letting Hochmeister help him up. The admiral tried to speak, then coughed. Shaking his head, he pointed toward the blasthole. John nodded. Together, they staggered toward the tunnel.

"Out!" L'Wrona ordered over the commnet. "Fall back!"

Feeling their way along the wall, John and Hochmeister made it to the blasthole.

The smoke wasn't as bad in the tunnel. Others staggered after them, choking and coughing, throwing themselves to the floor and the fresh stream of cold, clear air.

It slept, dimly aware that it was many yet one. Sleeping, it grew, the bonds between it entwining and thickening. Sensed but untested, it felt its strength also growing—strength it perceived as a warm glow, having no concept of strength, no concept of anything other than itself. Soon it would awake, an odd child of power, hungry and curious.

The pain struck without warning, a searing, devouring pain.

Wounded, it awoke, child of a warrior race. Terrified and angry, it lashed out.

Wheezing from the smoke, Shalan-Actal dropped Corporal N'Tron. The commando's head lolled to one side, neck broken, eyes blue and startled, staring sightless into the fire.

They are falling back through the blasthole, reported a warrior. *Pursue?*

One file only. All others, deploy foggers, tiers one through . . .

The fire went out, like a light turned off. The smoke was gone. The S'Cotar watched, unbelieving, as the breeding chambers repaired themselves, a green blur of speed.

The pain easing, it sought the source. There. Down there.

You are a fool, Shalan-Actal. You were warned about the growth accelerant.

Guan-Sharick? The Tactics Master followed that tendril of thought—within range. He tried flicking himself at it. He couldn't teleport.

It won't let you leave, will it? taunted Guan-Sharick.

What is it? he asked desperately.

Your children, Shalan-Actal. Your children becoming something Else. An angry child, Tactics Master.

The walls began rippling with cold green glow.

Out! ordered Shalan-Actal. *Use the K'Ronarin blasthole.*

Last one into the drainage pipe, L'Wrona turned, eyes streaming, and rolled a grenade back in. It detonated with a loud blast, blowback exploding into the tunnel, collapsing the blasthole.

The cold green fire left the wall in small clusters, drifting down to where the S'Cotar milled in confusion. Touching warriors' weapons, it released their potential just as the grenade detonated.

19

"Move, you hulk, move!" N'Trol stood at the Engineering station, glaring at the image of *V'Tran's Glory* on the main screen. "Half our mass, one-third our power, and it won't budge." The engineer looked down at the tractor-lock readout, not believing. The telltale read force seven—the destroyer should have been trolling toward the cruiser like a hooked game fish.

"Full power," said D'Trelna, watching the screen. The portal continued turning and growing.

"We're at breakpoint, Commodore," said N'Trol. "Tie in more power, we'll be breathing vacuum."

D'Trelna swiveled around, facing the engineer. "Objection noted, Mr. N'Trol. Execute."

"Your ship," he shrugged, engaging override.

Implacable groaned, engines straining against a seemingly immovable object. Vibrations shuddered down the long miles of the cruiser as the engines whined higher, pressed beyond design tolerance.

"Negative movement!" shouted N'Trol over the din.

"Hull sensors show fault lines—first, third, seventh through . . ."

"Cut down," ordered D'Trelna.

The engineer's fingers flew over his controls. The whining shuddering died.

"I'll take your damage control reports in a moment, N'Trol," D'Trelna said into the silence.

"Strange energy scan on the Maximus site," reported T'Ral.

"Define 'strange,' " said the commodore.

"Overlapping N-17 and N-30 groupings," said T'Ral, compiling separate readouts. "Fluctuating—every third series peaking five percent higher than the last."

"The portal's stopped dilating, sir," said K'Raoda.

D'Trelna glanced up. "So it has."

"Well, we know what happens after that, don't we?"

"Sir?" said K'Raoda.

"Birth, idiot," said N'Trol, busy at his station.

"That portal's half the diameter of Terra's moon," said T'Ral. "The baby should be impressive."

"We're just going to sit here and wait?" asked N'Trol, transferring the damage control reports to the commodore's station.

"Mr. N'Trol," said D'Trelna, looking balefully at the engineer, "we may die in a few moments. So let me say that you are one of the finest technical officers I have ever seen—and I've seen a lot."

N'Trol grunted.

"You are also as ungracious, unmannered and selfish as you are competent. Had I my way, you'd be freely discharged and sent home."

"Why, thank you, Commodore."

"But I don't have the authority."

"Captain L'Wrona on tacband, sir."

D'Trelna switched into the pickup. "H'Nar! What's going on down there?"

L'Wrona leaned against the tunnel wall, survival jacket torn, flecked with green blood. His six surviving commandos were behind him, tending their wounds. "We torched and sealed the vault, J'Quel," he said, "but there's something weird happening in there." He stopped, covering his head as the ground rumbled, showering the party with bits of cement. The rumbling ceased. "There's seismic activity—seems to be centered in the vault."

"What's your assessment?"

"The mutation process Guan-Sharick was afraid of—it's here, I think—out of control. Way out of control." He turned his back to the wind knifing down the tunnel. "Maybe we triggered whatever's happening, maybe it's spontaneous."

Across the passageway from L'Wrona, John slumped wearily against the wall, then jerked away, back stinging. "H'Nar!" he called. "This wall's hot!"

Turning, L'Wrona's saw the wall further down the tunnel glowing a sullen red—the air seemed to ripple in the heat. Rivulets of molten rock and cement were forming into fiery streams that inched toward them, slowly swelling.

"Everyone out!" he called, pointing to the entrance. "Make for the river and the opposite shore!"

"She's had it," said Hochmeister, throwing a jacket over a gut-shot commando. He and John followed the others into the night and storm.

"J'Quel, we're out," reported L'Wrona, scrambling down the embankment and out onto the ice. "Commvector a shuttle down to us."

The wind had dropped, but the snow was coming thick,

dry and stinging. They trudged in a ragged line across the cleanswept ice, making for the opposite shore.

Hochmeister slipped, starting to fall. An arm shot out, catching him.

"You're taking good care of me, Harrison," he said. "Why?"

"You're going to keep your word to the gangers, Admiral," said John, guiding the other around a suspiciously dark patch of ice. "And for that, you have to be alive."

D'Trelna nodded at a thumbs up sign from K'Raoda. "Your shuttle's on the way, H'Nar," he said over the commlink.

"Acknowledged."

"Here it comes," said T'Ral, looking up at the main screen.

"Gods of my fathers," whispered D'Trelna, rising from his chair.

It was huge—a black sphere hundreds of miles in diameter, emerging slowly from the rippling obsidian of the portal. Not a single light shone from its darkness.

"Computer," said the commodore, finding his voice, "search all data sources for any record of a vessel similar to the one now approaching us.

"K'Lana, give me ship-to-ship, all bands. Gunnery, lock all but one missile battery on that monster. Target that one battery on *V'Tran's Glory*."

"Commodore," said computer through the chair speaker, "there is an archival reference to ships of this configuration."

"Summarize."

"The data is in the classified portion of the Imperial Archives on K'Ronar. Requests must be made through channels."

"That's it?"

"Yes."

"You have ship-to-ship, all bands, Commodore," said K'Lana.

D'Trelna opened the commlink. "This is K'Ronarin Confederation cruiser *Implacable*. Halt and identify."

Something flashed from the black sphere, now half through the portal. Every screen on the bridge blanked as it exploded against the shield.

"The shield's gone," said T'Ral, incredulous. "Like something swatting a fly."

"N'Trol?" said D'Trelna.

"It somehow used our own shield to conduct a charge to the hullside shield relays. They're fused lumps." For once the engineer looked impressed. "It'll take months to repair."

"We may not have to worry about repairs," said D'Trelna.

"Switching to secondary scanners," said K'Raoda.

Their view of the outside came back.

"Burned out all exposed scanners," reported N'Trol, surveying the damage readout.

"Why doesn't it finish us?" said K'Raoda.

"Perhaps we're beneath its contempt," said D'Trelna. "Let's see if we can change that."

"Gunnery, open fire on the sphere—everything we've got."

"Move us in front of that portal, T'Lei."

It had saved itself, becoming flame even as the flames took it. And it had learned, taking the minds of the S'Cotar as they died. Integrating their memories, it saw what they'd attempted and understood their error.

It searched out *Implacable* and the portal. Finding them, it rose from its fiery creche.

* * *

They were halfway across the river when the top blew off Maximus, a sudden flash of emerald light sweeping away the dark.

Unbearably bright, a flaming green orb soared into the night and the storm, taking away the light and sending a shock wave crashing across the mountains.

"What . . . ?" asked S'Til, rising from the ice, vision still blurred by dancing specks of green.

"The end of the Maximus Project, certainly," said Hochmeister, brushing off his jacket.

The weather was closing in again, the wind throwing the snow into their faces.

There was a sudden loud snap! then a series of groans and cracks beneath their feet.

"The ice is breaking up!" John flashed his light ahead of them. Ice and snow were being replaced by a widening stretch of black water.

"Back! The way we came!" shouted L'Wrona. "Quickly!"

"Forget it," said S'Til, flicking her light along the network of cracks spreading from the Maximus side.

"Upriver," ordered L'Wrona, turning left.

Behind them, the cracks were widening to fissures, triggering more faults that began snaking up and down river.

They'd covered perhaps a hundred yards, their race with the dark water almost lost, when a yellow halo appeared out of the storm, resolving into a shuttle that hovered on n-gravs just above the ice, access port cycling open as a ladder descended.

"What's that?" asked Hochmeister.

"The cavalry, Admiral," said John as they joined the rush for the ladder.

* * *

D'Trelna shook his head, disgusted. "Not even slowing it," he said, watching red fusion beams and silver missiles strike at the black ship. The beams were splashing harmlessly against it, the missiles drifting unexploded along the sphere's equator, engines dead. "Cease fire," he ordered.

It was almost through the portal, a featureless black mass that filled the screen, only the drifting silver needles of *Implacable*'s missiles providing contrast.

"Message received on all bands," said K'Lana from the commstation.

That brought D'Trelna out of his chair, staring at her. "What?"

" 'Catch.' "

"Catch?" He turned back to the screen, just as all of *Implacable*'s missiles came alive, coming home on tails of pale blue fire.

"Gunnery! Destruct those missiles!"

"Negative response, Commodore."

"Get us out of here, T'Lei."

"Never make it," said K'Raoda, slamming in full reverse engines.

"Humor me," said D'Trelna. Gripping the back of the command chair, he leaned forward, watching the screen.

The black sphere's image shrank as they retreated. The missiles drew closer, then turned as one, heading away from Terra Two and the cruiser, driving in toward the sun.

"Whatever else they are," said the commodore, "they're cruel.

"Get us back on station," he ordered, taking his chair. "Gunnery, he's almost here. Destroy *V'Tran's Glory*."

N'Trol began whistling a tune popular when they'd last put into Prime Base—"Upship and Home No More."

"Commodore! Wait!" K'Raoda transferred a fresh pickup to the screen. A brilliant speck of green was rising from Earth's nightside, growing nearer as they watched.

"Gunnery. Countermand that destruct order.

"What is that, T'Lei?"

"The Maximus anomaly," said K'Raoda. He sent the targeting data flowing across the screen.

"Star plasma," said N'Trol. "Nothing else stays that hot."

"Headed right for us—and the portal," said D'Trelna. He studied the target projection. "Computer, assume us to be target of object approaching from planet. Give us standard audio count to impact."

"Acknowledged."

"Is it after us or the portal?" said T'Ral.

"Let's not find out," said D'Trelna.

"Thirty to impact," said computer, voice filling the bridge.

"T'Lei, at five, jump us just outsystem—about where we'd put a skipcomm buoy."

K'Raoda was suddenly very busy. "Cycling to drive, Commodore."

"Twenty to impact."

"Drive cycled."

"All decks, stand by for jump," said D'Trelna.

"Ten, nine, eight . . ."

"Hazardous radiation!" reported T'Ral, shielding his eyes as blinding green light swept the bridge.

"Five . . ."

The ball of green fire passed through where *Implacable* had been. Missiles and beams flashed from the black ship as she cleared the portal. Green fire devoured them. Reaching the portal, the Maximus entity passed through layers of wondrously intricate defense screens, penetrating the hull.

The black sphere exploded, a fierce flash of primary colors sweeping out from the portal.

The gray beam from the destroyer winked off as the explosion touched it. Freed, *V'Tran's Glory* drifted slowly toward Terra Two.

20

Warsuited, blaster in hand, K'Raoda stood alone on the bridge of *V'Tran's Glory,* talking to *Implacable*. "Bridge and Engineering are secure, H'Nar," he said. "S'Til's force is searching the rest of the ship—N'Trol's checking drive and engines."

"And those alien machines?"

K'Raoda looked at the small piles of gray ash littering the deck. "They couldn't handle defeat—they appear to have self-destructed."

The captain shook his head. "If we reacted like that, T'Lei, we'd be a long time dead.

"Advise when the ship's secure. Volunteer crew is standing by."

"Acknowledged."

Security seemed as deserted as the rest of the ship. S'Til walked past the central guard station and down the corridor, glancing into each of the ten detention rooms. The first four held no surprises—doors open, beds neatly made, a dresser, table, entertainment equipment, food unit, lavatory.

The door to the fifth room was shut. "Room five, Detention, is locked," she said over the commnet. "I'm going in."

"Wait for reinforcements," said K'Raoda.

Ignoring him, she stepped back, aimed carefully and fired, blowing the lock controller away without fusing the lock. She went through the door as it slid open, M11A levelled.

"And who the hell are you?" said the redhead in the brown K'Ronarin uniform, ignoring the blaster aimed at her chest.

"English," said S'Til, not lowering the weapon. "Is your name M'Kenzie?"

"MacKenzie." She took a step toward S'Til.

The commando officer held up a palm. "Stay there.

"Commander," she said into the communicator. "I need a decon team down here. They had a Terran prisoner."

"Machines have poked, prodded and probed me," said Heather, cheeks flushed. "One especially vile metallic thing was shoved into my . . ."

"Enough!" John held up his hands. "Did Q'Nil tell you *why*?"

Oblivious to the two Terrans, the medtech was busy at the exam room's lab console, reading Heather's final workup.

"Something about biological vectors," she said, glaring at Q'Nil.

"She's clean," announced Q'Nil in English, looking up from the console. "You can send her home."

"Q'Nil," said John, "tell Heather why you did outrageous things to her body."

"I tried," he said, stepping around the console. "She was shouting too loudly."

"I'm listening," she said coldly.

"Our machine friends could have turned you into a carrier of some very deadly latent bacillus," he said, meeting her look. "Anyone coming in contact with you would also have become a carrier. After a year, the bacillus would activate, killing you, everyone you'd passed it to, everyone they'd passed it to, on into infinity. Not so long and your world would be free of people."

Heather had grown very pale. "This has happened before?" she asked in a small voice.

Q'Nil nodded. "Long time ago. The Machine Wars. But under strikingly similar circumstances. Captive found, taken home, embraced by family and friends."

"And a world died?" she said.

"A quadrant died. Over two hundred inhabited planets, half a trillion people." He walked to the food server, punching up a cup of soup. "It's still there, on the star charts—the Plague Quadrant. The corpses are dust, the buildings and machines in ruins, cities overgrown. Fleet sends robot probes in now and then, taking samples—the Plague's still there, latent, awaiting a carrier. Formidable automated defense networks keep those planets and their buried wealth safe from greedy madmen—and us safe from the bacillus. Ironic that machines protect us from what machines wrought.

"Something to eat?" he asked, blowing gently on hot, clear liquid.

They shook their heads.

"Come on, lady," said John. "I'll give you a tour of *Implacable*."

"Fine." She turned at the door. "Sorry I was such a jerk, Q'Nil. Thanks."

"Happiness and long life, MacKenzie," he said, saluting her with upraised cup.

He stepped to the commlink as the door closed.

"Well?" demanded D'Trelna.

"They dosed her with a binary agent, Commodore. I almost missed it."

"What is a binary agent?"

"A war bacillus harmless in itself. Call it type zero. If type zero meets the other half of the equation, though . . ."

"Type one?"

"Yes—type one. Each mutates the other into the same deadly, highly communicable killer."

"So what good does it do for them to have just type zero walking around on Terra Two?"

"They must have seeded the locals with type one when they held Maximus, Commodore. MacKenzie's type zero would spread from person to person, remaining in their systems, even as type one is now spreading. They'd inevitably meet and the Plague would start."

"We came that close," D'Trelna held thumb and forefinger slightly apart, "to another corpse world?"

"We did."

D'Trelna sat silent for a moment, looking at the status board without seeing it. He turned back to the commlink. "She's clean now?"

"More than clean." He sipped his lukewarm soup. "She'll be spreading a counter bacillus that destroys both binary types."

"Thank you, Q'Nil."

"Oh, Commodore?"

"Yes?" D'Trelna's finger paused over the comm switch.

"The primary bacillus—the killer—it's the one used against the Empire. It's the Plague Quadrant bacteria."

* * *

"You look good," said John as they walked down the corridor, heading for the lift. "Especially for someone who's been held in the brig for about a month."

"When I came tumbling through that portal, I was sure they'd kill me," she said. "Instead they put me in detention—and ignored me. I learned how to use the food machine. And the entertainment link was a godsend. It's programmed for English. Anything you want to know about the S'Cotar, the biofab war, I can tell you, as long as it was in ship's computer. I can even read some K'Ronarin.

"When can I go home?" she asked, as they reached the lift.

"A couple of hours," said John, pushing the calltab. "D'Trelna wants to get back to Terra One." The lift arrived, announcing itself with a faint ping.

"You'll be delighted to know," he said, as they boarded, "that an old friend will be joining you on the flight home."

"Come," called Hochmeister as the door chimed. He sat at his cabin's small desk, looking at a page of closely written notes.

D'Trelna came in, attired in his usual rumpled brown duty uniform.

"Ah, Commodore," said Hochmeister. "Have a seat." The drab K'Ronarin uniform seemed made for him.

"Thank you, no," said D'Trelna. "We've finished testing the portal device aboard our destroyer, Admiral. We're leaving this charming universe almost immediately. Where would you like us to set you down?"

"Berlin. Midday, midweek, atop the Brandenburg Gate. I'd appreciate it if the shuttle could approach booming out Wagner—'The Ride of the Valkyries,' I think."

"Admiral . . ."

"Just joking, Commodore," he said with a smile. Taking off his bifocals, he set them atop his notepad and looked up at D'Trelna, hands folded. "My home is Dresden, a quaint city of the baroque. There're a number of parks. Just slip me into one at night. I'll take a cab."

"Fine." He stepped to the door.

"You don't like me, do you, Commodore?"

"Like you?" frowned D'Trelna, turning back. He shook his head. "No, I don't like you, Admiral. Oh, you're a cultured, intelligent man—you can be quite charming when you want to be. But you have the soul of an Imperial Security Master—you're a tireless and ruthless servant of Order. Happily, people like you are rare. Perhaps you kill each other off."

"Peace, Commodore," said Hochmeister easily. "I serve the peace."

D'Trelna shrugged. "Call it what you will.

"Please be ready to leave in an hour. I'll send an officer to escort you to hangar deck." He left the room, the door hissing shut behind him.

As Hochmeister picked up his glasses, the door chimed again.

It was D'Trelna. "You've piqued my curiosity, Admiral," he said before Hochmeister could speak. "You've been on board for a week, have left only once, and are logging almost continuous computer time. What the hell are you doing?"

"Just being a policeman, Commodore—serving Order. You have a S'Cotar on this ship."

D'Trelna glanced out the armorglass. The stars shimmered faintly, their light distorted by the shield. "Impossible."

"Guan-Sharick is on board. Probably since you defeated the S'Cotar off Terra One."

The commodore sat down facing the desk. "Explain."

"Certainly. I've spent my time reviewing your records. First for my own information, then to quell a suspicion. The suspicion merely grew.

"Who told you about Maximus, Commodore?"

"Guan-Sharick, of course."

"Yes. Guan-Sharick. Teleported aboard and walked into your cabin with a bottle of premium brandy. Shock. Amazement. Consternation."

"Yes."

"Guan-Sharick's briefing was interrupted. Remember?"

"Someone called." D'Trelna shook his head. "It's been a while."

The admiral reached for the desk complink. "I envy you your technology," he said, entering a command.

"The prophylactic that protects our civilization from infectious creativity," said the commodore as Hochmeister swiveled the monitor to face him.

"I like that," said the admiral.

"As true now as when first written, four thousand years ago.

"Half the screen's my log entry of Guan-Sharick's visit," said D'Trelna, reading the data. "The other half's a maintenance downtime log for the shield."

"Note the times."

D'Trelna saw it. He looked up, startled. "The S'Cotar arrived while the shield was up, he *left* when it was down."

"Correct," said the admiral, swinging the monitor back and disconnecting the complink. The screen folded itself neatly into the desk top, blending with the yellow t'raq-wood veneer. "That was the only time your shield had been down since you first arrived in the Terran system."

"One of us," said D'Trelna, pinching the bridge of his nose, looking pained. "One of us."

"Yes—if it's true the S'Cotar can't teleport through a shield."

"They can't."

He looked at Hochmeister, eyes narrowed. "Who?"

The admiral spread his hands. "I didn't know, but I thought an alien clever enough to infiltrate an enemy ship for so long would know where to set tripwires—early warnings of an investigation. Matching of those two log entries we just viewed would be a logical tripwire. An alert has no doubt now been triggered to someone on this ship." He touched the beverager, producing a cup of t'ata.

D'Trelna glanced at the door. "Someone who'll come to silence you."

Hochmeister shook his head. "No. Someone who is already here."

"You're very clever, Admiral," said Guan-Sharick.

"You're not D'Trelna, are you?"

"No. That capable lump's on his way to the bridge." The transmute looked around the room, then at the door. "No rush of commandos, Admiral?"

"No." He grimaced as he sipped the t'ata. "Hideous drink." He set it aside.

"Herbal. Very healthy.

"Why did you ferret me out?" The blonde replaced D'Trelna's image.

"Amazing how you do that," said the admiral. He rose, walking to the armorglass window and its view of Terra Two. "I need you. I promised the gangers I would help them—negotiations, profound changes in the way

America is run. Many in Germany fear a united America. I don't—they're no threat without the bomb. I can influence our side into neutrality while the gangers talk with their government." He faced the blonde.

"It's the American side that I can't control. For that, I need you. How many effectives have you left inside their government?"

"How did you know?"

Hochmeister shrugged. "Something was happening at the second-secretary level. In light of later data, it had to be you."

"I see. There're three that Shalan missed. Why?"

"I want you to use them in any way necessary to see that an accord is reached between the gangers and the government. A fair and equitable accord—UC is to be disbanded, the cities rebuilt."

"I'd have thought you had a warm spot for Urban Corps, Admiral."

The admiral shrugged. "Just playing a role. I was there to investigate suspicions regarding Maximus. Colonel Aldridge was a superb cover."

"You fooled a master," conceded the S'Cotar. "So, I do what you say, and then what?"

"Then you're free."

"Did I miss something?" asked the blonde. "Why shouldn't I just kill you?"

Hochmeister walked back to the desk. He stood, looking down at the S'Cotar. "Because I've recorded and hidden my suspicions and evidence about you deep in ship's computer. A routine report to computer of my death or disappearance would trigger a wide dissemination of that file. D'Trelna and L'Wrona would tear this ship apart with their bare hands to find you."

"I could steal the access code from your dying mind."

The admiral shook his head. "Probably not before my mind died." He tapped his teeth with a fingernail. "L-pill in a hollow tooth. Fast."

The S'Cotar was silent for a moment. "Very well, Admiral. It costs me nothing.

"I must return with this ship. However, my transmutes will report to you upon your return. When their mission's accomplished to your satisfaction, you will give them the access code to that file."

"They'll be leaving the portal open for a while, then?"

The blonde nodded. "The plan is to post a few ships off Terra Two—just to make sure there are no slimy green bugs left."

"I'm leaving tonight," the admiral said as the S'Cotar stood.

"I know. They're putting you and MacKenzie down on a scan-shielded shuttle. With the Maximus site obliterated, there's no trace of an alien presence on the planet."

They walked to the door. "It's probably being explained as a secret project gone wrong," said Hochmeister.

"Not a total lie."

"So, do we have a deal, Guan-Sharick?"

"We have a deal, Admiral," said the S'Cotar.

They shook hands, Hochmeister feeling the S'Cotar's grip as firm, dry and human.

Guan-Sharick was gone.

Bemused, the Admiral looked at his hand, then went back to the desk and stuffed his notes into the disposer.

"Well, this is it, then?" said Heather as they stopped at the foot of the shuttle. Hangar deck was back to normal now, blaster gouges along the walls the only trace of battle.

"This is it," said John. He handed her the green backpack he'd just taken from his quarters.

"What's in here?" she asked, unlacing the nylon cord.

"A belated gift from Prometheus," he said, watching her remove the thick, black bound book. "One of the oddities of our civilization the K'Ronarins were shipping home. They can always get another."

"*On the Construction of Atomic and Thermonuclear Weapons,*" she read. "But we know bomb theory."

"Theory." He tapped the book. "This tells you how—bomb casings, fissionable materials, detonators.

"You do have fissionable material?"

She nodded, thumbing excitedly through the manual. "Five German-managed power plants reprocess PU-239 through us." She looked up. "We've been saving a small percentage of it—conditioned the auditors to believe that five percent of any run is MUF—Material Unaccounted For.

"In a year, we're going to have our own nuclear force." She slipped the book into the backpack. "There's going to be a big geopolitical shakeout." She kissed him on the cheek. "Thank you."

"My pleasure," he smiled. "Luck to you."

"And to you," she said, holding out her hand. John shook it, looking for the last time into those cool green eyes.

Hochmeister arrived, wearing his old UC uniform and escorted by K'Raoda. "So, it's good-bye, then?" he said to John.

"For now, Admiral. But who knows? We're only a reality away."

"May I take your bag, Captain MacKenzie?" asked Hochmeister.

"Thank you, Admiral," she said, handing him the

backpack. She winked at John, then turned and bounded up the stairs. Hochmeister followed.

John watched the shuttle drift silently down the deck, penetrate the air curtain and vanish, a silver ship dwindling in size against the blue-green bulk of Terra Two.

He was halfway to the bridge when the battle klaxon sounded.

''Shuttle launching,'' reported K'Lana. ''And *V'Tran's Glory* advises ready to intitiate portal.''

''That was fast,'' said L'Wrona. ''One watch and N'Trol's removed the alien device? And tapped its secrets?''

''Get me N'Trol, K'Lana,'' said D'Trelna, looking at the screen. The destroyer stood well away from *Implacable*, Terra's moon large behind it.

''We're amazed at your speed, N'Trol,'' said D'Trelna as the engineer's face appeared. ''You're certain that alien portal thing will work?''

Smiling, N'Trol held up a familiar black cube. ''What alien thing?''

D'Trelna stared at it. ''Imperial,'' he said, seeing it all. ''Those killers are from the Machine Wars.'' He shook his head. ''All these ageless, deadly toys roaming about. And those fools back home think it's safe again.

''How long before you can have that portal ready?''

''The drive influx setting's made,'' said N'Trol. ''I just have to insert the cube.''

''Do it.''

''Yes, sir.''

''N'Trol, we'll send you a relief ship as soon as a task force arrives. Just sit here with your shield up until then.''

''Don't worry about us, Commodore,'' said N'Trol as D'Trelna switched off.

"That's the only time he's ever been civil to me," said D'Trelna. "Command must agree with him. Frightening."

They waited, watching the screen. It wasn't long before the portal returned, coming to life at the end of the gray beam.

"Battlestations, Captain L'Wrona," said D'Trelna, fingers drumming his chair arm. "And forward. Let's go get us a corsair."

21

"Marvelous ship," said K'Tran. "Wonderful how war spurs creativity." He stretched, luxuriating in the spacious bridge, the compact controls and most of all in the delightfully warm air.

"The finest and latest from Combine T'Lan," said A'Tir. She sat at the XO's station, scrolling through engineering specs. "Same old jump drive—they've just automated the hell out of it."

"We about ready?" he asked.

"Yes." She looked up. "Jump plotted and set. Navigation automatically reads jump point and engages drive. A few moments and we're on our way home."

K'Tran sat in the command chair, fingertips pressed together. "If I were Captain G'Ryn," he said, "I'd have broken out of *New Hope*'s brig . . ."

"Of course she has. We all but destroyed the locks."

"And would now be on the bridge, awaiting ship's status report." He punched up a tactical scan of the inner planets, hesitating for an instant over the new console.

The projection came on the screen. One bright green dot circled Earth. Another blip, red, marked the corsair speeding toward jump point. "There's the old barge," said K'Tran, not bothering with the targeting data. "G'Ryn's found the ship armed and operable. She'll be after us in a moment, murder in her heart."

As they watched, the green blip broke orbit, moving out.

Now he read the targeting data. "Coming right for us."

The green blip was gone, leaving only the red one marking the corsair's position.

"Good destruct," said A'Tir, going back to her reading.

The scan on the board changed to a larger scale, the planet Pluto in the center. Five more green blips were showing, just the other side of the planet, heading in. They and *Victory Day* were about to meet.

K'Tran stared at the targeting data. "Five heavy cruisers, just clearing jump point."

"Coming up on visual," said A'Tir, watching the board.

Five long, gray ships moved in close formation, surrounded by the faint glow of shields. They were L'Aals, the same class as *Implacable*, resurrected Imperial war machines that could turn *Victory Day* to scrap in minutes. They vanished as the cruiser shot past their formation.

"If we jump now, we'll only deviate two percent from ideal."

"They're challenging," said S'Kal from the commstation.

"Let's go for jump optimum," said K'Tran. "It's spring back at our little hideaway. Can't catch the last of the planting festival if we deviate.

"S'Kal, send a battlecode burst. 'Leaving system under special orders. Scan-shielded enemy flotilla in pursuit.' "

"You're amazing, Y'Dan," said A'Tir as the red-bearded

corsair made the transmission. "You flirt with destruction so you can watch straw-skirted girls dance the planting."

"A short but happy life." He smiled. "We all need to get away from ships for a while, breathe pollinated air, feel the warm wind in our faces."

"And then?"

"And then . . . the universe awaits."

S'Kal laughed, turning to K'Tran. "Task force commander acknowledges and requests last known position of scan-shielded flotilla."

The jump alert sounded, two long blasts of the klaxon.

"Tell him zero point," said K'Tran. Zero point was the standard reference for the heart of a system's star.

K'Tran opened shipwide commlink. "All personnel, stand by for jump. We're going home."

"So, he got away?" said Zahava, nibbling a chocolate croissant. She sat curled up on the sofa, her elegant dancer's legs tucked beneath her.

"Clean away," said John, tossing another log into the fire. On the other side of the living room's French doors, an early December snowstorm was covering their patio furniture.

John rose, dusting his hands.

"And the machine things?" she asked as he sat down beside her.

"Gone—for now," he said, finishing his coffee.

"If they're Imperial . . ."

"They are."

"Then how can they be the machines that killed the Trel, millions of years before the Empire?"

"If they're the same," he said, "the only way to find out is by going to the Trel cache—where we were supposed to be going when this madness started."

"Sorry I missed it."

He pulled her close, an arm around her shoulders. "I missed you," he said, kissing her.

"It's a cold day," she said after a while.

"Heat rises. It'll be warmer in the bedroom."

They were halfway up the old oak stairway when someone pounded on the front door knocker, ignoring the bell.

"I'll get rid of the sadistic creep and be right back," said John. Letting go of her hand, he went down and opened the door, letting in a rush of cold air and snow.

"J'Quel!"

D'Trelna filled the doorway, a stout snowman in hooded white survival jacket and battle boots.

"Sell you a weather-control unit?" he said, stamping his feet.

"Come in!"

Zahava bounded down the stairs. "J'Quel!"

He hugged her. "Long time, Zahava. You're looking well."

"Let me take your jacket," said John.

The commodore shook his head. "No time. I've been trying to reach you all day."

"I was picking Zahava up at the airport."

"So McShane said."

"Do you two still want to go on the Trel Expedition?"

They exchanged puzzled glances. "Of course."

"Good. We're leaving now. I've got a shuttle over in Lincoln Park. Get what personal things you want to bring—the Fleet of the Republic will provide clothing and toiletries."

Twenty minutes later they were trudging unplowed streets, overnight bags in hand. "What's the rush?" asked Zahava. The snow was ending with the day, the sun trying to briefly appear.

"The cruiser K'Tran pirated was assigned to the Trel Expedition," said D'Trelna. "It has a full mission briefing in its computer, including coordinates. We have to get there before he does."

The two men stood on the roof of the CIA building, looking across the river to the city. Low in the east, between the clouds, the first stars were appearing. In the grove beyond the parking lot, an owl hooted.

Suddenly the younger man grabbed the other's arm.

"There!" said Sutherland, pointing to where a shuttle rose above the city. It crossed the Potomac, coming in low and fast over the CIA complex. Passing the roof, it barrel rolled, then climbed high, silver hull catching the brilliant red sunset.

The two found themselves waving.

"God go with them," said McShane, as the shuttle vanished.

"Amen," said Sutherland.

"Buy you a drink, Bob?"

"Certainly."

They went inside, leaving the night to the snow and the stars.